Which Way To Go

Published in Great Britain in 2021
by Big White Shed, Nottingham
www.bigwhiteshed.co.uk
Printed and bound by Ben's Books, UK & Totem, Poland

ISBN 978-1-9163105-9-9
Copyright © Sue Traverso
Cover Design by Richard Heaven
Cover illustrations by Lillian Shaw

A CIP catalogue record of this book is available from the British Library.

To my grandchildren:

Megan, Aaron, Rachael, Immy and Lilly

CHAPTERS

ZOE

I pocketed my new mobile phone walking towards the bus stop. My trip back to the village I have called home for the last eight years, would only take twenty five minutes. I hadn't taken my car. Parking was so difficult in the City.

Amy, my daughter, newly graduated from university, would be staying in Cambridge working as a trainee journalist. Long before finishing her course, she had told me in her usual forthright manner that she had no intention of returning home to 'Recluse Cottage', her name for our house. She was right. I had hidden myself away there for too long.

I have got used to living on my own now. The empty nest syndrome has passed and if I am honest with myself, deep down, I had known Amy would not return. She wasn't going to follow in my wasted footsteps. The early promise I had shown had long dissipated into single motherhood. My bitterness at the departure of Jake, Amy's Dad, and my university love, had resolved itself into years of trying to shut the world out of my personal life.

I know how disappointed my sixties-loving parents had been, although they never said so. My other siblings had all gone forth into their own chosen worlds and, apart from one divorce, had still managed to achieve most of their goals. Our hippy parents, unshackled from the dreary post war fifties, spent their hours talking of free love, female emancipation, anti-Vietnam protests, and sang of peace. None of this had rubbed off on me. Our home was chaotic with four girls, one boy, a musician father and artist mother.

The house had been partially derelict. The elderly roof let water into most of the upstairs rooms. Leaks were slowly repaired, when money was more plentiful, so we moved into the bedrooms. Sometimes my parents were solvent, especially if Mum had sold a painting. She had studied at the Slade and taught art at a local private girls' school. Concealing her politics at work, she was avid in supporting all left-leaning activities in her spare time. Banners protesting all sorts of different causes decorated the house.

Our musician Dad worked nights, often on the road doing gigs, for weeks on end. It was a very hedonistic time and chimed perfectly with his views on life. He didn't belong to one group but hired himself out as part of backing groups to visiting singers.

I cannot hear the music of Fleetwood Mac, Bob Dylan, the Eagles or Chuck Berry without recalling my childhood years. The 80s music just passed me by. Not for me Madonna, Punk or Glam Rock, although I do have my Mark Bolan posters. Shamefully, I would leer obsessively at Mark on the wall above me whilst masturbating under the bed covers. Being the youngest, I was treated as a pet by my older siblings.

I was fascinated with their casual talk of snogging the latest squeeze, or wondering what Roger, the local idol, would be like in bed. Our brother treated us all with contempt. Stuck in the middle of this gaggle of females he didn't really 'get' us girls.

His contempt didn't run to ignoring the fact that twins,

Jennie and Frances, were beautiful with dark curly hair, slim athletic bodies and very long legs. They were also extremely popular with his mates. Lizzie and I were slightly younger and totally different. We were both studious and hated the clutter of the house. Our bedroom was neat, everything in place, with more books than the rest of the house and we were never late for school.

Lizzie's creativity emerged very early on. She would transform the displays in our room with gusto. Hand-made creatures would float from the ceiling, the walls covered in arrays of brightly coloured paintings. I slept under a dusty fairy floating above my head, refusing offers of an updated model.

I was the most studious child, preferring to read books, rather than participate in the hectic activity in the house. I had an old chair my grandmother had recovered for me in William Morris fabric and I would curl up for hours engrossed in the worlds created for me by brilliant writers. I devoured Jane Austen, the Brontes, struggled with George Eliot but loved Thackeray and Mrs Gaskell. Charles Dickens was to be endured but I did manage to read a few. The peculiar names he used for his characters confused me at times. A level French introduced me to Camus, Zola, Moliere, Racine, Dumas and Victor Hugo. Sadly, I found Germanic writers too stodgy and only really read Thomas Mann.

My other love was the local library and there, apart from reading my way through most of the fiction section, I discovered my obsession with history. I spent hours, long before Google, researching medieval history, the Anglo Saxons, the Scots, Vikings, Normans, right up to the end of the Second World War. My mind would conjure up the past. There was no romance in it. Life was brutal but fascinating. Mrs Maclean the librarian who had family back in Scotland, near Inverness, prodded me into discovering more about Scottish history and would order books for me from other libraries. My hero king was, and probably still is, Robert the Bruce.

I should explain that I have also kept, not exactly a diary, but notes of memorable items and facts and places. Many people have found their names recorded too alongside descriptions of the role they have played in my life.

My parents had produced an eclectic mix of children. Frances and Jennie decided they wanted to study drama. They had been involved in producing, acting and singing in numerous school plays. One teacher, Anthony, had spent years playing bit parts in war films and had many stage productions under his belt, decided, at the age of fifty, to teach English and Drama. He bullied and encouraged the girls mainly because both of them were inherently lazy. His work did pay off as they got into drama school – Frances to RADA and Jennie to LAMDA. Charlie became an accountant!

Quite obviously, Lizzie was going to follow in Mum's artistic footsteps but opted for St Martins College of Art rather than the Slade. She wanted to work in advertising as an art director.

I had dreamed of going to university from childhood. Not that I knew anything about what they offered. I was in love, mostly with their beautiful buildings and ancient surroundings. Of course, I am speaking of Oxford or Cambridge or Durham whose heritage appealed so strongly to the historian in me. I didn't fancy attending one of the newer colleges. Looking back, I was totally naïve and wholly unprepared for university life. I had spent my life under the cover of a book. I had no reality to draw from. I was, unbelievably dull.

I did expect, with the onset of puberty, that I would start taking an interest in the local boys but somehow this never happened. It wasn't that I had no male school friends but they remained just that, friends. I was the girl who could be trusted to go around with the gang and fit in with their antics whilst not demanding anything other than to spend time with them. I was popular only because I made no demands on their developing masculinity. It was always me the other girls approached to find out if one of my gang fancied them. I was the go-between. I could be relied on to keep their secrets too.

I went to the school dance with five boys but walked home alone until Charlie and his girlfriend caught up with me. I am not pretty as I think my face is too serious but I have large green eyes, thick dark hair, olive skin and a slim figure. I expect people would describe me as pleasant looking. I tan very easily. Mum says I look like her Italian mother. Unlike Grandma, I rarely smiled even though Mum said it transformed my entire face and I should do so more often. I am emotional and cry easily. Compared to Frances and Jennie I am small at only five foot six.

Musicians, singers, roadies and managers haunted our house. My father was talented and in demand. He played several instruments and backed up most of the groups and singers on the circuit. The house had a battered old room at the rear which looked like it might at one time have been a small ballroom with a tiny stage. It was cold and draughty. Over the years it was cleaned up, the parquet floor polished and, when funds were available, properly heated. It became Dad's session room. They would jam together, smoking weed, drinking beer and wine then disappear off leaving a mess.

My mother, whose own career was taking off, with exhibitions in the West End at Gimpel & Fils and regular submissions to the Summer Exhibition at the Royal Academy, refused to clear up the mess. Her studio at the front of the house, filled with light from the wonderful large window, was well away from what she called the 'Shack'. It was rather too large for a shack but the word certainly showed her disgust. A regular cleaner was needed.

Now Rosaria entered my life and she became my staunchest ally in this turbulent household and remained so until she died, far too early, of breast cancer. Originally from Santander, she had followed her brother to the UK to work. They lived together in a flat above a parade of shops. She cleaned for half the local community with an exhausting workload but was always cheerful and bubbly. Her deep throaty laugh could brighten up the most dreary day. I loved her to bits. Her brother was moody and sometimes very cruel to her but she never complained and was very stoic.

When she wasn't cleaning the Shack, she would do the washing and ironing for the family. My mother appreciated this Spanish gem and we would all gather round the kitchen table as she chattered away in her broken English, giggling when she got the words wrong, steam bellowing out from her iron and drinking hot chocolate (her favourite). I think she worked for us for nearly 10 years. She had a fount of basic common sense and could always be relied on to see a clear way through our many juvenile mistakes. She was a wise woman. Even today I miss her and frequently chat to her in my head.

I can still hear her saying, 'Zoe you look inside too much, you need to stop being unkind to yourself', and when I asked what she suggest I do, she would giggle and say, 'you dance, you laugh, you stop reading books and love life'. She should have been a therapist. I should have listened too. I seemed incapable of letting go, even though as a young girl I remember evenings of near hysteria with my parents when I was very young, playing games, running around the house dancing to records my father had played on as a session musician. Lizzie and I would dress up in floaty net curtains and, with our hair covered in flowers from the garden, we would both sing along to Hotel California, San Francisco or American Pie. That time of abandonment seems dreamlike to me now.

CHALLENGES

Running home from school, my brown envelope clasped tightly in my sweaty hands, (Mum had sprained her ankle and couldn't come with me and Dad was away, again) bursting with excitement, terrified too, I caught up with Rosy as she was opening the door. Being totally unfit I could barely speak but managed to gasp out that I had three 'A's and would most likely be able to take up the place I had been offered at Cambridge to study Modern European History.

'I did it Rosy, I did it. I am going to university'.

'Of course you are my darling. You will be a new person. You will make me most happy'. She enveloped me in her arms pressing me against her large breasts, kissing me all over my face. She was one big smile and her eyes were wet with tears of joy. We danced around on the doorstep until my mother hobbled into the hall. I felt a little ashamed that I had not rushed in to give her the news but she was never disturbed by my deep affection for Rosy. She was a generous spirit rarely getting upset at our love for Rosy.

She had a splodge of paint on her cheek, her hands were covered in coloured stains but this didn't stop her hugging me. For the first time I felt I had actually achieved something. Little did I know that getting a place at uni was only the beginning. Rather like the realisation that giving birth was just the first step of life-long commitment to the little body you are holding in your arms. Surviving Cambridge would be the next challenge. I was totally terrified. Whether it was excitement or fear that kept me awake for most of the night for a few days I was never sure. Eventually exhaustion took over and I slumbered again.

I was the last of our family to leave home. All the girls were renting a flat in Bloomsbury and Charlie was at Southampton doing Economics. My parents never made us feel that we should be worried about flying the nest. My father now worked at Abbey Road Studios and De Lane Lea as a resident musician so he was home more often. He still held his jamming sessions but the artists that came to the house were much younger. Occasionally we would have a visit from an American singer he had backed and they would blather on about the 60s.

An old friend, who was producing a film, asked Dad to put together the soundtrack. He loved this departure and before long it became his main source of income. With all his children in further education it must have been challenging financially so this regular extra income was a relief. A whole transformation was going on in the film world and musical soundtracks had finally caught up.

I was totally immune to the famous people who came to our house. Mother also had her own circle of artists. She designed the covers for many record albums in the days before CDs and DVDs became popular. As always, my parents evolved easily into the next phase of their lives. Trips to Los Angeles became commonplace. This flexibility seemed to pass me by. I was the opposite of my parents: timid, almost scared of my own shadow. I had no female friends. I had my sisters, so who needed girl-friends?

My male friends loved coming to our house and were always made welcome by my mother. None of them could understand my blasé attitude to the numerous famous performers who could be found lounging around in the Shack or drinking strong coffee at our large kitchen table.

One thing didn't change. Mum and Dad still dressed like sixties hippies. I found this excruciatingly embarrassing on my first day at college when we drove up to the halls. There was a reasonable smattering of early 4x4s and posh cars. Dad had borrowed his friend's VW camper covered in psychedelic graffiti, to transport all my belongings and our arrival did create quite a few turned heads. We disgorged ourselves from the campervan and it was obvious that my parents were in a different league completely from my, soon to be, fellow students' families.

Most of them seemed horribly overdressed for such manual activity as lifting boxes and carrying bags. Loud braying voices instructed the students to help unpack. My preparation, as you would expect, had been exhaustive and everything was labelled. Before departing, my mother had gifted me a magnificent handmade Welsh quilt for my bed which she had commissioned from a girlfriend. Mum's blouse was a glory to behold full of vibrancy and colour. My father as usual was wearing jeans. I carried my quilt and tried to hide my face in its beauty.

We struggled up the staircase to the room the Bursar had allocated to two of us. My new roommate had not arrived so we were able to unpack my boxes without interruption. Rosy had prepared tapas for us to snack on and we shared some wine. Dad refused his drink as he was driving. Remembering the days of drugs and drink when we were growing up, it was quite alarming to cope with such sobering changes. Already I felt guilty about choosing the bed with the view but silently told myself that if my new room partner wanted it, I would consider the request. I never had to make that choice because at 2 p.m. on that memorable day, my future best friend Varena blasted in, closely followed by a chauffeur, carrying all her bags. No parents though.

It was as if a bomb had exploded. I felt flattened against the wall by her personality. Like me, she had a pleasant rather than a beautiful face but, unlike me, she had an amazing figure. Her smile wrapped the rest of us in and before long we were all sitting down on the beds (not the chauffeur) finishing off the wine and Tapas.

Mother looked at her watch and said they must go to avoid the traffic on the M11 and I felt my stomach heave and a lump jumped into my throat. My fear was palpable. I had spent the day being brave but now I was just very apprehensive. Dad looked at me and I could see the sympathy in his eyes as well as something else. It was as if he was wondering how they could have produced a child so timid and he didn't know what to say. Mother spoke for him, as she could see his consternation, by being overly positive, and breezily wished me a terrific time in my new world.

'It will feel strange for a while but you have worked for this and deserve to be here. Do try to enjoy this experience as well, darling. Life is not all about study. Live and have fun too', she said and turning to Varena she smiled and said she felt sure we would be the best of friends. With a kiss on my cheek, they waved goodbye and disappeared down the staircase and jumped into the campervan. Most of the other cars had long since disappeared although Varena's grandfather's chauffeur was still sitting in the Jaguar. She had followed me down the stairs, apologised, then sent him on his way. They had driven from Yorkshire.

FRIENDSHIP IS FOR LIFE

26 October, a few weeks after my arrival, I was feeling much braver and settled and decided that Varena and I should go out to celebrate my birthday. She had already established a group of friends and we managed to get ourselves extremely drunk, staggering home making a lot of noise. We had spent most of the first days being inducted into the quaint future lifestyle we were to embrace. Although we were doing different courses – me: Modern European History/French and German languages – Varena: Anthropology - the induction for the first morning covered all students. We had already got lost several times but eventually found our way to the modern block across the river near our halls. Most of the lectures took place there anyway.

As luck would have it my period started that day and I was desperately seeking out the facilities without really taking much care about what I was doing. I rammed myself hard into the back of a student surveying the noticeboard. He shot round and gave me a furious look and I remember backing off into the Ladies which was just next door to the board. I yelled an apology and took a quick glance at the irate young man. He was truly, and I mean truly, beautiful. He had a mass of dark chestnut hair, penetrating blue eyes, an aquiline nose and broad cheekbones and a strong jaw. His mouth which was spouting his fury was more difficult to describe but it certainly showed his white teeth. I ran hoping for the ground to open up and swallow me. The Ladies would have to do.

Varena had spotted the altercation and followed me in.

'Good lord, Zoe you picked a beautiful specimen to bump into', she grinned. Her voice was full of laughter and she fell about in amusement at my obvious distress. 'I think you should go out there and throw yourself at his feet and beg his forgiveness' she giggled. I have a non-existent London accent – it is neither posh nor common – just ordinary. Varena's accent is pure plum.

I remember once visiting some American friends of my parents and the host mentioning that one of the dinner guests who was late arriving had a speech impediment but that she was very good fun. When the said guest walked in it became obvious that this lady did not suffer such an indignity. The only impediment was hereditary and was commonplace in posh circles. That said, she was very good fun once you got used to her extreme manner of speaking. She also had the filthiest sense of humour.

It had taken about an hour in Varena's company for me to fall desperately in love with her. She was everything I wasn't. Confident, friendly, open and generous. Although full of life she was just as likely to sit in contemplation for hours on end. Her parents were affluent and her father was in the diplomatic service in India. She had learned to meditate on a visit to Delhi on holiday from her boarding school. She hated her time at school and would have loved to stay in India but had used the meditation to help her cope. It was a particularly bitchy school from the many incidents she described. We spent hours talking about our childhood and friendships, hopes, and also about some of the sadder aspects. Her brother was also at boarding school and they only saw each other in the holidays at their grandparents' stately home in Yorkshire.

We were socially at totally opposite ends of the pole but that never worried us. Our friendship blossomed over the next few months and I forgot how scared I had been on my arrival. We bolstered each other up when we felt down. Alongside her good humour she was also extremely thoughtful and caring.

I made connections with some of the male students on my course and soon became another one of the boys. I seemed still to struggle with female friendships, other than Varena, who had already become part of several girl gangs. If we went out in groups I invariably ended up in the middle of the boys and Varena with the girls. Gradually partnerships were getting established and there were occasional bust-ups but there was so much choice it seemed wrong to get too hung up on one person at this time of life. We were pretty shallow and self-serving but none of us worried about that much.

There was a lot of money around. Most of us did not have to take a job to pay for accommodation. Two of the girls in Varena's group worked as bar staff during term-time and I often thought it would have been good for me to expand my confidence by helping out from time to time.

This thought had been zooming around my brain for a while. One of Dad's old rocker friends was appearing at the student club and, surprisingly, the tickets had been sold out very quickly. I offered to help at the bar that night so that Gina the barmaid, could watch the show using one of the two complimentary tickets I had been sent. Varena took the other. The warm up band was pretty atrocious but that didn't seem to bother the crowd who were bopping and screaming along. I must be a bit of a musical snob as I have been so used to the professional musicians and singers my Dad has worked with over the years. The bar was quietish when the first band was on, and surveying the dark hall, I saw the student I had accosted all those months ago.

He was looking around with his arms draped over a girl so I quickly bent over the glass washing machine to avoid being seen. During the break in the bands the bar was frantic and I was too busy to see where he had gone. The roadies were setting up the stage for the main attraction and everybody turned around in anticipation. He was on the fringe of the crowd in a group and I had the chance to really look at him. He was smiling, not snarling, and his whole demeanour had changed. He was tall, certainly over six foot and had a muscular body.

The last-minute rush for the drinks occupied me and then Dad's friend Jimmy and his group came on. I had spent many hours listening to them practising in the Shack and apart from looking slightly older Jimmy seemed very much the same. He had always treated me with kindness. The first song caused the hall to erupt and the place became alive. Faces were glowing in the lighting and I knew this was going to be a great success. Varena was jumping up and down with a tall young man I hadn't seen before. The bar was quiet and I looked to see if I could see snarling man again but he had gone.

Halfway through the session Jimmy took the microphone and said my Dad had asked him to sing the next song for Zoe and sent his love. He looked around the room and saw me at the bar and waved. He blew me a kiss and grinned. I swear all the room turned and looked at me and I think my face must have matched my red blouse. They gave a cheer and Jimmy and the group started up again. I don't remember the song because, stood in front of me was snarling man who had moved up towards the bar. He was looking straight at me wondering where he had seen me before. I knew the moment he remembered because his face changed. His mouth went from a slight smile to a grim line then unbelievably turned into laughter. I am not sure which I preferred. Both looks completely unnerved me.

'Why did you run away', he asked?

I was not going to tell him that it was because I desperately needed the toilet. I just couldn't think of anything else to say. I am not good at conversation with people I don't know and our encounter had not been exactly friendly. I stared dumbly at him and refused to respond.

'Well Zoe, now I know your name, here is your chance to apologise for nearly shoving my face into the noticeboard'.

'I didn't do it on purpose, it was an accident'. My voice came out like a squeak.

'Didn't your parents teach you any manners? Don't you think it would have been polite to say sorry?' He had a slight accent but I couldn't immediately place where from.

'I did say sorry – it is not my fault that you didn't hear me say it'.

He looked above me at the bottles of drink and then back and shaking his head turned around and walked towards his girlfriend, kissing the back of her neck when she smiled at him. I was dismissed.

After the gig, Jimmy invited Varena, me and some of our gang, backstage and we all trouped off into the dressing room. I had gone up in the pecking order because of my link to Jimmy with most of them asking how we knew each other. He explained that my Dad was the best backing musician in the business and he had worked with everybody. We were all offered drinks and spent about 20 minutes just chatting before we departed off back to college. The walk back was peppered with questions about my Dad, who he had worked with, had I met these stars and so on? I had moved from the background into the foreground without much effort on my part. Despite the unsettling scene with snarling man I slept very well that night. Life was improving.

THESPIAN SUCCESS

Jennie had finally graduated and their end of term performance was going to be King Lear at the Barbican. She had landed, unbelievably, the major role of Cordelia. Mum and Dad were ecstatic. We were all ordered to come up to town to see the performance, no ifs nor buts. If I wanted to, I could bring Varena along. Mum wrote. They would be delighted to see her again. Any chance to get away from our studies and ordered life was to be welcomed, even if it was just prior to exam time. Mum said it would be a sensible break for us.

Cambridge to London is a one-hour train journey and we could travel into Liverpool Street close to the Barbican. No university uniform, we must dress to impress. As I had no decent clothes, it fell to Varena to sort us out. She dragged me off to Cambridge City Centre and we trawled the shops for something suitable for me to wear. After hours looking, with the occasional break for cups of strong coffee, we found this amazing midnight blue dress. Even better it was in the sale. We dropped into a shoe shop and bought some matching ballet pumps which cost more than the dress and I was all set up. Needless to say, even in college, Varena always had the right clothes to wear. She attended many more dress up functions than me.

I had gone back to the bar and asked for work and spent

several nights pulling pints. My gift of the gab had improved tremendously even if it was somewhat shallow. I had also gone out with a couple of dreary nerds which had hardly improved my social standing. I still hadn't found anyone worth losing my virginity to.

We jumped on the bus for the station giving ourselves plenty of time to get to London. How foolish of us to think that the Great British Transport system would work on time that day. The bus got stuck in traffic, which is quite a strange happening in a city where bus lanes and cycle tracks were starting to dominate, and then our train to London was cancelled. We had to wait for the Kings Lynn to Kings Cross train and travel by underground into the City.

We eventually arrived at the Barbican with 5 minutes to spare, angry hot and flustered, (this was way before mobiles could track your every move) to see Mum at the entrance anxiously gazing around. Charlie had an equally difficult time travelling up from Southampton. We raced to our seats as the curtain went up and I spent the first acts thinking about the pressure on my bladder. Would I have to jump up just as Gloucester gets blinded to ask the elderly gent next to me to let me through, or would I cope?

By the time I got to the ladies in the break I was nearly screaming and my bladder released itself in a torrent. We had drunk several cups of coffee whilst sitting fuming in tunnels on the trip from Cambridge. I was sure the entire queue could hear my urinary explosion.

Jennie was amazing as Cordelia – Lear is my favourite Shakespearean play – and the young male actor playing the elderly king made me want to weep. I realised then how much I missed not going to the theatre. We had been regular attenders when living in London and frequently got offered free tickets for some of the shows. My particular obsession was musicals. I have lost count of the visits to see Phantom or Les Miserables or Cats. Despite our dreadful journey we spent a fantastic time and soon forgot our travails on the train. Dad had arranged a small minibus to take us all home and we celebrated with pizza around the kitchen table with Jennie laughing with relief. She had already been approached by an agent.

Returning to Cambridge the next day we both felt extremely flat. Exams loomed and I was still struggling with my history studies. Frequent conversational sessions in French and German were improving my pronunciation but the lecturer on European history was dreary beyond belief. I had found myself sleeping in several lectures jerking myself awake and wondering if I had dribbled or snored in my sleep. I mentioned this to my German tutor who was a neat, precise man with a total gift for languages. My sessions with him were zappy, fun and informative. It was such a contrast to my main subject. He suggested I speak to the faculty organiser and see if I could get on a different rota for next year.

Meanwhile, Varena was storming ahead with her anthropological studies and was planning a trip to Borneo in the holiday, travelling back via India, to see her parents. She was keen to study a group of indigenous tribes. We were so in tune with each other and the year had flown past. She had the same level of commitment to her studies but she was also encouraging a love of life in me. I found myself laughing several times a day and realised that university was good for me. It had expanded my horizons.

We both got good results in the exams and started packing up our belongings to return home for the vacation. We were planning on renting a flat in the town with two other students rather than stay in halls in the autumn. The family were off to France for the summer and I was joining them. Jennie had been offered a small part in a play so couldn't join us and Charlie was bringing his girlfriend. I was looking forward to catching up with Lizzie who was in her last year. Frances had been unsettled at RADA and was considering moving to the technical side of the profession. She preferred a behind the scenes role and had dropped out by the time we all arrived in Brittany.

It was the first time the family had been together since Christmas and, ever the observer, I was noticing how much we had all changed. Sitting by the pool at the gîte we had booked, it was clear how confident Lizzie had become and Charlie had changed too from a good-natured soul into a slightly arrogant control freak. He spent his days ordering us and his girlfriend around and became quite stroppy when we refused to be bullied into activity. He should have known better, especially in relation to our totally laid-back parents. I suspect they had noticed our differences too.

The purchase of the blue dress had changed my persona. I no longer dressed in tatty jeans and sweatshirts and had improved my wardrobe with the addition of strongly coloured tops and skirts. I did still wear sneakers but I also had some beautiful ballet pumps to put on when we were going out to eat. I had found a splendid bikini in the sale and realised that my figure too had filled out. My breasts had finally matured!

I had stopped hiding behind my fringe and learnt subtle ways of improving my makeup to highlight my green eyes. A few days in the sun and I felt almost goddess like! In an attempt to build on my French conversation I had borrowed the car and driven into town. This was quite an experience as I had passed my test the year before but hadn't driven for at least 8 months. Starting off I nearly forgot to drive on the correct side.

I parked in the town square, bought some bread for Mum at the boulangerie and then plonked myself down at a seat outside the café. The waiter, having sussed I was not a local and probably a tourist, was clearly surprised that I spoke to him in reasonable French. Delivering me the espresso he stopped to chat and I soon discovered that he was keen to improve his English. I explained my desire to become more fluent in his language and we agreed to meet up after he finished work. He was very fair with deep blue eyes and only slightly taller than me.

He explained whilst I drank my coffee, 'I have worked in Paris for a couple of years, but when my parents moved to the town and opened a café, I offered to help get it off the ground, as I was between jobs. I plan to go back to a new marketing job in Paris at the end of the summer but have not ruled out the option of going to London to work in the future'.

We spent evenings in a mixture of English and French discussing politics, art, history and, above all, music. Not rock or pop, but classical. We sat in the evening sun at the rear of the café chatting and listening to his classical music albums. I was transported, once quite literally, by some of the pieces we played and was frequently very emotional. I would go home with the sounds ringing in my head writing down the names of the composers or the orchestra or the opera or the singer in my small note book .

Yves took a long time to kiss me. He was quite shy and my almost complete absence of life experience with the male sex didn't help our relationship along. Our evenings were full of joy and laughter and on one occasion I had fallen back out of my rickety chair laughing when a loud bang from a car exhaust made me jump and I narrowly missed landing into the small pond. Jumping up to help me we clashed heads as I desperately pushed my hands down to cover my fully exposed lower body.

Taking my head in his hands, he said 'Zoe I am so sorry if I have hurt you but it gives me the chance to kiss you better'. Just like that he started kissing my forehead, my cheeks, then my nose and eventually my mouth. By this point I had stopped laughing and was revelling in his closeness. I wanted to nuzzle him and rub my face alongside his. I had never felt this reaction to any male and it was electrifying. Now I knew what people talked about being overcome by passion. I wanted to touch every part of him.

Driving home that night I realised I had finally come alive. I felt breathless and my whole being was throbbing. I wanted desperately to turn the car around and go back to him. I would have to wait until Thursday on his day off when we planned to spend the day together. I had no idea what would happen if we had sex, whether he would use precautions, but I didn't care. I was 19 years old and in the grip of my first passion.

My French was improving in leaps and bounds too. Probably not the vocabulary which would be much use to me in my chosen career though.

Thursday morning arrived and I was already wondering if I had imagined what I had felt and as usual my nerves had taken over. Rosy always told me to think of practical solutions but I am not sure, good Catholic as she was, she would have approved of my first reaction, which was to drive to the local pharmacy to purchase some condoms. Yves was waiting for me as I drove up and hopped in with a basket of food and a small blanket. He pecked my cheek and started issuing directions.

We could have gone to the beach (I had bought my beautiful bikini) but he suggested it would be quieter if we went alongside the river. He knew of several amazing spots and pointed out many places which had been recorded for posterity by the Impressionist painters. Remembering the bookcases full of art books in our room I could well imagine one view we passed having been painted by Pisarro, my absolute favourite artist.

Eventually Yves directed me to a narrow lane just past a magnificent chateau which was clearly in the process of renovation. No doubt it was some English banker, having made his fortune in the City, trying to become a local Seigneur. I wondered if the family could speak a word of French. I expect these days they would be making a TV programme about it and Dick and Angel would be coming along to support them. Of course, they would run out of money and have loads of children just like all the property developer programmes. I could write the script in my head.

Conversation in the car took a while to move from pleasantries. It seemed we both were nervous after the passion of two nights ago. Maybe we were worried that the reaction had been a one-off. Yves pointed to a turn-off and his arm brushed mine. I felt as if a jolt of electric volts had hit me and I had to grab tighter hold of the steering wheel. I started to feel this was going to be OK and that my reservations were a result of my cautious nature.

It was warm, quiet and deliciously fresh with a slight breeze when we got out of the car. The place Yves had directed me to park opened out onto a lush green bank alongside the river. The area was popular with long-boat holidaymakers but we only saw one pass dreamily along that morning. You could hear the hum of the engines chugging along in the distance. We waved at the family hoping the dog wouldn't fall off into the water in his excitement.

I can recommend losing your virginity to a polite, charming Parisian on the edge of a slow-moving river. The whole atmosphere was dreamy and slightly surreal. I wondered at what time I would have to admit my virginity and inexperience but somehow my body started to overcome my brain and I found myself desperate for Yves' lovemaking. Sheltered from view by some low growing bushes, we removed our clothing, all the time exploring with our hands and mouths.

Clearly Yves was experienced. His shyness had disappeared and he took me with care and kindness having brought me to a blinding need with his subtle moves. I was desperate for him to be inside me. He had stroked almost every part of my quivering body from head to toe and I had surprised myself with my own lack of inhibition. I had no need to worry about taking precautions as he had come prepared.

Looking back, I am amazed at my reaction. Charlie and Dad rarely covered up at home so I was well aware of the male body but amazingly I had no hesitation in stroking Yves' penis demanding that he enter me and release me from my torment. When he finally did so the sharp pain I felt disappeared immediately and I was able to at least meet his passion with my own.

On that glorious day we made love again twice and I will be forever grateful for his sensitivity. He treated me with respect and gave me so much pleasure. He knew exactly how to make me respond to his lovemaking and his patience helped me to have a really fulfilling first experience.

We met up the following week at the same place but I

was dreading our return to England at the beginning of September. Yves was due back at work in Paris too. Those final days became a very precious memory. We were not in love as our time together was too short for such a development, but our mutual affection ensured we made amazing memories for each other. Yves hoped one day to work in London and promised to write. For the first time I was actually unenthusiastic about returning to Cambridge.

We had spoken of my aim to work for the EEC when I graduated and laughed about my next year's holiday which would be spent in Germany. Would I find a German Yves? I think it was the light-hearted relaxed time which made my first experience so memorable. Talking to friends, later, I realised I had been lucky. So many had suffered disappointment at their first experience. For that I will be forever grateful to Yves. I even forgave him for not keeping up our communication. I was sad that he had moved to London a year later and hadn't contacted me. He met Frances at Victoria Station one evening and briefly filled her in with what he had been doing. He asked if I was well but made no attempt to get in touch.

'C'est la vie', was Varena's comment when I reported this encounter to her, arranging her serious face, she asked if I was upset by his neglect?

'No'. I had genuinely moved on in my life although I had had only one relationship since Yves. The problem was that I hadn't felt a strong physical reaction and, despite liking Steve a lot, I needed the whole package. I never actually told him this was the reason I broke it off.

I FIND MY CAREER PATH,
BUT NOT THE ONE I EXPECTED

Back at college, happily ensconced in our flat, I turned my attention to changing my lecturer and getting myself on a different rota.

Professor Weaver was ageless. I couldn't tell you if he was 60 or 80. I knew he must have been nearer 70 with his wealth of experience and also I had been told of his war record. My German tutor had explained that he was a brilliant educator but that his personal social skills were limited. They had been friends for a long time. I remember reading Goodbye Mr Chips many years ago and my next venture on the ladder had a certain resonance.

I found myself sitting outside his rooms rehearsing my reasons for wanting to transfer on to his course. I had already started a one-year business course alongside my other subjects. Was it right to tell a fellow colleague that your lecturer was so abysmally boring that you slept through his lectures and you weren't even tired?

I knocked and was answered with a very gruff 'Enter'. I poked my head around the door and slipped quietly into the room.

'I expect you want to transfer onto my course because you can't cope with your current lecturer' he muttered?

'Well yes' I replied. I was so relieved I hadn't needed to offer my explanation.

'You realise I can't take everybody who makes that request, don't you?'

My heart sank. I would be condemned to sleeping through lectures for the remainder of my course. I wondered if, when I finally got a job, I would need a nap in the day just to keep up. My power naps would be as long as two hours!

Prof Weaver had barely looked at me. He just shuffled his papers around his desk, then turned to look out of the window. It gave me a perfect view of his bald patch which closely resembled a monk's tonsure. I wondered if I should quietly exit and was about to do so when he turned to face me. His expression was unreadable.

'In your case I am prepared to make an exception. I have looked at your work and believe you have a great deal to offer if you are prepared to put in a lot of effort'.

I realised I had been holding my breath and let it out with such gusto that the papers on the desk flapped around. I told him he wouldn't regret his decision. He looked down then back at me. I am sure he had heard those words many times. How often had students failed to do what they promised. I was determined not to be like that.

He gave me a list of his lectures and I left his office feeling so positive about the future.

Three months later I was still so pleased that I had transferred to Prof's rota. My dreary sessions had turned into mind-blowing adventures. Prof Weaver, so closed off and shut down, delivered brilliant enthralling lectures. He challenged his students in a slightly sarcastic tone and could be devastatingly abrupt if he felt you were being lazy in your answers. He bullied and chivvied us into using our minds, opening up a European world none of us knew existed.

One afternoon two of us had been sat in the beaten-up old leather chairs in his office discussing the Italian Risorgimento, when the phone rang. He stopped abruptly and waited for the ringing to end, making no attempt to answer it. This actually happened several more times. He clearly resented the intrusion and took time to reconnect his thoughts.

My fellow student departed and I waited to collect my essay. Apart from admiring the man with his brilliant intellect I was still no closer to understanding him. Most of our communication was in short, matter of fact, sentences except when he thought I was being lazy. I would be challenged by caustic and sometimes witty comments which, initially, confused me. But slowly, I found my voice, giving him back as much as he handed out. As my confidence grew our exchanges expanded and developed into real dialogue.

Before I left, I turned round and suggested that if he found the calls intrusive he should install an answerphone to pick up when he didn't want to be interrupted. It is often my experience that great minds are never very practical and he looked astounded at the suggestion.

'But I would still need to listen to the messages'. I was not sure if it was the technology that he was unsure of or the fact that he had to communicate with the outside world.

Most of the Professors had remote secretarial assistance and many did not have individual help, with their work going into a typing pool. Prof Weaver had a diary secretary but nothing else and clearly she must have had difficulties connecting with him. He was notorious for shutting himself away. I had mentioned this to his friend my German tutor and he had told me confidentially what he felt the problem was.

In these days of Google it is easy to look up people's past lives, or what Wikipedia thinks are the facts, which of course is debatable, but before technology really took hold, that was more difficult. I really knew nothing about his history. Prof Weaver's brilliance had been noted as a student and he was offered a junior post upon graduation following his return from the war. He was from a Welsh mining village and had moved up through the grammar school system. One year into his university course and war was declared and he was called up. He had no hesitation in serving his country and duly reported for training in Aldershot. A short while later and he was a member of the British Expeditionary Force desperately trying to get back to Dunkirk. His unit was picked up by the Germans and he spent nearly five years as a prisoner of war before being liberated.

Returning to the UK he found his elder brother, who had been a conscientious objector, was dead. Killed in a mining accident. His parents were devastated by his death. His colleagues at Cambridge to which he returned, no longer recognised the bright outgoing friendly man they had seen go off to war. The only time he came alive was in his lectures. He rarely mixed with his fellow Dons. His concern for his students ruled his life. He had not married, living alone with several cats. Four years as a prisoner of war had done its damage.

Rosy always told me that finding practical solutions was what made her so positive so I gave some attention to the Prof's difficulties with the phone. Without consulting him, because I had worked out by now how contrary he was, I purchased an answerphone and arrived at my next tutorial with it in a bag. Waiting until the end I stood up and walked to his desk. I had realised that even if he didn't answer the phone he would still hear the messages so decided if there was an electric plug in his book room that would be the ideal place for the machine. This was crammed with books, documents and other paraphernalia and I had also seen a telephone point in there. If I could set up the answerphone he could shut the door and not hear the dreary recorded message.

He stared at me in confusion wondering why on earth I was suggesting this option. I explained that I had observed how the phone calls clearly caused him a loss of concentration and that all he had to do was check the machine when he wasn't writing or lecturing. You would have thought by his terrified expression that I was suggesting he walk barefoot on hot coals. OK, I thought what would Rosy do? Clearly this poor man was a technophobe.

'Would it help if I came by at lunchtime and checked the messages for you and then wrote them down on a pad for you to read later?' I queried.

The look of relief which swept over his battered old face was immediate as he absorbed my offer.

'Would you do that for me?' He stammered, looking away over the mountain of paper on his desk.

'You will still need to ring people back but this could happen at a time to suit you', I suggested.

'Yes, yes, I understand. Let us set an experimental period to see if this works'.

I was wondering what I had let myself in for but as I often had tutorials near his office in the mornings, doubted it would impact on my routine. It might delay meeting up with Varena for our snack lunch but she wouldn't mind. She was busy planning her next trip to Namibia and spent much of her time talking about a region called the Skeleton Coast. I couldn't imagine how many living specimens she would find in an area with a name like that.

He got on with his writing and I shut myself up in the bookroom and put a recorded message on and set the machine to kick-in after two rings. I had warned the Prof if he wanted to answer the phone he would need to be quick.

I moved to the door when I heard him say very quietly 'You are a very kind girl Zoe, thank you. Please let me know how much the machine cost'. Up until that point he had only referred to me as Miss Chapman. I said I would find the receipt. He didn't look at me as I waved goodbye.

Little did I know it but I had taken one step on my career path but it was certainly not the one I had chosen, but more about that later.

CAFÉ RELATIONSHIPS

Summer in Bavaria, perfecting my German, had proved quite dull with no German lover turning up at the local bar where I worked. Most people spoke impeccable English so I was not getting as much German conversation as I had hoped. Still I was often complimented on my accent. At least the family I lived with spoke constantly in their language so some benefit had accrued from my stay. The countryside was magnificent.

Returning to Cambridge and, for my final year, I decided to work only at weekends as, invariably, I got back late from the club. I took a job at a small, but popular, café down near the river. Any money I earned was being squirrelled away in my bank account. I planned a trip overseas after graduation although I hadn't decided where. I was certainly not the Far East back-packing type so I always imagined I would 'do' Europe possibly by train or coach.

I don't know how many students attend college but it is many thousands and I had never seen snarling man again. Obviously, he wasn't a regular at the bar. Maybe he was a fan of Jimmy and his group. Despite being from the 60s they seemed to have quite a young fan base. Jimmy had a return concert but it was at a much larger venue on a night I was working.

I digress. Here is the scene. Café is full and I am weaving my way through the tightly-packed table arrangements when Marie, the other overworked waitress, started losing a bottle off her tray. I bent down to catch it and promptly stuck my butt into the face of the man sat behind. Blushing furiously and saying sorry I turned to apologise only to discover that snarling man had returned to my life.

'Wow it is Miss Calamity again', came the sarcastic response. 'I am amazed the café takes the risk of employing you'.

I glared at him, turned on my heel and rushed off with the orders I had taken. I asked Marie to cover my tables and I concentrated my rather flustered efforts on the ones near the river. I did not look in his direction again.

The café shut at 5 o'clock and Marie and I were sat with our feet up on some chairs in the back indulging in the best hot chocolate in Cambridge when I realised he was coming through the door. Tom from behind the bar yelled that we were shut but he just kept moving in my direction. I actually had nowhere to run even though I had plonked my feet back on the floor. I wanted to slap Marie as she was clearly enjoying my discomfort and then, to my horror, she picked up her drink and moved over to talk to Tom.

Snarling man sat down replacing her. He must have been around for some time waiting for me to come out of the café and, when I didn't, decided to find me instead.

'If you think my apology wasn't profuse enough then I will say it again but you do seem determined to continue your aggressive behaviour towards me and I am at a complete loss as to why you are so hostile', I said.

He shuffled on to the chair and I realised that he was extremely well built with broad shoulders under his smart, fitted, shirt which highlighted his powerful muscles. His whole body appeared to be threatening and then in the blink of an eye he burst out laughing throwing back his head. He had dropped his bag on the floor when he sat down and I noticed the logo was Cambridge Rowing. So clearly snarling man was also rowing man who had turned into laughing man in the last few minutes.

I waited, staring at him, for an explanation of his hilarity. When it came I wasn't sure how to respond.

'I have often wondered if I would come across you again and without warning you present me your bottom in the most unexpected place'. He moved slightly closer and lent towards me.

'Have you always been so disaster prone?'

'I certainly wasn't sticking my rear end in your face on purpose and I rarely make mistakes, except when you are around. Fortunately for me I haven't come across your friendly path for quite some time', I retorted.

Marie came over to the table to say they were locking up and we needed to move. I jumped up to grab my bag, caught the edge of the table, and overturned my left-over chocolate plop into his lap covering his immaculate trousers and then splashing the rest down onto his rowing bag. Marie grabbed some tea towels and threw me one as I repeated, 'I am sorry, so sorry', over and over until snarling, laughing, rowing man told me to stop. I was dabbing him dry in the most inappropriate area and blushed furiously as I removed my left hand from very close to his most intimate parts.

He turned to Marie asking if he could change in the toilets before we shut up and disappeared with his bag. We cleared up the fallen soggy chocolate mess and I was just thinking

I ought to make a run for it when he reappeared from the toilets wearing knee-length wet suit bottoms. The vision of his muscular thighs caused me to have a massive sexual response and I am sure my wide-open mouth must have betrayed me. Since Yves, I had not experienced anything like it, much to my disappointment. Marie and Tom beamed from the doorway and ushered us all out of the café.

Our flat was only a few minutes' walk away across the bridge and, having got control of my reaction, I offered to go there and clean his clothes up enough for him to get home. He looked slightly baffled by my offer but realised he would look quite strange walking through the town in his smart shirt and wet-suit bottoms so agreed to take up my offer.

We turned and walked towards the bridge in silence. What do you say to somebody you have just covered in hot chocolate? Apart from 'Sorry, I promise not to do that again', which seemed a dangerous precedent from our previous encounters. I bet he was glad he hadn't bumped into me more often.

'I know you are called Zoe from that night in the club, but maybe I ought to introduce myself'. He held out his hand which I took rather gingerly. 'Jacob Campbell'. Edinburgh Scottish – that was my betting on his accent. His grip was crushing my fingers together.

For some reason I was still clutching on to his hand. It was possibly the fact that I had experienced a second bolt of lightning, my first after Yves touched me in France, my second just now. It must be my fate to develop my sexual side with men I picked up in cafés.

I managed to wrench my hand away. 'Zoe Chapman', I responded and could think of nothing else to say. Unlike with Yves, with whom I had spent hours chatting, I knew absolutely nothing about this giant of a man with his massive muscles and sarcastic manner. Apart from rowing I didn't even know what he was studying. Maybe it was the time to ask.

'What are you studying?'

'Environmental sciences, and you?'

'European history and German and French. I am also doing a short one-year business course'.

'You must be pretty busy and also managing to work at the café must eat into your study time'.

We had by now reached the flat which would be empty of its occupants apart from me as two of us had gone home for the weekend and Varena was on yet another course. I indicated the front door, unlocked and pointed to the lounge. His sheer bulk made the place seem quite small. I turned to hang up the key and he moved closely past me through the door. Another strong reaction on my part as his back brushed past mine – what on earth was wrong with me?   Had I turned into a sexual fiend?

This man had been rude to me from our very first encounter but I was massively sexually attracted to him. He sat down and removed his anorak. I asked him to let me have his trousers and I would try to remove the stains. We had a tumble dryer in the utility room. He pulled them out of his bag and handed them over. I offered him a cup of tea whilst I rummaged in the cupboard for the hand washing powder. I picked up a damp cloth and started dabbing uselessly at the stain.

He got up. 'Yes, I would like a tea but let me make it if you tell me in which cupboards I will find the cups', he actually smiled as he said this and I felt like my legs were turning to jelly. He would soon be wiping me off the floor. I pointed out the cups and the tea bags and went on with my hopeless attempts to remove the chocolate stains. This was not working and I was going to have to admit this. The trousers needed to be soaked in stain remover and then washed.

He lent across me to fill the electric kettle and I shot backwards. He asked me if I was okay. I felt it was only fair now to tell him that I was unable to remove the stain properly so I did so.

'I knew they would need a good soaking and wash but I just wanted to talk to you'.

'Why?' I whispered without looking at him. I dropped the cloth, dried my hands and turned to switch on the kettle. Silently he put his hands on my shoulder and made me face him.

'Because you interest me. You are very unlike girls I normally find myself attracted to – I find you intriguing'.

'You have a very strange way of approaching somebody you are attracted to'.

'Let's make the tea and start again, shall we?'

'But what about your trousers?'

'Wring them out and let me have a plastic bag to carry them in. I only live about a mile away and can easily walk home'.

We made the tea, found some biscuits shoved at the back of the cupboard, and sat down on the sofa in the lounge. We had been particularly lucky to find a flat with decent furniture as most of our friends frequently told us. They spent their time lounging around on dirty, shabby chairs which would have failed any fire-inspection, if they ever took place.

Jake, as his friends called him, then asked me several questions about my life before college and how I had known Jimmy the singer. I started to relax describing my father's musical connections, explaining about the Shack, my mother's successful art career and my siblings' potential career choices. Jennie was getting regular work and Jake had actually seen her in a recent Indie film. Lizzie had found a job after graduating, as a trainee art director at one of the new smaller advertising agencies which were opening up all over London. Charlie was taking his accountancy exams whilst working at one of the big five accountants and was based at London Bridge. I never could remember the name of the firm.

It was my turn to find out about him. As I suspected, he was from just outside Edinburgh across the Forth Bridge but had lived most of his life at South Queensferry. His parents had moved a few years ago. His father was a vet. Another brother was still at school. His mother had been a concert pianist. He and his brother had attended a Rudolf Steiner school in Edinburgh. He loved sport but had broken his leg playing rugby and was encouraged to start rowing to build up his muscles again. From the size of the muscular leg inches from mine this route had been successful. He had rowed for Cambridge earlier that year in the Boat Race. They lost but he didn't seem too worried. I pointed out that sport was not one of my areas of interest although I loved swimming. I was not remotely competitive. He said what he liked most about rowing was that all the guys depended so much on each other. It was very collaborative. He appeared to have a wide circle of friends both male and female. He was a follower of 60s music which is why he was at Jimmy's concert.

We had both relaxed and sat back on the sofa. I was afraid to go too close in case I received further electric shocks but I was supremely aware of his physical presence. I couldn't imagine this god-like creature having any interest in me. This just didn't happen. He was by no means a gentle soul, his remarks could be caustic and some of his judgements seemed harsh but I didn't care. I was half-way in love already. How blind I was. If Varena had been around she would have shown him the door but by the time she returned I was well and truly enthralled. With Yves I had got to know him gradually but Jake was a completely different kettle of fish.

Two hours later and we were stripping off his wet-suit bottoms and I was lying naked under my sheets. It was pure lust and I was loving every minute. We did things to each other with abandon. I had no modesty whatsoever. This was absolute joy. When I reached my climax my whole body was on fire.

I realised I was extremely hungry not having eaten since the morning so we ordered a takeaway and some beers and filled the time waiting for the delivery man with Jake reducing me to a quivering wreck. This was so much better than Yves even though I was only slightly more experienced. Unlike Yves, Jake was far from gentle and he had tremendous control. He delighted in bringing me almost to my climax and then withdrawing so that I was reduced to pleading with him to release my tension and come back to me. He would hover over me tormenting me. When I finally reached my orgasm it was so overpowering I felt my entire body shudder with relief. He had obviously had many sexual encounters and was far more experienced than me.

At 10 o'clock Jake decided he needed to go home. It was probably a good decision. I doubt my body could cope with any more sex. My lips were bruised, my face was red from his stubble and my lower body was something else. I could barely walk.

As he kissed me goodbye Jake whispered 'I always knew you would intrigue me. You have such hidden depths – I will ring you tomorrow', he laughed and waved me goodbye strolling off in his wet-suit bottoms into the night.

When I eventually fell asleep I was dead to the world. It was lucky I had set the alarm for work or I would have still been tucked up by lunchtime. Groaning as I tried to walk, I wandered into the bathroom. I shuddered at the vision. I actually looked as if I had been shagging all night. I showered, washed my sweat soaked hair and searched in Varena's make-up supply for enough to make me look less of a slapper. The eye make-up was wonky but I didn't care. I did look slightly more presentable.

Marie and Tom smiled covertly at each other as I arrived and laughed as I winced when I sat down. How could I be so different when sexually aroused. I was Miss Jekyll and Mrs Hyde. Introverted Zoe had transformed into a sex-addict overnight. It was a struggle to stay upright for most of the day and by lunchtime I was desperate for food and a sit down. I walked around the back with a sandwich and sat in the rickety old deckchair Tom used when he wanted a smoke. It stank but I was pretty oblivious. After eating my sandwich and downing loads of water I found myself drifting off only to be woken by Jake leaning over me and shaking me. I complained he was too rough but he pointed out that it had taken a good five minutes of shaking to arouse me from my stupor.

He said he had needed to see me and couldn't wait until later that day. Oh god, I thought, he wants more sex. I felt certain my sexual organs would need plastic surgery if I kept up that level of activity regularly but I was wrong, he just wanted to see me. I only had a few minutes before I went back on duty. He kissed me very gently (unusual for him) and said he would ring around 7 p.m. waved goodbye and I returned to being happy Miss Wonder Waitress.

We managed to see each other most days and sometimes when our flatmates were out, to have sex, which still continued to be amazing. My loss of concentration was causing consternation in my teachers. I had taken my eye off the ball and Prof Weaver was firmly of the opinion I needed to start stepping up to the mark again. I am sure it was also having an effect on Jake's studies. We needed to talk.

Fate, or rather a deluge of heavy rain from a thunder storm, solved the problem. One evening a terrifying downpour raised the level of the river and Jake's flat, which was in the basement nearby, was flooded. His room was at the back and had the least damage and the other occupants had time to move their belongings into it as the waters rose. They were able to salvage at least their clothes and music systems but the kitchen and lounge were awash. The landlord had offered alternative accommodation which the other two had accepted but Jake felt it was sub-standard and decided not to transfer. The landlord offered him a rebate.

The two girls Varena and I shared with never seemed to be happy at college and one had already dropped out and we were in the process of finding a new share. The other spent more time at her boyfriend's place than she did at our flat so I suggested that maybe Jake would like to rent one of the rooms for the remainder of the academic year. I checked with Varena. She was fine about it. She too was away a lot staying over in town with an old boyfriend who lived in Cambridge. The landlord had no objections so Jake moved in. Problem solved. We wouldn't be chasing all over the town seeing each other, we could both study and work towards our finals and still have sex!

IGNORANCE IS BLISS, OR IS IT?

On one of my trips to check Prof Weaver's answerphone I was standing waiting for the tape to rewind when I heard two girls, sitting on a bench outside chatting. It was a still day, quite warm for late autumn and their voices carried. I recognised the girl Jake had been with at Jimmy's gig.

'I put up with the other girls because I thought deep down that I was the one he really cared for and that sooner or later he would stop seeing them but he dumped me so cruelly with a brief telephone call. It was humiliating. Okay, he never spoke of love, but we were together for almost 12 months. Surely I deserved better treatment'. She was crying and the other girl gave her a handkerchief from her pocket.

I felt guilty at listening to her distress and was about to look out again when Prof Weaver put his head around the door saying he couldn't read my writing on one of the messages. By the time we had finished the two of them had moved off through the quadrangle.

Jake's undoubted good looks had always worried me. I imagined half the women wanting him and the conversation I had overheard hit a chord. Clearly, he had had many other girlfriends during his stay at college and I had just become one more. Would our relationship last or was it just another fling for him? He did not indulge in endearments and was rarely gentle in his lovemaking but he was always willing to make sure I got the most out of our times together. I was falling in love with him but what did he think of me? I was too scared to ask. Varena too had her doubts I knew, but she refrained from voicing them.

Christmas came. I was home in London in the bosom of the family. Jake went back to Edinburgh. He phoned me regularly. My mother was acutely observant and she made it clear that in her eyes I had blossomed into an attractive girl and felt my relationship with Jake had matured my womanhood. Charlie was engaged to a really strange lady he had met at a drinks party. I know my parents weren't keen but preferred to let things go along (Charlie did marry Helen but the marriage was doomed with him moving out within six months). Dad had just come back from Los Angeles and seemed quite exhausted.

It was the first time Jennie had managed to spend some time with us. Her career had taken off. She had appeared in two major blockbuster films and was reading for auditions all over the place. She had done a 'chemistry reading' just before Xmas with a young actor we all fancied. It always made me laugh. Chemistry reading - it sounded like a dreary chat in a laboratory. Jennie pointed out laughingly that the best audition she ever had was with an actor who left her feeling absolutely cold. She was amazed when she was offered the part. Obviously, she was an extremely good actor. She felt it was fortunate that funding dried up on the project.

At times she seemed quite sad. When I asked what was worrying her she pointed out that an actor's life is so transient and made it difficult for relationships. She had gone out with an American actor she met on set for a few months while she was working but when the film was 'wrapped', she returned to the UK and he stayed put. She had tried to seek work based in the UK for some stability but this had limited her choices. So many projects were now being filmed on location and with less studio work.

Frances, too, spent weeks away working on different film sets. She was responsible for continuity, whatever that meant. Her attention to detail had always been a defining part of her character so I imagine that role would be perfect for her. She was also engaging with all the other specialisms that combine to make successful programmes. She was seeing a cameraman at the time.

The Xmas period passed by so quickly and is one of the most memorable in a long list of happy times with my family. We had all toasted and recalled our memories of dear Rosy who had died in November. I saw her one last time at the hospice and was shocked at how thin and drained she looked. My Mum had nursed her at home but had finally accepted Rosy needed better palliative care so, reluctantly, Rosy was moved to a beautiful Victorian house overlooking Clapham Common for her final days. After she died, I cried myself to sleep for several nights wrapped up in Jake's arms.

Jake and I had agreed to return to the flat early in the New Year but he had nearly killed himself getting drunk at Hogmanay. He had fallen off a bar stool, smashed his head open and had to visit A&E for stitches to the nasty gash and was kept in overnight with a bad concussion. I am sure in these days of mobile phones he would have sent me a ghastly picture to look at. Fortunately for me no such technology was available. I was extremely squeamish and the amount of blood he had lost was awe inspiring. Our return was delayed but we managed one night at the flat before Varena and our other flatmate arrived back.

Living together with other flat sharers, out of respect for them, our sex life had toned down slightly. It is not endearing listening to your house mates having rampant sex. I had stopped work at the café and Jake was not rowing so much in the bitterly cold weather. The minute the flat was empty of the others we would indulge in our favourite sport with relish. It was one particular Saturday afternoon in the early part of January, after an hour of unrestrained activity, that Jake realised his condom had split slightly. Today I would have gone for the morning after pill but it was not available as an option. We sat on the bed and agreed it was time I visited the Family Planning Clinic to get the pill.

Varena, Jake and I took our studies seriously so the months leading up to the finals were a more sober time with all of us revising. I still visited Prof every day to sort out his messages and he gave me some extra lessons as a thank you. We were very calm and I felt much more secure in my relationship. Truth be told Jake had little opportunity to pursue other females. When we weren't in lectures or study sessions we were living together at the flat. Now I no longer worked at the café and with his rowing restricted by the weather, we practically spent our entire lives together. Varena and Jake seemed to have reached a compromise in their relationship too. If she was still dubious about him she never spoke to me about it.

Two things happened before my exams. My father had a heart attack and I missed my period. My distraught Mum had rung early one Sunday morning to say he was in St George's Hospital. Jake and I rushed up to London on the first train out and went by underground to Wimbledon. Mum collected us from the station. She had been told to go home as Dad was heavily sedated and she had been with him most of the night. She had been reassured he would be okay.

Throughout the morning Charlie, Lizzie and Frances turned up. Jennie was filming in America and was waiting to hear if Dad was OK before she booked a flight back. For the first time in my life Mum was not on top of the situation. Although they were both extremely demonstrative with us, their relationship always seemed more like good friends than husband and wife. It was casually affectionate. Dad's heart attack had totally disrupted this calm state of affairs. She did not cry but looked at us all with a haunted desperate despair. They were both strong characters but now I realised they were a true partnership.

We were all pretty much useless. Jake took charge making cups of tea and walking down the road to get some milk. This was his first meeting with the family and nothing about our disarray fazed him. Amazingly Charlie did not object to Jake taking this role. He seemed to have lost his need to control. Charlie would normally have been the one reassuring the girls, but not this time.

It was Jake who sat with Mum when she rang the hospital. She had only ever spoken to him on the phone at Christmas. He held her hand, which she couldn't stop shaking, and when she heard that Dad was going to pull through, he stopped her from collapsing into a heap on the floor. This was a side to him I had never witnessed. We were told Dad could have visitors one at a time later on that day so Jake suggested he stay at home and, when we were leaving to come back, ring him and he would order a take-away Indian from our favourite curry-house up the road. We all chose what we wanted even though Mum said she didn't think she would be hungry.

Charlie drove off with Mum and Lizzie. Frances and I held back for a further half-hour knowing how awful it was to park at the hospital. Dad was never ill and I felt strangely reluctant about visiting him. I was envisaging him all linked up to machines. I am glad I knew nothing about the fact that they had used the electric paddles to restart his heart.

We must have driven around the car park six times before we found a space. Neither Frances nor I were good at parking and it seemed all the available ones were for cars half the size of her Volvo. She carried a lot of boxes around for work so it was a big estate. I had to scramble over to her side of the car to get out.

We met Charlie and Lizzie on their way out. Mum was waiting until we arrived. Both of them looked better. Apparently, Dad had a stent inserted into his artery in the morning but would need to have a by-pass once he had recovered. Frances kissed them and said we would meet back at the house with Mum. Frances' excellent sense of direction got us to the ward in no time. Dad was in a small room off the main section. The nurses let both of us go in.

I had to control my shock when I looked at Dad. He was deathly pale and his cheeks were sunken. His thick dark hair seemed to have gone grey overnight and hung over his ears. He still refused to have it cut, often wearing it in a ponytail. Frances held my hand and we put on our brightest smiles. This didn't fool Dad for one moment and he insisted we come either side of him for a cuddle. Mum looked exhausted. We had to be careful as we moved close to him as he was still wired up. I managed to settle myself next to him desperately trying to avoid strangling myself with the drip. Frances took his hand opposite me.

'You are not to worry about me you two. I am going to be fine. I am determined to leave this hospital as soon as I can. You know how I hate them'.

'Zoe, you need to get back to Cambridge and work for those

finals. Can't waste three years of your life by flunking them now. The doctors have said I can go home in a couple of days. Mum tells me your bloke Jake is a good sort and has been really helpful but both of you need to go. Lizzie has said she will take some leave and be with Mum until I get back home'.

We could all see that the effort of cheering us up was draining what little energy he had, so we decided it was time to go. We cuddled and kissed him and left Mum to say her own farewell and waited in the corridor. We just beat the nurse who came along to say we needed to leave Dad to rest.

Mum joined us. For a family who spent their lives chatting, the silence walking back to the car was weird. But what could we say to support Mum? She had always been a realist and I think she could see big changes were ahead of us all. Dad's frenetic lifestyle may well have caused his heart problems. I found the phone boxes near the exit and rang home. Jake said he would put the food order through. We would call in and collect on our way back.

Ali handed over six bags of assorted curries, rice, poppadums, naan bread and several bottles of Kingfisher beer and we loaded them into the car. Frances complained laughingly that it would make the car stink for weeks.

Lizzie and Jake had laid up the table and put the plates on to warm up. I flung my coat down and he took my hand, then enveloped me in a large hug. I was momentarily taken aback. He was not the demonstrative type at all. This was another awakening. How much more was I going to learn about Jake?

Although she had said she wouldn't be able to eat, Mum realised she was actually very, very, hungry even finishing off some of the spare curry. Jake had found a frozen cheesecake in the fridge and had defrosted it for our pudding. The beers helped to reduce our tension. I was sorry Dad couldn't be with us. He so loved our family gatherings.

Jake had taken several calls from friends who had heard the news about Dad's heart attack. He seemed quite impressed with some of the famous names that he had written down. Chatting at the table he said he envied us our big family. His brother was several years younger and his parents rarely sat down for meals. Being a vet meant his father was frequently called away at meal times so mostly it was just his mother and the two boys.

By 10 o'clock we were all completely knackered. Mum suggested Jake and I make up the bed in the spare room so we duly trundled off, found some sheets, and literally collapsed into a heap on the bed. I lay thinking about the day with Jake snoring lightly in my ear until I drifted off. I woke around 5 a.m. and it was still very dark. I watched Jake sleep by the light of the clock-radio. I needed him very badly and kissed his cheek. He stirred and pulled me towards him. I wanted to feel alive. I buried my head in his chest to smother my gasp as he brought me to my climax. I realised I was crying and he bent to lick the tears away.

After breakfast Charlie dropped us off at the station and we caught a train to London, crossed over to Kings Cross by tube, and then the fast to Cambridge. We watched the Hertfordshire countryside give way to the flatter Cambridgeshire fields, holding hands but saying very little. I wanted to let Jake know how much I appreciated his kindness of the last few days but somehow, I felt it was not necessary. Our connection was so deep that we rarely needed to speak.

I had telephoned Varena to let her know the doctors felt Dad would make a good recovery following his by-pass operation later on in the month. We stopped off in Cambridge town for a quick snack. I had warned Prof that I might not be around to answer his messages but decided to call in on him before going home to the flat. Jake went on ahead.

I knocked and put my head around Prof's door to find him staring out of the window. He seemed to be completely oblivious of me. Very slowly he turned round trying to focus. I had only once seen this happen before and it took him several moments to gather his thoughts well enough to speak. Today was much longer. After five minutes I moved towards him and took his hand very gently. He put his feet firmly down on the floor and pushed his wheeled chair away from me and started to shake. He had continued to hold my hand so I was dragged forward towards him. I stretched out to get hold of his desk with my free hand to stop myself falling headlong into him.

This activity seemed to bring him back to reality and I disentangled myself and stood waiting to see if he recognised me.

'Zoe, Zoe, why are you here? Your father, your father, is he alright, is he alright?' He repeated over and over.

I pulled the chair I used when we had tutorials towards me and sat down. The wrinkled old hand I was still holding had started to shake and soon his whole body was reacting in the same way. I looked around for a glass of water and saw a jug on the window ledge. Dropping his hand, I filled a glass and held it for him to drink. He gulped down a few mouthfuls and then moved his head back. Without his glasses I noticed his deep brown eyes.

'My father will be fine Prof. He has had a stent inserted and they plan to give him a by-pass operation later. He told me to come back and finish my studies. I was on my way home past the college and decided to call in and sort your messages.' I was trying to sound as calm as possible but frankly I was really worried.

The shaking was less violent. I was now holding both his hands and he made no attempt to take them away again.

We sat in silence listening to his old clock ticking away. Finally, I decided I needed to mention what had just happened.

'I don't want to be intrusive Prof, but have you had other incidents like today before?'

He raised his eyes to mine and I could see them watering. He had stopped shaking and his breathing was more normal.

'Yes, yes, Zoe. I have had them since my return in 1945 when I travelled to South Wales to find my brother dead. I have no idea what it is that causes my blackouts nor do the doctors. I don't have epilepsy although the symptoms are very similar. Just when I think they have disappeared something happens to trigger an episode'.

I can't imagine what anybody walking in to the room would have thought. Me sitting close up to the Prof holding both his hands could easily have been misinterpreted. This realisation made me slowly draw back.

'Will you be OK or should I call somebody?'

'There is nobody to call', came the muffled reply. 'I will just sit here for a short while and then get on with my marking and you should go home. You only have a few weeks before the exam season starts'.

'I will just check your answerphone before I go'. I realised this would give me more time to ensure he was okay without actually sitting in front of him.

There were two days' worth of messages but none of them urgent so I wrote them on the pad and cleaned down the tape. I wondered what would happen when I finished college. Would somebody else help? I ought to look around the group and see if some kind soul could be persuaded to continue on the job.

I handed him the list of messages and walked to the door turning to make sure he seemed alright.

'Thank you, Zoe. I will be fine, off you go'.

Varena yelled from the shower and told me to come and fill her in on Dad's health. I closed the lid on the loo, sat down and briefly sketched out what we had done for the two days.

'Sounds like Jake was very resourceful. I seem to underestimate him. I wonder if it is because he is so beautiful. He certainly isn't shallow. So many deeply attractive men behave like complete arses to women'.

'Has he been home?'

'No, I haven't seen him and I have been around since lunchtime'.

I suddenly felt quite tired. I didn't mention Prof's episode feeling it would not be right to discuss it with Varena.

'Is there any food in that I can make myself some supper?'

'Loads of eggs and some frozen chips but not much else. I forgot to shop today'.

'Any bread?'

'Might be a few slices'. Varena grabbed a towel and sat down on the edge of the bath rubbing her hair vigorously.

We ended up with scrambled eggs on toast. By 8 o'clock I was getting worried about Jake and rang his old flatmate Carl but he hadn't seen or heard from him. The phone eventually rang just after 10 and I rushed to grab it.

'Zoe, I met up with some of the rowing crowd and have had a lot to drink. I think I will sleep on the couch here rather than come home now. I will come back tomorrow. Shall I call in and get some food from the local store?'

It was almost as if we hadn't spent two of the most dramatic days in our relationship, his call was so mundane. I really was quite dumbfounded, mumbling that we could do with some bacon, bread and mushrooms for breakfast. Oh, and maybe some fresh coffee. He said he would do that and rang off. I was really tired, rang my Mum to find out the latest news and then dropped into bed. I found myself tossing from side to side and finally gave up, turned the light on and found a book to read. Jake had been so great. Maybe I should have thanked him more profusely. Something had gone wrong but I couldn't work out what it was.

I crawled back into bed around 3 o'clock and was still fast asleep when Jake arrived back. I woke to the smell of bacon cooking and fresh coffee. Varena was already sitting at the table chatting with Jake who had an apron on cooking some eggs. The smell was welcoming but suddenly my stomach churned and I had to rush to the loo. I felt the bile in my mouth and I was sick, really sick. When I was sure I wasn't going to puke any further I stood and filled a glass with some water and gulped it down.

I had an appointment the day before for the family planning clinic but had missed this in our rush to London to visit

Dad however, it was blindingly obvious to me that I was pregnant. My breasts had been sore and I had missed one period. I had never been regular so hadn't been too concerned until a few more weeks had passed and nothing happened. I sat on the toilet wondering what on earth I was going to do.

Varena knocked on the door and asked if I was alright. I splashed my face and opened the door.

'Yes, I am fine. Must have been something I ate yesterday'. As I had eaten the same food with Jake at lunchtime and with Varena last night and neither of them had been sick this was a pretty lame excuse but she nodded and went back to the kitchen. I followed on behind her and Jake gave me a penetrating look but decided not to question me. He kissed the top of my head and pulled out a chair for me to sit. I drank the coffee but rejected the food, sticking with a piece of toast. Jake explained that he was talking to the crew and they were planning to get back on the water. He would need to get fitter and go back in the gym. He rarely asked my approval of any of his plans, always appearing to accept that I would be compliant and raise no objection. Today was no different. I said I would go shopping with Varena to get some food in. I wondered if he was going to totally ignore the fact that I had been sick and what this implied. I needed time to myself too as the realisation that I was pregnant was a blow to all my plans.

Jake showered and went off to the gym, Varena and I walked to the shops. It was no good I couldn't conceal my discovery and told her I thought I was pregnant.

'Well, thinking is not the same as knowing', she replied. 'We need to go to the chemist and get a test. We can work out what to do after that. I take it that Jake doesn't know?'

'I only realised it myself this morning although I have noticed some changes in my body shape and my breasts have been sore'. I couldn't really tell Varena that sometimes my breasts were painful after particularly active love-making. Jake was rarely gentle.

'I will need to talk to him this afternoon but frankly I am dreading his response'. We have never discussed the future as in terms of 'us'. It had always been that he would go off back-packing after graduation, before settling down to look for a job, and I would spend a month in Europe and then start looking at vacancies on my return. We were aware that most environmental scientists worked on projects overseas. I think I knew deep down what Jake's attitude would be to the baby's arrival.

The pregnancy test was positive. I sat on Varena's bed with tears of despair streaming down my face. How had my bright future become this dreadful prospect? She hugged me and coughing slightly said 'You could have an abortion'.

It took me a while to stop crying. Blowing my nose, I shook my head. I couldn't do that. We had often discussed abortion and women's rights at home. My mother had been an active campaigner and had been delighted when David Steel's Bill was approved in the House of Commons. No more back-street abortions. She would defend my right to choose but I knew this was not a course of action I could take, even if that was what Jake wanted.

I was lucky Varena was such a close friend. My mother would have been supportive but, with Dad ill, I couldn't land my problems on her shoulders too.

Jake returned in the early afternoon and Varena made herself scarce. I was hunched up over the sink washing up and turned around to face him. He pulled me towards him and hugged me gently whilst stroking my hair. My nose was pressed into his chest and my head fitted neatly under his chin. Without saying anything he picked me up and took me into the bedroom.

'You are pregnant, aren't you?' He whispered very quietly. When I nodded he took my hand and raised it to his lips. Looking back afterwards, I think he needed time to find the right words to say to me. He lay back against the wall pulling me against him. I struggled to look him in the face. When I finally plucked up the courage, I could read the confusion in his eyes.

'Before you say anything Jake, I must tell you that I refuse to consider an abortion'.

'I wouldn't have asked you to have one but I am struggling to work out where this leaves us'.

I could have stayed wrapped up in his arms for ever. He was my rock. Oh, hang on, so far, he hadn't actually said a word that would give me any reassurance that we were in this predicament together.

'Do you love me Zoe?'

'Yes, I think I do. Why is that relevant?'

He swallowed and looked down at me. Very quietly he said 'Because I am not sure I love you enough to give up my plans. I have lived my life up to now with one big aim and that is to see the world and work overseas using my skills. I am not ready to settle down with a family, even if it is with you'.

I extricated myself and got up. My heart was racing and I felt slightly nauseous.

'We always knew that after graduation we would be going our separate ways'.

'So, I am just a college fling to be discarded at the end of term and my pregnancy is just a minor complication. You act as if you had no part in this activity' I shouted at him.

'I do have a responsibility and I freely accept it but I cannot, just cannot, give up my dreams'.

'But it is okay for me to pass up on my career, though?' I screamed. The urge to hit him was so hard I had to press my hands down my side to stop myself from lashing out.

As if he understood my fury he took hold of both hands and dragged me back to the bed. 'I am so sorry Zoe, I don't want to hurt you any more but I would regret not going and might even come to resent you for making me stay'. As ever he was being brutally honest. He had never promised we had a future. He hadn't lied to me in this respect. I knew my anger was futile. I was too devastated to cry. I was mute with loss. He kissed my face and stroked my hair and before I knew what was happening I found myself aroused and was responding. It felt as if I wanted to absorb him and make him a part of me so he couldn't leave. We didn't even manage to remove our clothes such was the urgency.

We made love, but this time was different, oh so different. We were gentle with each other. It was almost as if we were scared to hurt the foetus. His gentleness was almost more difficult to cope with. It unnerved me. It was like a farewell. Our unrestrained sexual joy in each other was a thing of the past. Responsibility for the little being I carried had become paramount. For me at least.

Days of discussion followed and finally it was agreed that he would not leave the country until after the baby was born.

We both needed to finish our degrees even if mine would be lost to single-motherhood. It was only a few weeks until the exam season started. Jake spent more time away from the flat either studying, visiting the gym or rowing. Varena became my replacement rock. I couldn't burden my parents with my pregnancy even though Dad was on the mend. I planned to go home for Easter and tell them. Jake was flying to Edinburgh. He had offered to come with me but I needed to see my parents alone, so I refused.

Being slim, my pregnancy was starting to show. I could no longer wear jeans and changed to loose-fitting smocks and elasticated waisted skirts. We found some pretty tops in the large Oxfam shop in the city centre.

I hadn't found anybody to replace me, after my departure, to help out Prof Weaver. On one visit I had got soaked and arrived with my clothes clinging to me. My pregnancy was obvious. I rushed in to the office and flung myself into the book room hoping he would be buried in his paperwork. Some days he barely spoke. I was hoping that would be the case today.

Writing down the messages, I felt him standing behind me.

'When were you going to tell me about your pregnancy?' He asked.

'I was hoping to be able to conceal it for a few more months until after the exams but my body decided otherwise. Being pregnant wasn't what I planned'.

'Fate often does that you know. Come and sit down and talk to me'. It seemed bizarre that I should be discussing pregnancy with this elderly professor but it was almost as if a dam had broken. I explained about Jake's decision to continue his career out of the country; that he would remain with me until the baby was born.

'Have you spoken to your parents?'

'No, it is too close to my Dad's heart attack. I just couldn't load something else on their shoulders. I am going home for Easter and will speak to them then'.

'Will they be supportive?'

'Oh yes, but I also know they will be enormously disappointed too. All my siblings have been successful in their careers and my parents are very proud of them'.

'Life rarely goes along in straight lines. I never envisaged going to war, becoming a prisoner and, on my return, finding my pacifist brother dead. It should have been me. I had wanted to get married and have children but the woman I planned to marry realised I had changed. She married a German prisoner of war who had been helping on her parents' farm'.

Professor Weaver had put on an electric fire to warm me up and partially dry off my clothes. He had made me a cup of tea and I was hugging my hands around the cup. The whole place was an oasis of peace and calm. For two years I had visited it daily during term time and I was going to miss it. Prof had become part of my life and his quiet presence seemed to envelope me as I sat there. He didn't offer any advice, he just let me sit. He let me be.

'Taking a degree is not just about getting the requisite knowledge to get a job, you know. It is much more than that. It opens up your mind and helps you make sense of the world even if it appears chaotic at times. Your study will never be wasted. You will draw on your experience for years to come'.

'I guess you are right Prof but just at the moment I am struggling to concentrate. What is happening to my body is overpowering'.

'When is the baby due?'

'October'.

'Well you have quite a few months ahead when you can make decisions after your exams. Useless worry at the moment will get you nowhere'.

I thought of dear Rosy and knew she would be saying the same thing. It reminded me of the night after her funeral when I had cried myself to sleep in Jake's arms. Although not generally demonstrative, at times of crisis, he would step up to the plate.

'You are right Prof. By the way I still haven't found a young student who will help out when I leave'.

'Ah, I think you will be the first to know that I have decided to retire at the end of the summer term'.

'Really, but what will you do?' I had imagined he would be teaching for many years to come.

'Well, at 73 it is time I handed over to somebody younger. When my father retired, I moved my parents to a small house on the Broads. After they died, I rented it out to a friend of theirs on condition I could keep my dinghy in the garden so I could sail at the weekends'.

'Wow – do you still sail?' I wondered if he had any blackouts when sailing but didn't say so.

'No, not for several years now but I spend many weekends birdwatching near the water. The house needs some renovation but will hopefully be ready for me to move into in late summer. My elderly tenant has had to go into a home in the city'.

It was starting to get dark so I got up to leave. I promised I would try and put my woes behind me until I really needed to make decisions. He told me to let him know if there was any way he could help.

Walking home I felt calmer. My childhood had been happy and unchallenging but in adolescence Rosy had been only too willing to offer me advice. Now at college I knew Varena was there for me too. I laughed to myself. Who would have thought that my elderly professor would also offer his support! Prof was right. First things first. Get that degree and then… well that was in the lap of the gods.

I think Jake was surprised that we didn't talk more often about what would happen after the exams but I realised I needed to avoid negative thoughts to get me through this bad patch. It was difficult enough thinking about my trip back home for Easter. I knew there was no way I would change his mind. Men like Jake don't compromise.

When we were at home in the flat and Jake was studying at the table I would look at him and wonder what I could do to make him love me enough to remain in the UK.

EASTER

Mum collected me at Wimbledon. I had a coat on and so my pregnancy wouldn't be immediately obvious. She regaled me with all the news. Lizzie had a really nice new man, Frances had been promoted and Jennie was home at the moment so we would have a chance to catch up. Charlie hadn't been in touch for a while but she didn't seem worried. Dad's by-pass operation had been a success and he had been commissioned to put together a new soundtrack. This was much less challenging work and Mum felt it would be good for him to be occupied.

I was somewhat relieved to see Mum was her usual calm self. She was letting her grey hair grow out and there were small white streaks mixed in. I had never thought of her as beautiful but her bone structure had become more defined as she got older, making her look distinguished. I wondered if Lizzie could be persuaded to do a portrait for us. She had painted Dad playing guitar in the Shack years ago and it was hung above the instruments on the stage.

We lived in South Wimbledon in what I always thought of as rather like the Addams family home. It was late Victorian, detached, red brick and had two turret rooms on either side of the front entrance. The hallway was pure magic. During the renovations, we had uncovered a beautiful mosaic tiled floor which had been protected by the grubby old carpet.

Dad came out to greet me. His face had filled out and he had a healthy glow. I grabbed him and felt I would never let go. It was time to remove my coat. Mum had walked ahead into the kitchen. I looked Dad straight in the eye opened the flap of my coat and placed his hand on my swelling stomach. He shot me a look wonderingly then his eyes widened in shock.

'Oh my love, how many months?' He whispered.

'Three at least but we aren't actually sure of the dates'.

'Is Jake happy with this?'

I shook my head silently. Mum called out to ask us why we were whispering in the hall and I turned to walk towards the kitchen. She took one look at me and lifted her hand to her mouth. She rushed forward and pulled me into her arms. Dad followed after me.

'Why haven't you told us before?' She asked.

'I could hardly add to your problems until I knew Dad was on the mend'.

'and Jake?'

'He doesn't love me enough to put his future plans on hold. He has been kind but there is no chance of him changing his mind'.

'Why isn't he here with you?' Dad retorted angrily!

'I didn't want him to come Dad. I need to be with you. He isn't going to be around after the baby is born. He has agreed to stay until October but I need to work out my life without him. He is talking to his parents to see if they will advance him some money to support me whilst he is travelling. He has promised to send money when he starts work wherever he is. I am hoping it will be alright with you if I move back

70

until the baby is born. I need to get my degree so I have put any decisions about my future on the back-burner, until after the exams'.

Mum had made some tea whilst Dad and I were talking in the hall and we sat down at the kitchen table. I was still holding on to his hand. I felt a bit silly so quickly pulled it away. He placed my hand back on the table and covered it with his own.

When I had suggested I return home I noticed Mum glance at Dad then drop her eyes and turn round to pick up the mugs.

'We were planning to tell you all at Easter that we have decided to sell the house and move. It is far too large for the two of us especially now Dad no longer needs the Shack' she said.

'Where were you planning to move to?' I asked.

'East Anglia'.

We had spent many summer holidays renting converted barns in Suffolk and Norfolk when we were children. Other times we had travelled to Denmark, and Zeeland. The light was perfect for Mum to paint so I wasn't surprised at this suggestion. It was always a struggle to return to the metropolis with its noise and pollution after summers away in the peaceful surroundings of the coast. It had not been discovered by the 'Chelsea by the Sea' gang and was still relatively undeveloped and perfect for our needs. We had all struggled along the breakwater ridge carrying Mum's collapsible easel and chair to get out to the sea at Burnham Overy Staithe so she could paint while we played in pools or ran the miles to get to the distant water.

'When did you plan to do this?' I asked, when I had recovered from the shock. I always thought my parents would live in London for ever. This was silly because I had known that Dad's heart attack would change the balance of their life. Both of them had careers which would continue wherever they lived.

'Sometime in early May but we may delay until the baby is born. We have had the house valued and it will be enough to buy a slightly smaller place and still have quite a good deal of money left over. Property here is very much in demand. It won't be such a wrench as many of our friends have already moved away'. Mum replied.

'We plan to look around in the next week or so after Easter. You will be welcome to come and live with us of course. I am quite looking forward to my first grandchild'. Mum gave me a beaming smile and leant over to touch my shoulder.

At this point, before I could say any more Jennie breezed into the room. She had obviously been in the shower and not heard us arrive. She flung herself at me and wrapped her arms around my neck from behind. Kissing my cheek she looked down.

'Oh lord what is that bump, Zoekins?' She yelped and lent round to grab a chair. 'How long have you been pregnant and am I the last to know?'

We all started to say 'No'. Mum explained that this was news to them both before I had a chance to respond.

'I was just asking if I could come home and live when Mum told me their news'.

'About their move?' She said.

'Yes, it is quite a shock but actually just the right thing to do now I think about it. It is nice to be here at celebration times with us all around but the rest of the time Mum and Dad must be rattling around the place'.

Jennie was the only member of the family not to have met Jake and all she knew about him was from Mum and occasionally a remark from me in our calls. When she wasn't filming we spent hours catching up. Because of this she hesitated to ask the next question.

'Before you ask, Jake is not going to allow the arrival of the baby to interrupt his plans, so I am looking at the realms of single-motherhood not long after graduating'.

I could see she was confused as Mum must have told her how caring Jake had been on our visit after Dad's heart attack.

The phone rang and Jennie raced off to answer it. It was her agent and she spent some time chatting to him and writing notes as he was speaking. When she put the phone down she muttered about needing a secretary.

Easter came and we had the egg hunt on the Sunday although only Lizzie, Jennie and I were at home. I had many discussions with the girls about my options. What could I do to bring in some money? Lizzie suggested I do some translations when I came down at the end of my exams. She offered to get a copywriter at work to write up some blurb and she would do the artwork. I could then compile a list of local companies and mail them offering my services. I had no idea if there was such a need locally, but then, we suddenly stopped. Could I do this in East Anglia? Surely, I would need to be near a city. Norwich was growing and obviously Cambridge was expanding rapidly. Would I be able to persuade Mum and Dad to live further inland?

I returned to college feeling much more energized. The girls had shown me that I wouldn't have to ask for state help as soon as the baby was born. I went for my twelve week scan and Jake came along too. The young woman carrying out the scan took one look at Jake and almost became a shivering wreck. I looked from her to him and wondered how I had managed to have any sort of relationship with such a beautiful creature. All was well and we went out for a meal afterwards.

'I have spoken to Dad. He was not impressed by my desire to continue with my plans but has reluctantly agreed to advance me £6,000 so that I can support you whilst I travel'. He had rested his hand on my leg and I felt an immediate response. My body continued to betray me. What will I do when he isn't around? I felt tears well up but quickly blinked them away. I was not going to be pathetic.

'I will pay him back when I get a job'.

I was too cowardly to ask what happened when he stopped his travels. Would he come back to me? Would he ask us to join him? As Professor Weaver had said there was plenty of time so why worry needlessly. My way forward was to pass my exams, nothing else mattered.

It was good that Jake had returned to rowing and training because the atmosphere at the flat was not pleasant. Helen had moved back in having broken off with her boyfriend but she did not have finals until next year and Varena was extremely cross. Cross with me for letting Jake get away with his behaviour and furious with Jake for his callousness. I pointed out to her that he had never lied to me. He had always made it clear he would depart off on his travels as soon as he had his results. Now, he was at least staying until after the birth.

'That is some consolation' she expostulated! 'What a selfish brat. It is immoral. Departing off to swan around the world and leave you to bring up his child alone'. She realised that she was not helping the situation and stopped. Putting her arm around me she mumbled an apology and said she hoped my patience would pay off and he would come back to us.

I had extra revision with Prof and he had kept me up to date with his plans. I told him of my parents' desire to move to East Anglia too. He gave me details of villages that they should avoid but also many more that might fit the bill. They already had buyers for our house who were happy to wait until they found their perfect move. They were moving back to the UK from France just before Christmas.

My exam dates were earlier than Varena and Jake's. I had already done one paper. I was surprised at how relaxed I was. Jake was much less so. He was grumpy and offhand so I kept well out of his way spending more time in the library. Confident Varena thoroughly enjoyed her first exam. She absorbed facts with such ease.

When he wasn't studying, Jake spent large amounts of time in the gym. After my final exam I went into town to get a couple of maternity dresses as I was expanding considerably. As I stood waiting for the bus home I saw Jake sitting in the café opposite. I was about to cross over and bang on the window when I noticed a girl was sitting down with a drink. It was his old girlfriend. He put his hand out and took hers. Before I could think about moving away he turned and looked straight at me. He was too far away for me to see his reaction but I know he had seen me.

A bus arrived and I jumped on so I never knew if he had come out to speak to me. Running to the flat with tears pouring down my face I arrived just as Varena came back from another exam. She took one look at me and shoved me through the door and into the lounge.

'I was in town and I saw Jake with his old girlfriend holding her hand. I was at the bus stop'. I was sobbing and my face was wet with tears that wouldn't stop.

'Here is a tissue and wipe your face. Take some deep breaths'.

I looked around the flat and knew I couldn't stay. I couldn't face seeing him again. I told Varena I was going to pack a bag and go home. I would collect my things later with Mum after Jake had left the flat. He only had one exam to go. I would ring Prof Weaver and let him know I was going home. We had arranged he would let me have his new address in Norfolk when he moved and I had given him my parents' address and phone number. I couldn't face him either.

We slung some clothes in a suitcase and Varena ordered a taxi. She offered to pack up the rest of my things if Mum wanted to drive up and collect them. After two hours I was on the train to London. I had stopped crying. He was never going to make me cry again.

Varena rang Mum to tell her what was happening. She had an evening engagement at a show in Bond Street but would meet me at Wimbledon. Dad was away. I was in a cold fury by the time I came out of the tube station. It is impossible to park nearby so we had a special place where Mum would collect us. The journey had brought realisation. So many visits to the gym, drinking with the crew. Our sexual activity had dried up, not because he was afraid of hurting our baby, he was being offered an alternative. His consideration was not through love, but guilt. What a stupid fool I had been.

She was at our usual place. I put my bag on the back seat, opened the door and kissed her cheek. She took my hand

and drew it to her mouth.

'I am angry that I have to go to this event but I will get home as soon as I can' she promised. 'Varena did not tell me what has happened but you can let me know when I get home. We will get through this'.

'I know we will but just now I need to eat and relax. I hadn't fancied the dried-up sandwiches on offer on the train and the coffee had been stewed'.

'I remember that feeling, I was eating the whole time when I was pregnant. There is cold chicken and loads of salad in the fridge and plenty of fruit. Ring Varena too – she left a number and it is on the pad'.

She dropped me off and I rummaged in my bag for my keys. I waved her away blowing her a kiss and turned to open the door. As I walked in, I heard the phone ring in the distance and then heard the answer machine click in with its message. The voice at the end of the line was Jake's.

'Hello Sarah, has Zoe arrived home? I really need to speak to her so could you ask her to ring me. I am at the flat. Thank you'.

I had to eat some food as I was feeling very shaky and I was dying to pee. After I had completed both activities, I rang the number Varena had left.

'Hello, Varena Hesketh' came the answer.

'Varena. I am home. Mum dropped me off. Sorry I haven't rung sooner but I needed to eat. I have a message from Jake on the answerphone. Have you seen him?'

'Oh yes, I have. He was home when I got back from the station. He wanted to know where you were. I told him you had left and were on your way home to Wimbledon and that you wouldn't be returning now that your exams were finished'.

'What was his response?' I asked.

'She can't be serious. We have so much to discuss'.

'Seeing you holding hands with your ex didn't help, frankly,' she had shouted at him. 'The last thing Zoe needs is you messing her around still further. Your decision to go travelling is bad enough, without her having to know you are betraying her with other women too. What kind of arrogant brute are you?'

'So you didn't mince your words then' I laughed. Her fury had released my tension and I was mildly hysterical. 'You really are the best of friends, defending me. I need to start looking after myself from now on so I can assure you I won't be answering his calls. He has already rung here'.

'I know I heard him making the call. I told him I doubted you would be ringing back anytime soon. To be fair he seemed genuinely upset'.

We agreed we would speak again when I had settled back in. I would need to arrange for my parents to collect my belongings which had grown quite considerably since my arrival two and a half years ago. I was longing for my safety quilt.

I never spoke to Jake before he left college. My mother cleared his many messages off before I heard them but, strangely, she never removed the very first one. I missed the end of term balls – I had nobody to go with and would have had to buy a maternity ball gown to attend. For the same reason I didn't attend the graduation which was very sad for my parents. Not very impressive watching their heavily pregnant daughter stumble up on the stage to collect her first class Honours degree. They had cleared everything from the flat. Jake had moved out so there was no problem. Varena, thrilled with her result, was going to spend some time at her grandparents before flying to India. She would pass a few days with me before catching her flight from Heathrow.

Time seemed to have come to a halt. The only thing changing was my waistline. One day, when Mum was out and Jake had long since stopped trying to speak to me, I answered the phone. It was a soft-spoken woman with a slight Scottish accent. I had never met Elspeth, Jake's Mum, but I knew it was her. Our conversations at the flat had been minor, mostly message taking, when he was out. I sometimes listened to his calls. He clearly was very fond of her.

'Hello Zoe, its Elspeth, Jake's Mum, please don't hang up. I need to talk to you'.

'I am not sure why', I replied.

'Because I know my son has behaved badly to you and I am so distressed that he has done so. My husband and I both want you to know that we want to support you'.

I couldn't imagine what help a couple, based near Edinburgh, could offer to a single mum in Wimbledon, but I let her finish.

'Jake has gone to France on a short consultancy trip but he will be back and we want to make sure that we have agreed how to support you financially before he departs to South America. I know you are refusing to talk to him and frankly, I don't blame you, so I am hoping talking to me will be easier'.

'I am living at my parents, so I doubt I will have financial difficulties'.

'I know that, but Jake must shoulder his responsibility towards you and the baby not just now but long-term. He cannot behave as if neither of you exist. He is at fault here. I doubt I should be saying this as it feels like a betrayal but his desire to follow his dreams at all cost is wrong, plain wrong'.

'Elspeth, the problem is that he doesn't love me or feel enough for me to stay and would resent us stopping him from achieving his ambitions. I cannot deal with that so my only option is to let him go and I move on with our child on my own'.

'I know how strong minded he is but he must not walk away without acknowledging the need to look after you both. This is our first grandchild too and we want to be part of your lives'. She asked if she could ring me from time to time and I told her I didn't mind.

Slowly life returned to normal. I wrote a long letter to Prof Weaver apologising for my abrupt departure. He replied enclosing an invite to his leaving party. He said it would be a rather dry affair but would be so pleased to see me. We had already made several outings to East Anglia looking at property so we decided to make another visit and drive back via Cambridge. There was a nice hotel just on the outskirts.

That day my overriding concern was not the house search. I had been asked by Prof's friend, my German tutor, if I would say a few words. Standing in front of a group of Dons who I hardly knew, six months pregnant, was not my idea of fun but for Prof Weaver who had helped me so much I just had to do it. I had written, re-written, and scrubbed out reams of paper before reading it to Jennie and had finally managed a brief but honest little speech.

We found the perfect property south of Norwich. Turnpike House was a Victorian farmhouse in a pretty bad state. The agent was quite apologetic when he opened the door. The layout offered plenty of choice and there was a small set of outbuildings ripe for conversion. The rest of the farm had been sold off but there was a tiny thatched barn across from the house. The grounds were about two acres. There was a five hundred year old oak tree in a field at the edge of the property. To Mum and Dad it was perfect. They put in a cheeky offer straight away. The agent drove off saying he would be in touch with the executors and get back to us.

They dropped me off at the college and I found my way to the ancient dining room used by the Dons. Herr Scherman met me at the door as previously arranged. He did a double take at my swelling stomach but was too polite to mention it. Obviously, Prof had not passed on the information about my pregnancy to him.

He got me a soft drink and we moved over to where a group of men and one woman were chatting to Prof Weaver. He was gazing vaguely around the circle and suddenly noticed me.

'Miss Chapman, so glad to see one of my star pupils, do come over here'. He moved over to let me stand beside him. 'You are looking very well' he said lifting his eyes from my lower body to my face. 'When is the baby due?' His eyes were full of laughter.

'Oh, not until October' I whispered, hoping that somebody would start the conversation rolling again.

I had been warned that the event would be dry but it turned out to be positively arid. Conversation was desultory and I was wondering if I could make it to the toilet before I had to make my speech. Just as this thought entered my brain, a senior Don clinked his glass and asked everybody to gather round. There were more than forty or more people in the hall. I was glad so many had come, especially as term-time was ending. It showed me that my Prof was a respected member of the community.

'Normally, it falls to me to thank retiring members of our fraternity for their long and dedicated commitment to the aims of our college. However, this year one of Professor Weaver's students Miss Zoe Chapman, who has achieved a First, has been asked to give the speech of thanks' he said and turned to me moving aside to let me step on to the slightly raised rostrum. A lectern had been provided but I knew my speech off by heart by now.

'Thank you for giving me the chance to wish dear Professor Weaver a happy retirement. He certainly deserves it. It saddens me to think of all the students who will arrive next year who will not have the chance to attend one of his inspiring lectures. I wasn't coping well with a previous lecturer (I had made sure he wasn't in the room), spending more time dozing off than being awake'. The guests laughed rather self-consciously probably trying to remember if I had been one of their students.

'I asked to transfer to Professor Weaver's classes. I am so grateful he accepted me. I have loved history since childhood. Studying European history has been truly absorbing. He has challenged me, annoyed me, praised me, in equal measure. I learnt how to deal with his occasional caustic comments and how to give back as good as he gave. Without his encouragement I would not have achieved my First.

I am here to speak on behalf of the many students over the years who have benefitted from his absolute dedication to their education. There were never any easy answers! Thank you, dear Prof, for allowing us to be a part of your world'.

I looked over at Professor Weaver and smiled. His face was unreadable but he gave me a small nod.

'I don't intend to say too much as I have been assured by Prof on many occasions, that my brevity was one of my more popular traits. I have no intention of allowing you to disappear into the East Anglian countryside. My family will be moving there soon and I hope to continue to meet up and explore the wonders of European history with you for many years to come'.

'Thank you Miss Chapman, may I now ask you to fill your glasses to toast James (I had never known that was his Christian name) and wish him a full and happy retirement'.

They all gathered round and toasted Prof whose face was now a dark shade of puce. I can imagine this was excruciating for him. One of the reasons I had kept my praise to a minimum.

After that, people started patting him on the back and saying goodbye. As the crowd thinned out I walked up and took his hand.

'My mother is picking me up in a short while. We are staying at Grantchester. We found our perfect new home today and have made an offer. When I say perfect I mean it might be in a few years' time when it has been partially rebuilt', I laughed.

'If you need a good builder I can recommend one to you. He has just finished my work'.

'Let's speak tomorrow'.

I stood on tiptoe and kissed his cheek. No mean feat when you have a bulging stomach like mine!

'If you decide to install an answerphone at your new home, maybe I will be nearby and help out'. I smiled at him hoping he would understand how deeply grateful I was he had taken me on as his student. More people were coming up to speak to him so I caught up with Herr Scherman for a few moments before walking out to find Mum.

NEW BEGINNINGS

Our cheeky offer was accepted and my parents set to organising funds to carry out the basic building works. Prof's builder was a god-send. He knew the planners, architects, sub-contractors (and those to avoid) and within a month or so, the house became ours and work started. At the rear of the building were three largish outbuildings. They were to be rebuilt and converted into a small separate annex for me and the baby. I suspected Mum was not too keen, having successfully reared her own brood, to get too involved in my untried motherhood by having me live in.

The new owners of the Wimbledon house were moving back to the UK in early December so we would have to decant to Norfolk by late November. This would allow time for the arrival of my baby at the hospital I had been attending for scans and clinics, and a decent time to pack up and clear away all the family detritus which had cluttered our rooms for years. If you walked into any of our bedrooms we might only just have left.

Mum organised a family weekend and we were all asked to take away what we wanted. The remaining items would either go to auction or be dumped. We had a fabulous time reliving all our childhood antics washed down with beer and wine. Stone cold sober, Dad and I looked on, laughing together at their antics. Mum was worse than the rest of us.

Music rang out all over the house. It was fantastic.

Two days later I received a letter from France in Jake's handwriting. I had kept in touch with his mother since our conversation. Gradually my anger was dissipating. I went up to my room and started to read.

Dear Zoe,

I hope this letter finds you well. Mum tells me she has spoken to you and explained I am in France.

I so desperately wanted to talk to you but understand your refusal. It was a big mistake meeting up with Jemma. I hadn't seen her since you and I got together but I bumped into her the night we returned from London. She was with the rowing gang. Nothing happened that night but I found she was around a lot when we finished training. On the day you saw us I was actually explaining that you were pregnant but that I was still leaving the country. I said there was no point in her pursuing a possible return to our relationship.

I hadn't wanted to admit to you that I was struggling with my studies which is why I spent so much time in the Library catching up. You are an extremely bright student, I am more of a plodder. Between you and Varena, I was aware that I had not worked as hard as I should have. I am not surprised that you got a First. You deserve it.

Training helped a lot. It cleared my head. I knew you were pregnant probably before you were certain. I didn't have the courage to talk to you about it. For that I am profoundly sorry. I know I have not been good to you.

We avoided talking about our goals, probably because we knew they wouldn't converge and that, long-term, we might well find ourselves in different parts of the world following our dreams.

I do love you, but freely admit that is not enough to stop me following my chosen path. I have to go.

I still do want to be part of your life wherever I am and I made the promise that I would stay around until after the birth of our baby. I can't bear to think of you hating me although I have provided plenty of reasons for you to do so. I have never lied to you and never will.

Well, here is the reason I am writing to you now.

I want to be with you when you have our baby. Please, please give this some thought. I hope you will find it in your heart to let me be with you. I return to the UK in late September via Gatwick and wonder if we can meet up?

I have angered and hurt you by my decision to go ahead with my plans and I know I am asking a lot, but I do hope you will let me be with you.

Love

Jake

By the time I reached the end of Jake's letter my mouth was dry and I was sobbing. I had to admit that he had never lied to me and maybe my insecurity in our relationship had made me misread the situation. Right from the start I had wondered what he had seen in me. I doubted his affection, feeling unworthy. I had assumed his training and gym visits were actually trysts with his old girlfriend. The conversation outside Professor Weaver's office had coloured my views. I should have talked to Jake. Our whole time together was built on what we hadn't had the courage to say. My emotions had been all over the place during the early stages of my pregnancy. I had to admit I was very slightly unbalanced, particularly after my father had his heart attack.

I needed time to take stock. I realised I didn't even know what Jake had achieved. I must ask Elspeth when she rings.

Eventually I showed my parents Jake's letter.

'What have you decided to do?' Mum asked. She had agreed to be my birth-partner.

'I think I need to meet him on his return from France before I make the final decision'.

The closer it got to October the more anxious I was about actually giving birth. I knew my mother would be staunch and was obviously experienced but Jake was the baby's dad. I also knew he had shown himself to be supportive and reliable during the crisis over Dad's heart-attack. I was torn.

I think Mum realised what was causing my confusion.

'I actually feel it should be Jake who is with you. It is his baby too. So, if you feel able to, I would advise agreeing to his request'.

So, here I was, sitting in a café waiting for Jake's plane to arrive. I had left plenty of time to park. I was not sure I would even manage to fit behind the wheel. I looked like a mini-elephant. In the toilets I had peered at myself in the mirror. Reflected back at me was somebody I didn't recognise. My face had filled out, I was brown from lazing around in the garden, my hair was glowing. Pregnancy in its later stages had proved good for me. My tan highlighted my white teeth. I had dressed with particular care.

The flight from Perpignan was overdue. I remember singing Peter Paul and Mary's *Leaving on a Jet Plane* earlier on that day and it stayed rumbling around my head. My neighbour kept glancing at me. Maybe I was singing out loud.

At last the arrivals showed the plane had landed. I had thought to bring a placard with Jake's name on it but decided against it. This reunion was going to be difficult. I stood near the gate and spotted him before he saw me. I could feel my heart pounding. He was dressed in shabby jeans, tight tee-shirt and carrying a large rucksack. His hair had been bleached by the sun and his eyes were gleaming beneath his tan. My legs felt like jelly. Was this a good idea?

Catching sight of me, he stopped, laughed and practically ran over to where I was standing.

'My god, you are enormous. Are you sure the baby isn't due much earlier?'

He didn't know whether to touch me or not so I reached out my hand and the next moment he had dropped his bag and attempted to envelope me in a gentle hug. This was not entirely successful, my distended stomach proving too much of an impediment. I lent forward and pecked him on the cheek conscious of the smell of his skin and wanting to do so much more. I was frightened of his impact on me even now after three months of being apart.

'Shall we go over and get a coffee in a quieter part of the complex?' He asked. I nodded. Picking up his bag he took my hand and we walked over to the Costa tucked away in the corner. Sneaking peaks at him, I realised that he was not as confident as he seemed. He was swallowing hard and was not sure what to say. It was almost as if he was scared to upset the balance we had achieved so far.

We found a table away from the busier part of the café and he went off to buy our drinks. I had forgotten how big he was. He dwarfed most of the customers standing alongside.

To add to my discomfort the baby had decided to play footie with my insides and my stomach was being pounded in all directions. Jake put the coffees down and sat beside me on the sofa. It was meant to be big enough for three people but certainly not for a massively pregnant woman and a well-built man. Jake looked down and spotted the movement in my stomach. He asked if he could touch me. Taking his hand, I laid it on the mound just as the baby went for a goal.

'Wow, that is amazing. Does it happen all the time?' He gasped. His hand had remained on my bulge.

'Pretty much. Mum is convinced it is a boy'.

'I have missed you Zoe. You went so quickly. I was completely thrown. Varena made it quite clear that she thought I was a brute. She was not keen to hear my side. What is she doing at the moment?'

'She has an interview with the UN to work in South America somewhere. I am waiting to hear from her'. Jake's Mum had told me he had achieved a First so his last-minute panic may not have been in vain.

'What were you doing in France?'

'I was part of a group project looking at the diseases which are affecting the vines. Good experience for my first job'.

I told him I was glad he had got the result he wanted and asked if he had gone to the graduation ceremony and the balls.

'The ceremony yes, the proms, no. I had hoped to track you down at the ceremony but you didn't come'.

'I didn't fancy prancing up on the stage in my maternity gown'.

We ordered more coffee and slipped back into our old easy way. By the time he caught the flight to Edinburgh we had agreed he would come back down to London two weeks before I was due. My mother had said he could stay with us but warned he would have to help with our continued clear out. I had told him of our planned move to East Anglia. I stood waving to him as he went through, my lips throbbing from kissing him many times before he left.

MY FOOTBALLER ARRIVES

Jake returned at the beginning of October. The house was changing daily with the family moving out their treasures. I had been sleeping in the double bed in the spare room as I was too large for my small single bed. Mum opened the door to him and I waddled along the corridor watching them. I thought she would be wary of renewing his acquaintance but she was really welcoming.

This was the first time Dad had met Jake. He stood in the kitchen entrance waiting for his women to let Jake through to greet him. Our entrance hall is large so there was plenty of room for mini-elephant and Jake the Giant to say hello. I took the initiative and started to aim for his cheek but he pounced and before I could object was giving me mouth to mouth resuscitation. I suppose when your partner is like an overblown balloon and sex is out of the question this was probably the next best solution.

Taking his coat, I shoved him through to meet Dad who shook his hand and ushered us both into the kitchen. If Dad is not sure what to say he usually offers a cup of tea. Mum looked at me and grinned.

Conversation was all about our move. We avoided Jake's imminent departure after the baby's birth but otherwise there was no constraint in our relationship. Dad showed him the plans and talked about progress. The main house would not be completely finished but the conversion of the outbuildings into a single-storey two bedroomed annex was virtually done, only the painting was outstanding. Our move was set for early November.

Those days before Amy's birth were some of the best of my life. Jake was loving and kind. He sat with me into the night when I couldn't sleep, with my head resting on his chest until I dropped off with exhaustion. He worked with Mum and Dad to clear the rooms making frequent trips to the dump. We had finally started to really understand each other. I knew he was afraid to talk about his departure, not wanting to hurt me, but I forced him to describe his plans and explain why he was visiting one particular country and not another. When he spoke his eyes would get a far away look and I knew I had no chance of changing his mind.

I was resigned but it didn't stop me being frightened for my future. I would have sole responsibility for this baby. I know I would be living with my parents but the choices I would make would be mine alone. I realised I was afraid to live without him.

Two days later my pains started. I kept this knowledge to myself. I didn't want to speak until I was sure. By lunchtime they were at regular intervals. Time to find my bag and off to the hospital. No going back now. Mum drove, Jake sat in the back with me, having rung ahead to warn them.

Eleven hours of labour and Amy decided to release my agony. I had alternately screamed, laughed, cried and sworn at Jake. It was his fault I was in so much pain. Even the pethidine failed. I was pink with the gas and air. He had patiently held my hand, rubbed my back, given me drinks, refusing to respond to my accusations. I apologised to the midwife during a lucid period but she just smiled back. She had seen it all!

9lbs 4 ounces of baby came out with a whoosh. Amy had arrived, a girl, not a boy as my mother had suspected. I am still amazed that my small body had managed to expel such a large baby. Wrapped in a cloth, with the blood wiped from her head, she nestled in my arms with Jake looking on. He stroked the crown of her head gently and kissed me. I tasted the salt from his tears. We had agreed on possible names only a few days before. Amy for a girl, Sam for a boy.

Amy went off to the nursery and I was moved to the ward. Jake had gone to ring our parents. I was exhausted but I couldn't sleep. I just lay in a haze. I had given birth. I was a mother. I was no longer frightened. I had responsibilities now. I had a future even if it was different from the one I had planned.

Today mothers return home the day after having a baby but I spent 5 more in hospital. I wrote letters to Varena and Prof Weaver. Determined to breast-feed Amy, I was struggling. I was too tense. One night a new nursery-nurse was on duty. I could hear the distant sound of music. Recognising Amy's screams, I walked along to do the night feed. Vaughan Williams' *Lark Ascending* welcomed me. A large black nurse smiled and brought Amy to me. Sitting down in the comfy chair she placed a soft cushion on my lap, all the while whispering to me in a hushed soothing tone. Amy was hungry and latched on to my sore breast, limpet-like. I felt the tension start to rise but was told to relax my shoulders and listen to the music, let it ease me. She massaged my neck too. My breast seemed to flow into Amy's mouth and released the milk she craved. We talked in whispers. She had been a midwife for 20 years. Loving the babies more, she transferred to the nursery. Lucky babies.

Mum fended off the family on my return home. Every now and then they were all in the UK and had demanded to see the new arrival. Jake's parents had flown down whilst I was in hospital. Amy screamed most of the time during their visit. Elspeth commented that Jake had been difficult as a baby for the first few months. Thinking of Jake, huge Jake, as a baby, made me chuckle.

Mum decided to organise a lunch-time party for the family. Some of our close neighbours were invited too. This would be Amy's welcome and our farewell to the house too. Jake was flying to South America on 8th November, joining up with his group in Rio. In the hope of distracting me, my parents had booked the removers on the 10th. Most of the house had been boxed up. The bedroom I shared with Jake and their room were the only bedrooms which had not been cleared. Mum and I had happily mooched around buying baby clothes, a pram and a Moses basket. Amy being so large, this would soon have to be replaced with a proper cot.

Working in France had been lucrative for Jake. He offered to pay but Mum refused saying he needed this to support his trip.

Jake was very hands-on. He willingly changed smelly nappies, walked around cooing to her when she was crying and, on a few nights, fed her with the milk I had expressed. My friendly nursery-nurse had said it was a good way to encourage babies to use a bottle even if they were being breast-fed. A full five hours of sleep were bliss, even if my breasts were pounding with milk when I woke up.

The family arrived with their respective partners. Charlie's new girlfriend was a definite improvement on his ex-wife. Amy was passed around and admired. Frances whispered to me that she might be pregnant but it was a secret. Lizzie brought her fiancé a fellow art-director. Only Jennie came alone, saddening me. Between jobs she was coming to help out with the move.

Dad displayed photos of the new house showing the changes the builder had wrought. Completely finished, my annex and Mum's studio looked amazing. Our elderly neighbour Annie remembered my parents' arrival next door before we were born. She described Dad emptying buckets of water where the roof had leaked and digging up the garden to clear the blocked drains.

We were all trying to put a positive spin on the move but it was tinged with sadness. 'Nothing stays the same', Rosy used to tell me. 'You must take your chances and move on'. In a few days' time my whole world was going to change. Jake was flying away. Neither of us really had the courage to discuss the future. We played it safe. We weren't brave enough. Even Amy's arrival had not succeeded in glueing us together.

Varena had rung from New York. We wrote and spoke to each other at least once a month. The time between was nothing. Each conversation ran on as if we had only been chatting an hour ago. Her father was retiring and would be living in Yorkshire. Her grandparents were keen to hand over the running of the estate. She hoped to fly over early in the New Year.

I had a long letter from Prof too. He had sent a massive bouquet of flowers to the hospital. I had to share it around some of the other Mums. He was keen to see Amy and wanted to know when we planned to arrive in East Anglia. He had sold the Cambridge house and was living full-time at the cottage with his cats.

So many positives but the big cloud hanging over me wouldn't shift. We both knew it and the last few days with Jake were surreal. We were winding down, losing each other. Always honest, Jake offered us no future, because he didn't know what his future would be. He could hardly take a new born baby with him trekking in the Amazon or climbing Peruvian peaks. Even without Amy I would not have followed him. I was not the adventurous type. My travels would be to European cities not the jungles of South America. Despite loving each other we were not compatible.

We decided not to take Amy to Heathrow. He had spent most of the morning holding her. We were running late, Mum eventually dragging her out of his arms. His bags had been loaded into the car, he turned to kiss her again and thanked my parents for letting him stay and then flung himself into the driving seat. I was hugging myself, wondering if he could see to drive as his tears were flowing freely. Handing him my handkerchief at the traffic lights, he took a huge breath and blew his nose. His control had returned.

The conversation was desultory. Parking was difficult so there was little time before he needed to check-in. The screen already displayed a departure gate. I handed him a picture of me with Amy that Dad had taken a few days before. I realised I had nothing to remember him, no photos. All I had was Amy. I would ask his mother if she had some pictures she could share. Time was running out.

'I love you Zoe. These few weeks have been amazing. Please don't hate me for leaving'.

'I don't hate you but I am sad that Amy and I have no hold over you, that you are still able to leave us'. I was struggling to hold back my tears, biting my lip. I didn't want his last view of me to be me crying. I knew I was losing the battle so I reached up and kissed him, trying to imprint the feel of his lips on my memory. My hands gripped his body, feeling his strength.

'I love you too'.

The tannoy message relayed the last call for his flight. He crushed me to him, kissed me again, picked up his bag and fled, not looking back. He was gone.

Once he was out of sight, my legs gave way and I collapsed on the floor. The lady from the WH Smith shop rushed over to me, helping me up. She gave me a chair and asked if I needed medical help. I refused.

'I will be OK in a few minutes, thank you'.

'I hate working on the departure side of the terminal. So much sadness. I much prefer the arrivals'.

I needed to be with Amy. I bought a coffee and sat quietly. I didn't want to have an accident driving home. My parents were too old to adopt Amy if I died.

I remember nothing of the drive home. My mother was waiting anxiously at the door holding Amy as I drove into the drive. Flinging myself out of the car I held my arms out. She was all I had of Jake.

LIFE GOES ON

The first year of Amy's life actually flew past. We were about to celebrate her first birthday. Our lives had settled into a routine in the peace of the beautiful East Anglian countryside. Dad's health had improved. Mum's paintings were flying off the easel. I had achieved a measure of solace. Once a week, Amy and I spent the day with Prof Weaver. Lizzie had produced my direct mail leaflet offering translation services. Start up was slow, but gradually, with word-of-mouth references, I was managing to earn some money. Technical translations were challenging. At least my brain wasn't slowing up. At the beginning of each month, money from Jake's parents arrived in my account. They made frequent flying trips from Edinburgh to see Amy.

Jake had travelled with his group for six months in South America and then wrote to say he would be moving on to Polynesia. At least once a month he would try to ring, sometimes waking me up in the night as he mistook the time zones. If he was based anywhere for a few weeks I would write sending photos of Amy.

During the summer the siblings visited. Mum complained we were a hotel now, seeing them more than the later years in Wimbledon, but I knew she loved having us around. Frances gave birth to their second grandchild in May. A beautiful little boy. She was on six months leave and her partner,

James, was going to share the child-care arrangements so she could return to work. He was a scriptwriter and mostly worked from home. The arrangement was ideal.

Lizzie was still with her art director. Their flat in Pimlico overlooked the river. Churchill Gardens was a massive council estate but the flats had been sold off courtesy of Mrs Thatcher's Right to Buy policy. The previous owners had made a killing of course when they sold on to Lizzie. Jennie had given up her flat and stayed with them when she worked in the UK. So much of her life was now lived in the States. Boyfriends came and went. Nobody lasted long.

Lizzie had always been my soul-mate. Jennie and Frances were such a complete unit, they had little time for us youngsters when we were growing up. However, on her last visit Jennie and I spent long hours talking. She had finished a run of two films. Desperate for more work in the UK, but being out of the country, she missed the chance to read for several films and one play. We talked around the need for her to have a local contact who could take messages and relay them on. This had to be somebody she could trust.

I offered straight away. No hesitation. By the time she left for filming in Hungary we had notified everybody who needed to know. I would fax through her messages at the end of the day. Most mornings I was up early, Amy was an early riser. Luckily, she went to bed at 6.00 in the evening. I did a lot of my translation work then. Jennie would fax her replies and I would ring the people back. Her new agent was delighted.

Prof Weaver laughed when I reported on my new role. He was a changed man. Gone was the haunted look. He looked years younger. He rarely suffered any blackouts, Amy's first word was 'Prop', her second 'no'. Even I started calling him Prop. He had become a part of our family. During the winter he would come for lunch on a Sunday.

Lizzie used several freelance artists and when she heard about Jennie's arrangement with me she laughed.

'I can never get through to book them. They rarely answer the phone. Maybe they should use you. What a good idea', she mused. 'I am going to do a re-write of your translation leaflet and offer telephone answering services to these creatives. For a small retainer you could be their off-site office assistant'.

By the end of the next month I had six new clients each paying me £10 a week to answer their calls. It was hardly a fortune. If this was going to be my way forward I would need to do some more marketing. Lizzie printed me off 100 leaflets. Driving around I posted these in shops and post offices. I felt like I had hit the jackpot when I got my first response.

Hadley was a freelance salesman working for several technical companies. His wife had been his backstop but she had re-trained as a teacher and had a new job. Mainly it was messages. He rang me in the evenings when he was on the road. His business card carried my phone number.

Lizzie always told me that to get a 30% response to an advertisement I would be lucky. Through Hadley's recommendation, I got six clients. From the advertisement, I got thirty five. The need was definitely there.

Communication was always by telephone. I rarely met up with the people I assisted. I made sure they knew that if they persistently refused to act after I had passed on their messages I would stop providing the service.

By the time Amy reached her birthday I was fully engaged.

She never objected when she was shut in her play-pen whilst I answered the phone. She would soon be walking! With my translations and this new venture, I was earning £100 a day. I paid my parents rent.

Elspeth was on one of her visits. Amy adored her grandparents. She was surrounded with love.

'I think it is time you stopped sending me the money, Elspeth'. She looked up.

'I am earning good money now and I think it is unfair that you should still be supporting me'. I replied.

'The responsibility is Jake's not yours. He has spent a year following his dream and should now be considering providing for Amy himself'.

I then uttered words I would live to regret. 'He should be working'.

Jake's younger brother Robert was off to university next year and it seemed wrong for me to be accepting their money.

Two days before Amy's birthday a courier delivered a parcel for her from Australia. I peeked in and saw the pretty wrapping paper and the card. I put it away for her to open. I missed the letter addressed to me.

The house was full for the day. Even Jennie was home. Amy, who had taken her first steps a week earlier, was attempting to run between us all, plopping down on her nappy clad bottom every now and then. She was pulling at Prop's trousers and jumping up and down to the Rolling Stones. She was the next generation to be inducted into the Stones.

Time to open the presents. Laughing as we helped her rip open the parcels, she looked just like Jake but her features were less defined, gentler. Despite the happy atmosphere I couldn't help wishing he was here to see her. The pile of unwrapped presents were discarded for the fairy Lizzie had created. Meant only as a decoration for her present it soon got pulled apart. Suddenly, I remembered Jake's parcel. I pulled it off the hall table and took the package into the room. The card and letter dropped out as I handed Mum the present. She was trying to stop Amy from bashing Frances' baby on the head.

A cuddly Koala emerged. Amy licked it but wasn't sure about the taste. She lay down on the floor and pulled it to her and closed her eyes. Just as quickly she opened them and grinned at us all. I think La La was a hit. Well Koala was a bit of a mouthful.

Amy's first birthday was faithfully recorded on video by Dad who had found a new hobby. I converted my copy to CD recently when I found it.

I decided not to read Jake's letter until later when she was in bed.

'Dear Zoe,

I hope the parcel arrives on time. I am sorry not to have written or telephoned recently.

I have been offered a job at the University of New South Wales. It will be my base although I will still travel from time to time. One of the Aussies in our group introduced me to the faculty. I was due to start in January and had hoped to get a flight home for Amy's birthday but they wanted me to start straight away. I am sure she will have a wonderful day with your family. Mum tells me she was down with you a few weeks ago.

She mentioned that you had asked her to stop sending the money. I am glad to hear that your new venture is proving a success.

Obviously, now I am going to be working, I will transmit a similar amount from here. You will need to let me have your bank account details.

Zoe, there is no easy way to write this. I am getting married. I planned to tell you this news in person. Clare has been a member of the group I travelled with. She was on a sabbatical from the University for a year. She is also an environmental scientist and recommended me for the job.

I am so sorry. I didn't plan for this to happen. I genuinely thought that when I found a job, I would be asking you and Amy to come and live with me.

I am conscious that, loving me, has caused you enormous pain. Your generosity in allowing me to spend those few weeks with you before and after Amy's birth, meant so much. The night you gave birth is engraved on my heart. Please believe that.

I really hope you will find somebody else to love. You deserve it. You certainly didn't deserve me. I know I have let you down in so many ways but a part of me will always love you.

I do hope, when you are less angry with me, that you will write and give me news of Amy. I carry around the photos you sent.

Love always

Jake

TROUBLED TIMES

I never replied to the letter. It was nearly six years later when a death brought him back into our life. Any news he received about Amy was from Elspeth. He had written to his parents at the same time. His father refused to speak to him for many years. He was ashamed. Elspeth was distraught. I realised that she, too, had lost her son. They had always thought he would return to work in the UK.

I have blanked out from my memory the days after receipt of Jake's letter. My mother said I behaved like an automaton. Elspeth rang regularly but I couldn't speak to her. I knew I would collapse if I did. I had to keep going for Amy's sake. As all children do, she picked up on my mood. I struggled not to lash out at her when she threw the bar of soap at my eye at bath time. I shut her in the playpen when she refused to eat the food I had prepared. I was on a knife-edge and my mother knew it. She would appear in the flat if she heard me raise my voice or if Amy persisted in screaming. Without asking me, Amy would be whisked away.

Anger is exhausting. I still had my translation work to do. I had to be charming to my callers. I had to function, but my body was slowly breaking down. Luckily Christmas was a quiet time when people retired to their family homes for respite from the daily grind. On Christmas Eve I woke up sweating. My temperature was 103. I had a sharp pain in my chest and was struggling to breathe. Staggering to the door I could see Dad at an upstairs room. He looked down and waved. I dropped to my knees holding on to the door frame. His face registered his concern and he disappeared. Seconds later he was running across the yard.

I had pneumonia. I spent a week in hospital. The doctors were less concerned about the fever and more about my state of mind. The psychiatrist was adamant I was suffering from depression. I missed Amy too.

Prop visited me towards the end of the week. I was in a side-ward. Taking hold of my hand he just sat. He stroked it gently.

'You need to listen to the doctors, Zoe. Don't ignore their advice. You can't get better on your own'.

'I am a mother with responsibilities, I can't let Amy down'.

'You need counselling Zoe. You need help to get over your grief. She needs you to be well'.

My parents found a clinic in Cambridge. Jennie was staying in my flat helping with Amy. She was also answering the calls and taking messages. After she left, Mum took over the role. I spent hours with a young therapist called George. He had long ago worked out that my main motivation was to be well enough to go back to Amy. The drugs made me feel empty. George described them as a temporary bandage to help heal what was broken. They were a not a long-term solution. That was up to me.

'How do you heal a broken-heart?' I asked.

'I am not sure you ever do, to be honest. You learn to live with it. What we can do is show you ways to cope, to prevent your grief from overpowering you again. We teach you to take care of your own mental state, to love yourself, to protect yourself'.

George made me confront my fears, he saw into my very soul. Slowly I revealed my entire relationship with Jake. I relived the times of extreme sexual gratification. The lengths we had gone to please each other. He took me back to my childhood, to Yves, to university. I sobbed, screamed, stormed out of the room in a rage, returning like a sulky child. I maintained a sullen silence at other times. His patience was magnificent.

By the time I left the clinic I had been shown ways to look after my mental health. I had resolved to go to Edinburgh to see Jake's parents. I would take Amy and spend some time with them. I loved Elspeth who had been so staunch during the last year and I needed to show how much I appreciated the love she showered on us. She had written a wonderful kind letter hoping that I would keep in touch with them. Amy was their link to their son too.

George had put me in touch with a counsellor in Norwich which was closer to home. I knew by then that depression does not leave you but you learn to live with it. I had not seen Amy for six weeks. How would she react to my return?

She was in the hall scooting around in a Noddy car when I walked through the door. She screeched, desperately trying to extricate her legs from the car and ran to me. I lifted her up, feeling her solid little body.

'Mummy'.

'What did you say darling?'

She repeated 'Mummy, Mummy, Mummy' over and over again. My parents were laughing in the background.

'When did she learn to say that?' I asked.

'About a week ago. We said Mummy would be home soon. She stared at us then repeated Mummy. Because we laughed, she thought this was a great game. Now she won't stop'. Dad replied.

It was the best homecoming. Here were the people who mattered to me. They had loved, cared for me and who else did I need?

After dinner with Amy tucked up in bed Mum brought me up to date with the news. Jennie had been asked to take over a role for a film in the UK. The lead actress had broken her leg badly in a riding accident. All the other siblings were well and keen to see me. My business had expanded. Not the translations obviously but I had acquired several of Jennie's friends in the film world. She had turned out to be a very good marketing initiative. I explained I was going to Edinburgh with Amy and would ring Elspeth tomorrow. Slightly surprised Mum asked if that was a good idea?

'George told me that I should stop running away and have the courage to face my fears. If I am honest, I knew all along Jake would not return. His letters and calls had become scarcer, shorter, and more impersonal as he moved on from South America. He had also spoken frequently of the people in his group and Clare's name had cropped up several times'.

It was good to lie in my own bed that night. I spent an hour just looking at Amy sleeping. She was Jake in repose. Strangely I didn't feel sad about this. The drugs seemed to have numbed my senses.

Elspeth cried when I said I wanted us to fly up and see them. Archie had visited a few times but it was normally

Elspeth who made the trip down. They both met us off the plane from Norwich. Amy was in seventh heaven on the flight. She should have been sitting on my lap but the plane was only half-full so the stewardess suggested she have the seat next to me. I was glad it was a short-haul journey of an hour. She would have broken into the cockpit on a long-haul.

Dunfermline was a short trip from the airport. Elspeth had purchased a car seat for Amy. The conversation was stilted with Archie concentrating on the driving. I was glad to arrive at the house. Amy was desperate to be freed from the car, running off when I unclipped her and put her down on the ground. She grabbed Archie's legs and hugged him and then took Elspeth's hand. The atmosphere changed. We relaxed. It was cold, so we rushed inside.

The house reflected Elspeth's personality. It was immediately obvious. Trailing after Amy running from room to room, we ended up in the kitchen. The house was packed full of beautiful antiques, cupboards of pretty china, elegant tables, a magnificent grand piano stood in one corner of the music room. No gleaming modern kitchen for Elspeth. A large oak dresser filled the whole of one wall.

'Time for a cup of tea, I think', Archie picked Amy up and stood her on the table holding tightly on to her chubby arms. 'Do you want a drink too, little lady?'

He settled her in an elderly wooden high chair whilst I rummaged around in my bag for her drinking cup and plastic bib. Amy's eating habits left much to be desired. I was glad the stone floor could be easily cleaned. She would dig her fingers into the bib's trough and stuff the food that had fallen off the spoon into her mouth, sometimes just as I was trying to feed her with the next mouthful.

A cot had been put up in my room. The view from the window across the muddy fields was probably better in the summer. Elspeth had kept all Jake and Robert's toys. Amy's bath that night in the deep Victorian tub with large claw feet was shared with ducks and plastic dinosaurs.

Exhausted by her day Amy went to sleep straight away. Archie had been called away for an emergency after dinner so Elspeth and I sat in the lounge in front of a roaring fire.

'Zoe I don't know whether we talk about Jake or not?'

'Well we can't pretend he doesn't exist can we', I replied . 'George, my counsellor, has urged me to be more open and not to bottle things away, even if it is hurtful'.

'Jake was always a free spirit. He has had his own agenda most of his life. It rarely coincided with ours, I have to say'. Elspeth put another log on the fire and sat down next to me. She rested her hand on mine.

'Thank you for bringing Amy to see us. It reminds us that we still have a part of Jake around. We love her for herself though, not just because she is Jake's daughter. I can already see she has a determined mind of her own'.

There were plenty of frames with selected pictures of Jake and his brother on the tables but I asked if she had a photo album and could tell me about Jake and Robert's earlier years. We spent the evening laughing at their crazy antics caught on camera. Jake, covered in mud after rugby and then one with his leg in plaster. Holiday snaps in the Orkneys. All the time Elspeth was filling in with background stories. I realised how little I knew about the man I had loved. Still loved. She was bringing him to life for me. This was therapy for her too.

Despite the cold, we spent three very happy days. We

struggled up the hill to the Castle. I was glad Archie was pushing the pram. I offered on the downward journey. When the rain started, we hid in the art galleries. Amy, trapped in the pram, was not impressed. I made a pilgrimage to Sir Walter Scott's statue in the Waverley Gardens. On the final day we walked around the perfectly laid out squares in the old town. I vowed to return in better weather.

'Has Jake actually got married' I asked at our last meal. We were sat around the dining room table. The joint of roast beef with all the leftover trimmings lay in the middle of the table. Archie had carved the joint in masterly fashion. Well he was a veterinary surgeon after all.

Elspeth looked at Archie. 'Yes, at the beginning of January. He rang us at Christmas to give us the date. I am pretty certain he knew neither of us would be there'.

'I would be very sad if Jake's decision to stay in Australia, and the hurt his letter had inflicted on me, impacts on your relationship with him. You have been enormously kind to us and I love you for it, but Jake is your son. Loyalty to me and Amy should not stop you loving him'.

'We are as angry with Jake as any parent would be, knowing how he has treated you. He has a child, he has a responsibility, to you both. Maybe we are too old-fashioned'. Elspeth's response was controlled.

'Jake never promised anything. He always made his goals clear to me. I could not bear to live with him knowing he was only with us because of duty. No relationship could survive that. He would blame us. The price would have been too high'.

As we left to check-in Elspeth handed me a large brown envelope. Inside was a silver frame with a picture of Jake at his graduation. A huge lump lodged itself in my throat. Amy grabbed for it. She pressed her sticky lips to the glass and kissed it. I told her it was Daddy. This was the first picture she had ever seen of him outside of Elspeth and Archie's home.

CHANGING SEASONS

She stood in front of the mirror, turning from side to side. It was her first day at primary school and she was delighted with her school uniform. All her young life Amy has loved dressing up and as far as she was concerned this was another outfit to dance around in. How the teachers would contain this bright hyperactive child for a whole day was beyond my imagination.

Before the advent of mobile phones, I was pretty tied to the house looking after my clients. Mum and Dad helped if we had doctor appointments for Amy. She was rarely ill though. I was particularly squeamish at vaccination time. It was Dad, occasionally Mum, who went to the mother and baby clubs or delivered Amy to pre-school. They knew all the young mums and became the taxi-service on play visits to friends. I lost track of all Amy's playmates, she was extremely gregarious.

Dad arrived to take the photographs, ready to answer the phone calls, so I could drive Amy to her first day of school. She would only be in for the mornings the first week. Her excitement was palpable. I soon lost her in the group of reception children standing with their mothers. A pretty blonde woman came up to me and introduced herself. Her son Angus was a particular favourite with Amy, they had met at playgroup. We were let into the classroom and the children were shown the pegs to hang up their bags and coats. After a brief chat the Mums departed.

Angie, Angus' Mum, asked me if I would like to come to her house for a coffee? She lived around the corner from the school. I hesitated only slightly, then said, 'yes'.

'You work from home, don't you?' She asked.

'Yes, I run an answering service and also do German and French translations'.

'I have known your Dad since mother and toddler group. He is a particular favourite. We love his stories. Your Mum donated a picture to raise funds for the group'.

I hadn't known that. How divorced I was from the life going on around me. My parents knew everybody and frequently entertained. Old friends from London drove up to stay at weekends. Once Amy was tucked up in bed I would join them for a meal and we would share memories about the Shack and the Wimbledon home.

Apart from my visits to Prop (Amy had struggled with Prof so now the whole family called him Prop), I had no social group to mix with. Working in the evenings after Amy was asleep made it difficult to develop new friendships. I longed for Varena's brief visits and loved the arrival of my siblings but I must have appeared very boring. I had deliberately closed down my life. When I relaxed, I read.

The semi, attached to Prop's house, was sold and the new owner Graham turned out to be a gay garden-designer. Between them Prop and Graham had transformed the gardens surrounding their houses. Graham would spend hours digging, rearranging, moving plants, watering, weeding. Prop was too old to do more than potter but he had a gardener who came in three times a week. It was rather an open windy spot so the first planting was hedges. Not too tall so the view was obscured, but enough to protect the flowers they planted.

The effect was stunning and my mother had spent many hours chatting to Prop painting different parts of the garden. She presented him with one particularly beautiful view. Amy and I loved Prop. We were the daughter and grandchild he never had. Our Saturday visits were part of our routine. He had become quite a local celebrity giving historical talks at the local village hall. His fame spread and he was much in demand. One week he gave four presentations, his carefully handwritten notes packed up in his battered old leather briefcase.

My father always produced spare copies of his photos of Amy and I sent these on to Scotland. If Jake knew anything of our life it was through Elspeth. Four times a year she and Archie would fly down to visit us. Amy loved Archie's tales of the animals he had cared for. I knew Jake had taken his Doctorate and that he had twin boys. He continued to send a monthly amount for Amy and presents for her birthday and Christmas. I had no contact. His picture was frequently kissed and had to be wiped clean regularly. She did ask me once if she would be able to meet Daddy and wondered why he didn't live with us. I said maybe, when she was older, she could fly to Australia and visit. I said that even Nanny Elspeth hadn't met her half-brothers.

'Would you come too Mummy, you must miss him, he has been away so long?'

I was so glad I accepted Angie's invite to coffee. We had become firm friends and she knew my history. Her husband was working on the rigs in the North Sea so she had weeks as a single parent too. When her husband was home and could baby-sit she came over in the evening if I wasn't busy translating. This part of my business was very spasmodic. Like buses, all the work seemed to come at once.

Dad was answering the phone one day whilst I got my hair cut. When I breezed in it was obvious that he wanted me to return. I immediately thought we had a problem with one of my less popular clients.

'Jake's brother has just rung'.

I felt my stomach lurch, not Jake, he must be OK. Amy needed to meet her Dad one day.

'Archie had a stroke yesterday and died this morning'. Dear Archie, Amy's beloved grandpa, who had only just restored his relationship with Jake, was dead. Poor Elspeth. Like my parents, they were a unit. Strong, indivisible.

I rang Elspeth but she was so distraught her responses were disjointed and I found it difficult to understand what she was saying. Eventually Robert took the phone and told me what had happened. Archie had been on a call and hadn't felt well. He asked for a glass of water and seemed better. Driving out of the farm gates his car smashed into one of the posts. He was unconscious when they reached him, dying in the early hours of the following day.

I asked if it would be helpful if I flew up to be with Elspeth but he said her sister had come down from Inverness and would spend the week with them.

Archie, so full of life, fit and energetic, was dead.

When Robert rang with details of the funeral, I asked him if Jake would manage to fly back. He wasn't sure if he would arrive for the funeral but had arranged for three weeks compassionate leave. My parents would have both wanted to come with me. They liked Archie but somebody needed to look after Amy. She was too young. Dad and I caught the early flight out of Norwich and picked up a hire-car. The funeral was at noon.

The flight was delayed and the church was surrounded with parked cars. We had to squeeze into the back of the pews behind a pillar. I could see very little. Archie had been a popular vet and some of the mourners were standing outside. The service was simple and beautiful. His best friend gave a witty affectionate speech and then said that Archie's sons would like to talk about him. I looked at Dad.

'Did he say son or sons?' I asked.

Without standing up and peering around the pillar we couldn't see the front row of the mourners.

In the silence, Jake's unmistakable voice rang out. I had assumed he would not be at the funeral and was caught off guard. Between them Robert and Jake had written a moving tribute to Archie . I was sobbing by the time they had finished. Dad took my hand and squeezed it hard.

The family were going alone to the crematorium after the ceremony and my first glimpse of Jake in six years was holding his mother up as they followed the coffin out of the church. His head was bent towards her so I couldn't really see his face. Robert stayed behind inviting the mourners to the hotel up the road then left the church with a relative.

The church was slow to empty and when we emerged into the grey wintry day it took some time for the cars to clear away. Not sure if there would be enough room to park, Dad and I decided to walk slowly up to the hotel.

Breakfasting early in order to catch the first flight, we were both hungry, and we moved to the buffet through the crowds. Old friends were greeting each other remarking on the sad occasion. There were no familiar faces for us. The waiter offered us a coffee and some food and we sat tucked away in the corner close to the door.

It seemed an age before the family returned. My heightened emotion had probably magnified the time lapse. They came into the hall to be surrounded by their friends, Archie's colleagues, local dignitaries, all wanting to offer their sympathy. Elspeth and her sister moved one way, Robert and Jake in opposite directions. I had a perfect view of Jake's back. The two brothers were so much taller than most of the guests. We remained seated.

Their arrival seemed to jettison the mourners towards the food. Gradually the groups separated and split up so we could see more clearly through the crowd. Turning, Elspeth saw us sitting near the door. She spoke to her sister and then walked towards us. Jake, who seemed to be monitoring his mother's moves, glanced over and saw us. He looked dreadful even with his tan. His eyes had dark shadows as if he hadn't slept for some time and he had a haunted bleak look. The person next to him reclaimed his attention.

Elspeth sat down between us and rested her head on my shoulder. She was heavily made up but her tears had left mascara streaks under her eyes. I pulled out one of Amy's wipes and gently patted away the damage. I think by then she was all cried out. Dad held her hand to stop it shaking. She seemed to have aged ten years. We didn't speak. She knew how sad we were.

'Will you come back to the house afterwards please?'

We were on the last flight out at 8.30 that evening so there was plenty of time. She gave me her keys.

The guests were drifting away. We had another coffee and then crept out. Jake made no attempt to speak to us. Robert waved as we left.

It was strange letting ourselves into the house. I had only ever visited with Amy and she had always rushed into the porch and dragged us in behind her. We went into the kitchen and cleared up the table, washing up the cups and made ourselves some tea. After the crush at the hotel the peace was refreshing. I showed Dad the piano and he sat down and found some sheets of music.

The family arrived back an hour later to the haunting tones of Finlandia. Our piano was an upright. Dad used it when he was composing. Elspeth's grand piano was something else, transforming the music. I was lost in the fjords, with the waves lashing the steep cliff sides. I could see Viking dragon ships rowing out to sea. I had closed my eyes, it had been such an emotional day, and drifted off.

We were expecting the sound of cars in the drive, but they had walked back, so we did not hear them come through the door we had left on the latch. I felt, rather than heard, movement close by and opened my eyes, momentarily wondering where I was. Jake was standing in front of the chair I was curled up in. Without hesitation I stood up and held my arms out to him.

He moved into me, leaning down and resting his head on my shoulder. I felt his shuddering sobs. Dad quietly shut the piano and left the room.

Wordless, we sat down on the sofa and I let him release his grief. Murmuring softly, I stroked his head, rested my face against his cheek, wiped away the tears that had mingled with mine, all the time trying to comfort him, as I had done so often, with his daughter.

If I ever thought I would see Jake again it was not like this. Of course, I still loved him, George had told me to live with that knowledge but I realised I no longer needed him. We sat wrapped up in each other's arms until his sobbing stopped.

'I thought you might have brought Amy'.

'No, she is too young. My mother wanted to come too, but one of us had to stay behind to collect Amy from school. Prop offered but she is too much of a handful these days'.

'Prop?'

'That is Amy's name for Professor Weaver. She couldn't pronounce it properly and the name stuck. We all call him Prop these days'.

'How is he?'

'For a long time, he seemed ageless but he is slowing down. He may soon have to stop driving as his eyesight is not good. He had a cataract removed last year which helped but he still needs the other sorted. He has become a full member of the Chapman clan'.

'How are they all? We have seen all Jennie's films'.

'Frances has two boys now. Charlie has a girl. Lizzie has just become a creative group head but has just broken up with her long-term partner. She doesn't plan to have children'.

'And you?'

'Not much to tell, really'. I brushed his hair back from his sad eyes and looked away. 'I have an established mixed-bag clientele. Several actor friends of Jennie, artist colleagues of Lizzie, film technicians, musicians, scriptwriters, accountants, salesmen, designers and so on. I can now translate some pretty technical documents in both German and French too'.

'It sounds busy'.

'Yes, it is and pretty full-on sometimes. My parents have been great with Amy, and Dad really enjoys helping out with the messaging. He has become friendly with a lot of my clients. I am ashamed to say he knows much more about their lives than I do'.

A knock on the door and Dad came in with drinks for us. We pulled apart self-consciously. Dad patted Jake's shoulder and reminded me we needed to leave soon to catch our flight. Jake leant back and put his arm around me holding me close. We drank in silence.

'Can I come down and see Amy?' He whispered. 'I need to be here with Mum and Robert for the next couple of weeks. I only arrived back yesterday but I would love to spend some time with you both before I fly back'.

'Of course, I am sure she will love that. I think sometimes she doesn't believe you actually exist'. I laughed 'She kisses the graduation photo your mother gave us. By the way I don't think I have congratulated you on your doctorate, Dr Campbell'.

It was time to go and I needed to say my goodbyes to Elspeth and Robert. She kissed me and whispered in my ear 'You and Jake are good, aren't you?'

'Yes, I think so. It is time he met his daughter again'.

AMY'S DAD IS REAL

It had been an emotionally draining day. Neither of us talked much on the way back. Dad had spoken to Robert to see if there was anything we could do to help. Elspeth's sister was going to stay for a while. It was too soon to decide what would happen. He and Jake would talk. Jake had been flying for twenty four hours in order to get to the funeral and was in no fit state, intellectually or emotionally, to deal with discussions about the future. He needed to sleep. He and his father had only recently begun to make up for the years they had been estranged. Jake had told me how guilty he felt.

We didn't tell Amy Jake was in the country. He rang to let me have the details of his flight from Edinburgh. We would have time to collect Amy on the way home from the airport. We had five days before he flew back to Edinburgh to catch his flight home via Dubai. He would sleep in the main house.

I was excited and worried about how Amy would react. We got out of the car and walked to the school gates. I could see the mothers' responses to this handsome tall man standing beside me. He looked better. The haunted look had disappeared. Maybe they thought he was my new boyfriend. Angie waved from a distance and walked over.

'Hello Angie, meet Jake, Amy's Dad'.

'Oh my god, you are real. Amy will be over the moon'. She replied.

'Zoe tells me you are a good friend and that your Angus is a particular favourite of our daughter'. I had filled Jake in on some of Amy's friends on the journey from the airport.

'Oh yes, without a doubt, they are a real pair of monsters', she laughed.

The school doors opened and the children filed out looking for their parents. Amy was always one of the first out of the class keen to get home to her grandparents. She stopped, saw me and Jake, then her mouth opened in a soundless 'Oh'. Dropping her bag on the floor she flung herself across the playground into Jake's arms screaming 'It's my Daddy, it's my Daddy'.

Holding on tight to Jake's neck she looked down at me 'He is real, Mummy. Isn't he big?'

I could tell Jake was finding it difficult to speak. He buried his face in her hair. Not sure if he was laughing or crying, I asked Angie to send Angus over to pick up Amy's discarded bag.

We turned to walk to the car. Amy refused to be put down. She wasn't going to let go of her Dad that quickly. He might run away.

At the car we finally extricated Amy's arms from around Jake's neck. I could see the marks where she had held on tight. He fixed her into the car seat. Angie whispered in my ear that she would ring, took Angus' hand, and walked off. Jake squeezed himself into the front seat.

My mother was walking from her studio to the main house as we drove up and laughed as Amy screamed out of the window. 'I have found my Daddy, come and look. He is real'. Jake unwound himself from the front seat and leant in to get Amy out. He turned warily towards Mum. She grabbed Amy's hand and put her arm around Jake.

'He has flown all the way around the world to see you Amy. Aren't you a lucky girl? Why don't you take him to see your flat'. Father and daughter walked off holding hands. Jake leaning over slightly to reach down. I had forgotten how tall he was.

'Dad has a problem which needs sorting and he asked me to get you to go round as soon as you returned' Mum said.

Jake was already being shown Amy's bedroom and I could hear them laughing. Amy's voice was slightly hysterical. We would have tears before bedtime.

I made the call to calm my client. He was particularly unpleasant and I had been considering asking him to take his business elsewhere, but this incident needed sorting. Ten minutes of hassle, trying not to lose my temper as he lobbed accusations at me, was not what I needed. When I turned round, Jake was standing watching from the doorway. He filled it. He was still well built and obviously fit. His hair was shorter which showed the scar from his Hogmanay accident.

I had rung the headteacher explaining that Amy's Dad had flown from Australia for his father's funeral and wanted to spend a few days with her. Would she allow her time off? I needed to complete a form but she said it would be unfair for Amy not to spend this with him.

On the next morning I woke to find Amy was already up. She often went in to my parents if she got up early. Wrapping myself up in a dressing-gown I wandered over into the kitchen. No sign of Amy or my parents. I made a drink and walked out into the hall. From the upstairs bedrooms I could hear Amy's voice in the distance. Making another cup of tea I carried the mugs upstairs. At Jake's bedroom door I put them on the table and knocked.

'Come in' he called.

I picked up the mugs and pushed the door open. Amy was in bed with Jake snuggled up beside him. He slept in a pale blue tee-shirt which highlighted his muscles. I would have loved to have snuggled up too.

I gave him his tea and sat down on the chair near the bed.

'She arrived about 5.30. this morning'.

'Amy knows where Dad keeps the key so she can let herself in'.

We all sat and chatted until Mum called out that breakfast was on the table. Dragging Amy away so Jake could put some clothes on, promising that he wouldn't be long, we bumped into Dad coming from the bathroom. He picked Amy up and kissed her.

The next four days followed a pattern. Amy would arrive in Jake's room, snuggle up and go back to sleep. I brought up the drinks and we would chat until she woke up. We talked more in those days than the whole time we were together at college.

We took Amy over to see Prop. Jake had never met him. Even in winter his garden had shape and the frost glistened on the seed heads Graham insisted be left for the birds. They had so much in common despite the age gap. I was so glad he had moved in next door.

Prop was working on his talk to the WI that evening and didn't see Jake straight away but Amy plopped herself on his lap and pointed to Jake standing in the doorway.

'Look Prop I found my Dad'.

Jake grinned self-consciously and held out his hand. Holding Amy with his other hand Prop shook it. He looked from Jake to Amy and back again and then at me.

'She looks like him doesn't she'.

'Yes, but I hope she won't turn out quite so large', I responded.

Amy jumped off his lap and asked if he had any chocolate biscuits. They wandered off together into the kitchen. Jake looked around at the shelves full of books.

'I can see you have built a very loving world for our girl. She is surrounded by people who care for her'.

'Well, you know the Chapman clan. The house is still regularly full-up with friends who have discovered the delights of East Anglia'.

'Have you found anybody else?'

We had still not really spoken about Jake's family in Australia. He had described his work, how he loved the variety. This was a new area to be faced.

'No, there is very little opportunity. I work evenings and visitors to the house are mostly old friends of my parents'.

'I am sorry about that'.

I was afraid to say that I was too frightened to commit to any relationships. My way of dealing with loss had been to avoid complications. On the whole I was happy, if sometimes lonely. Seeing Jake had reminded me that, once, I had been highly sexually motivated. I didn't want to admit that the only sex I had these days was with the help of a vibrator!

Prop and Amy came back with the biscuit tin and some fresh coffee. We spent the morning with him. He and Jake discussed the University system in Australia and how different it was. They compared the two but didn't come to any conclusions. Leaving Prop to complete his talk we drove off to find somewhere to eat. We decided Norwich would be the best place in the winter.

Those five days flew past. On the last evening I plucked up the courage to talk about his family.

His twin boys, Richard and Andrew, were four. They were identical but didn't look like Jake. Clare worked part-time at the university with the boys attending the creche. Jake had applied for a Head of Department post but his departure to Scotland might have impacted on his application. He wasn't sure. There was another candidate who was keen. Most of his work was in the Far East. He had spent time in Indonesia, Vanuatu and Polynesia. Later on that year he was exchanging with a colleague at Harvard for four weeks. He regularly submitted papers on his research to environmental institutes and had recently been invited to a high-level conference in Canada.

Jake knew he was young to apply for the post. It was rare to achieve that status at his age.

We talked well into the early hours the night before he left to catch a few hours sleep in the main house. As he wished me goodnight he turned and lifted me up. He kissed me hard on the mouth. I pulled back, afraid of the danger but he laughed.

'I will always love you Zoe. I still want you. I have not forgotten those months we were together. They can't be regretted. We have Amy to show for all that passion'.

He kissed me again and I lost myself in him. Then, abruptly, he stopped. This was too dangerous.

'I must go'.

He put me down gently, stroked my hair, kissed my forehead and disappeared into the dark.

We arranged for a taxi to take Jake to the airport. Amy would have wanted to come and we knew she was going to be distraught at his departure and we could better deal with her sorrow at the house. Jake promised to write and speak to Amy from time to time and I would send news of her progress. I couldn't bear the thought of another six years of no contact.

The taxi came and Jake picked Amy up. She knew he had to go to Granny Elspeth and back to his sons so she tried to be brave. I was trying to be brave too. Saying goodbye to my parents, Jake loaded his bag onto the back seat, all the time with Amy clinging to him. Still holding Amy, he crushed me in his arms and kissed me quickly whispering that he loved us both. Dad came forward and took Amy off Jake and he ducked into the taxi seat. We waved until he was out of sight.

Jake was true to his word. Each month he wrote to Amy and every now and then he rang. He did this from his office late in the afternoon when Amy was home from school to avoid upsetting Clare. Two years later he was in Geneva at a Conference and flew into Norwich to see us and then on to Edinburgh. Elspeth had sold the house and moved into a smaller, more manageable, bungalow. Jake had been trying to persuade her to fly out to see her other grandchildren but she was wary of the long journey. She still visited us regularly. The next year, he managed three short trips in between environmental conferences.

Elspeth was with us for Amy's 11th birthday. Amy was now at high school. Years of visiting Prop had engendered a love of education. She had a zest for learning. With Jake, who was now a young eminent Professor, a well-known specialist in his field, as her father, that was not surprising. I mentioned this to Prop one day.

'She has two very gifted parents'. He said quietly. 'You have a good mind, Zoe, you just haven't had the chance to fully display your talent'.

After supper Elspeth surprised us all by saying she was thinking of going to Australia in the summer holidays and would I be willing for her to take Amy along? She had waited until Amy had gone off to do her homework before raising the subject.

'I will be happy to pay for her trip although I am sure Jake would be more than willing to contribute if it gives him a chance to spend time with Amy'.

'I think Amy would love that', I replied, without hesitation. 'She is old enough to really appreciate the experience'.

'Good' she said. 'Now I need to make sure Jake and Clare are on board. I will phone him when I get back'.

I wondered to myself what Clare's reaction would be when Jake's love-child turned up. I could see Mum had had the same thought as she looked across the table.

It was some time before Elspeth rang. I had convinced myself that Clare had not been keen and the subject had been dropped. I was wrong, Jake had been away in America and had only just returned. He was delighted and offered to pay both their flights. They had a small annex where Elspeth and Amy could live during the stay. The dates were agreed so that he would be around and I went in to talk to Amy.

'Granny Elspeth is going to Australia to see Daddy'.

She was peering into her computer screen. 'Does that mean we won't be seeing him here next year?' Jake's irregular visits upset Amy's balance and as she got older she resented them more.

'Well, actually, Granny wants to take you with her'.

'What, are you certain?'

'Oh yes, she has realised she isn't getting any younger and it is unlikely Clare and the boys will ever come here, so she must make the trip'.

'Has she spoken to Dad about this?'

'Yes, he was delighted', she said. 'He even offered to pay both your fares'.

'Well I would be mad to pass up a chance to go to Australia, wouldn't I?'

'So, is it settled then?'

'Yep'.

Apart from school trips, lasting only a few days, Amy and I had spent most of our life together. When the time came for her to join the flight to Edinburgh to connect with Elspeth, before catching the plane to Sydney, via Singapore, I was decidedly nervous. Amy was very excited. She was on an adventure and her Dad was at the end of the trail. It had been two years since he had managed a brief three-day visit.

I drove back via Prop's house. He was becoming increasingly frail and I was visiting more often. Graham, his neighbour, kept an eye out for him too. He spent a lot of time reading and cataloguing his extensive collection. It was as if he was tidying up his life.

Sitting in his garden admiring the flowers, I sighed.

'In some ways I wish I could have gone too. I have often wondered what made Clare so much more of a wife, than me'.

'Mostly I would say she fitted in with his lifestyle. She was happy to travel around South America with him. Would you have wanted to do that?'

'Oh god, no. I can't think of anything worse. Jake knew I didn't fit the bill but hadn't wanted to tell me'.

Whilst Amy was away, I had registered to do a computing course in the evenings. It was three nights a week for a month. I needed to learn how to design and set up databases to improve my services. My little book of information on each client was so out of date.

I couldn't rest until I knew they had landed. Once I heard I could settle down. I was trying to work out the time zones when the phone rang. It was Jake. Their flight was delayed by 5 hours and he wanted to let me know. He knew I would be worrying. The next call was from Amy saying they had landed safely. Granny was exhausted but so pleased to meet Jake's family. She asked if I had seen Prop and was he OK?

'He is fine, don't worry. I hope you have a lovely time'.

'I wish you had been able to come too', she said, hanging up.

For Amy, that trip to Australia, was a dream come true. Clare, Jake and the boys had made their visit amazing. I needn't have worried. Jake showed Amy around the university campus with its modern buildings. He was keen to introduce her to his colleagues. I had thought he might not wish to acknowledge her.

Although the twins were younger, Amy hadn't minded. She had half-brothers. This was so important to her. They pranked her and it took a while for her to discover which twin she was talking to. She had seen that Richard had a slightly bent ear-lobe but didn't let on that she had discovered this.

Her stay in Oz flew past. In no time at all I was greeting her at Norwich airport. She was tanned and her hair was slightly bleached. She had stayed with Elspeth for a couple of days after their return. The flights back ran smoothly and there were no delays. Looking at this eleven year old, she seemed wise beyond her years. She handed over a letter from Jake and then flopped down on the sofa.

'I had a brilliant time Mum but I did miss you lot. How is Prop?'

'I called the doctor last week as he had chest pains'. Amy jumped up and grabbed my arm.' What was wrong?' She enquired anxiously.

'It turned out to be severe indigestion'.

'Ha, ha, he had probably been eating radishes again'.

'I will tell you all about my trip when Grandma and Grandpa are around as I don't want to have to repeat my stories again. Where are they?'

Mum was putting up a display in our local church helping

132

to raise money for the tower repair. Dad was in London meeting a film producer about a new soundtrack.

I opened the envelope. Several group photos dropped out. Pictures of Elspeth with her grandchildren, the whole family sitting down to eat or swimming at Bondi beach. Jake must have been taking the pictures as he was only in the family group. Nearly as tall as Jake, Clare stood with him near the barbeque, laughing. She was wearing shorts and a bikini top. Everybody else was sat down eating. Amy was in the middle with her arm around one of her half-brothers. I felt the tears well up but it was a good feeling too. She was no longer an only child.

Folded around the photos was a letter from Jake.

Dearest Zoe,

This last month with Amy and mother here with us has been so amazing. I am so grateful to you for letting her come. It is a long journey for an eleven year old even if she is with her grandmother. I think that Amy was the adult on the trip, personally.

It has been a wonder to see all my children together. Even now the thought brings me to tears. I never felt this would happen. Watching Mum with Amy, Richard and Andrew sitting out on the veranda chatting in the evening made me chuckle. I wish Dad could have been with us. I still bear the guilt of those long years of estrangement.

There is always something about your first-born child. I don't know what it is but, even though I love the boys to bits, Amy moves me in a way I can't explain. I will never forget her birth and that time we spent together.

I took Amy to meet my colleagues at the university. They were astounded at her maturity. Australian children are quite immature at Amy's age.

To see her talking to my fellow scientists about the environment made my heart swell with pride. She referred lovingly to her very own 'Prop' and his mass of books. In Australia there is a tinge of envy about the eminence of Cambridge Dons even if they are retired.

You have done amazingly Zoe. She is all yours. She loves you deeply and I am envious of that depth of feeling.

I hope it won't be too long before I make my way back to England via a conference or two. I have submitted papers to an environmental forum to take place in France later this year. Let's keep our fingers crossed one of them gets accepted. Thank you for letting her come to Oz.

Yours for ever

Jake

I placed this letter in the box containing the other one Jake had written telling me he was getting married. Sometimes I wonder if those few notes would be the story of my life.

On Sunday Prop came to lunch. I drove over and collected him. Amy regaled us with her stories of her time in Sydney. Dad asked her if she preferred Australia to England?

'No, it is just so different. I enjoyed the visit, getting to know my brothers, seeing Dad in his home environment but Granny and I agreed that we wanted to be back home. I so missed you all'.

'Would you want to go again?' I asked.

'Oh yes'.

DEATH OF A DEAR FRIEND

Three years later Prop died. He had been having trouble breathing and was diagnosed with cancer of the lung. He had never smoked but had been surrounded by men smoking in the prisoner of war camp and I suspect it may have affected his lungs. He refused to have any treatment. He told me he was too old. His book cataloguing was complete and he offered them to a reference library in Cambridge. They accepted with alacrity and sent two young history students to help pack the boxes. It took them five days (three days to pack and two days to chat with Prop drinking tea and eating chocolate biscuits). Prop and his two cats came to live with my parents for the last few weeks of his life. We couldn't leave him alone in his house even though Graham made sure he was okay but, as he was often away surveying, it was too risky.

He died, as he had lived, quietly with no fuss, surrounded by people who loved him and had become his family. I wasn't sure Amy should be present but she refused to leave his side as he lapsed into a coma. He slipped away holding our hands. We were both heartbroken.

Prop had asked Herr Scherman to be the executor of his will. He rang me after the funeral and asked to come round.

Prop had left his estate to "his beloved friend Zoe and her

daughter Amy, they are the family I never had". There were charitable bequests but the remainder, including his house, he had left to me. I also inherited £60,000. He left Amy £20,000 in a trust to be made available when she started university.

Probate for Prop's estate took six months. I had time to decide my future. I had lived securely in the flat with Amy. My parents' protection had been the bedrock for Amy's early years. I met up regularly with Prop's gardener to make sure all was well with the house and garden. On these visits my thoughts crystallised. Prop's legacy had offered me a choice. I spent long hours translating and my list of clients needing off-site messaging was full. I had little time to spare for myself. If I read a book it was normally into the early hours.

At fourteen, Amy was mature and independent. At school she was fully participating in all the extra curricular activities, particularly sport. She was a runner, competing in both short and long-distance events. She was an all-rounder. Like Jake, she was tall and well-built. She and Angus cycled to school in the summer months often stopping off at Angie's house on the way home. They were inseparable.

Prop's house was marginally closer to Amy's secondary school. It was time to move. I would sit in Prop's winged chair and feel his presence. My grief was still bubbling around under the surface and I had returned to counselling to make sure I didn't have another breakdown. Amy missed Prop too but she was young with so much to look forward to.

Minus Prop's books the house was sad. They had been such an intrinsic part of his existence. A few gardening books lay on the lower shelves. Prop rarely used the front room preferring the smaller library to the left of the entrance hall. He had no use for a dining room, eating in the kitchen. He had enlarged the kitchen by removing an old scullery, installing a downstairs toilet and a utility room. All the Victorian features had been retained as much as possible.

I kept a few of Prop's belongings. His worn old cardigan was wrapped up in tissue paper and put in my memory box along with his glasses and Jake's letters. I could keep him alive in my head by moving to his house. I now knew this is what he had wanted. My future was his legacy. His spirit would move me forward just as he had supported me for most of my post university life.

My parents were not surprised at my decision. Dad handed me Bob's (the builder, ha ha) telephone number and I arranged to meet up at the house. Most of the work needed was cosmetic but he suggested I install a new bathroom with a shower, update the Rayburn and improve the central heating. A small amount of roofwork around the chimney was required and the old woodburner in the library needed renovation. Graham helped me choose the paint scheme.

All villages change and East Anglia's population was expanding. Down the road from Prop's house a small estate had been built. Prop had not participated in the village's objections to the scheme, believing young families would keep the area alive. The benefit for us was that broadband in the area was far better than where my parents lived.

With money to spend, Amy and I went off to John Lewis in Norwich and ordered furnishings, carpets and curtains. The house was much larger than the flat and my few pieces of furniture looked sparse when the removers unpacked. At auction I bought an old pine kitchen table. A reconditioned electric AGA, at least twenty-five years old, looking immaculate after a respray, warmed the whole of the ground floor. I swear the previous owner hadn't used it other than as a heater. Nobody had ever cooked on it.

I set up my office in the old library. Unpacking my books I wondered how I had got so many. In the flat, one wall was top to bottom with books. Amy had a large bookshelf in her room too. With the better spring weather, Amy had started cycling again. She arrived back with Angus in tow. Angie was coming over later to collect him and his bike.

I was sitting at the kitchen table drinking coffee when they blew in. Neither of them did anything by half. They were so full on it exhausted me. Stopping only for a quick drink of juice they charged upstairs to unpack Amy's boxes. Apart from making up the bed I had agreed not to do anything more.

Mum, Dad and Jennie arrived just as it was getting dark, bringing food for the gang, followed closely by Angie. Two years before Jennie had damaged her ankle when filming in Ireland. It was not ideal for one of the main characters to be hobbling around, so they had arranged for physiotherapy on the ankle, to speed up recovery. Back in London a few months later she had bumped into her physio saviour in a bar. He was out celebrating his birthday and asked her to join the party. Together now for at least 18 months, she and Stephen, made a delightful couple. They shared a flat in Battersea overlooking the park. He seemed to cope well with her frequent absences filming.

Mum's chorizo, tomato and roast pepper soup, followed by a selection of cheeses and French bread, hit the mark. It was perfect. Her chickens sent me a present of six large brown eggs for breakfast the next day. I couldn't remember the last time I had bought eggs in the supermarket.

Over coffee, Mum nodded at Dad who smiled back, and disappeared to the car. He slipped back through the kitchen entrance with a painting covered in brown paper and passed it to me. Expecting one of Mum's signature landscapes, I was astounded to find she had painted a portrait of Prop. Between them she and Prop had managed the sittings before he became too ill.

Amy came and stood behind me with her hands on my shoulders. Here was the man we had loved and who had cared so greatly for us. My mother had captured his essence. Sitting looking out of the window of her studio with his glasses clasped in his hand, he looked so peaceful.

'I am not sure where to hang the picture. In the lounge or the library'.

'It should be the library which is now your office. He never used the sitting room. You will have a daily reminder of this gentle soul who has given you so much, Zoe', she smiled.

She admitted that her portraiture skills were rusty. She had painted us all over the years at varying ages and the pictures were hanging on the stairs leading up to the first floor. Dad called it his *Rogues Gallery*.

'It was challenging but I want to do more. I think it is time I painted the grandchildren, starting with you Amy, as the oldest'.

I wondered how on earth Amy would sit still long enough. I thought she would offer some excuse to avoid sitting for Mum but actually she liked the idea.

Mum and Dad had celebrated the long-awaited departure of their youngest child by getting themselves a dog and a new tenant. There were several rescued cats alongside Prop's elderly felines lounging around the house, failing to earn their feed by keeping the house mice free, but we had never had a dog.

A visit to the local animal sanctuary had resulted in the arrival of a small mixed-heritage brown and white puppy. Amy and Angus were ordered to come up with a suitable name.

"Chewy" would have been my first choice. His little sharp teeth chomped up the edge of carpets, legs of chairs, his toys and his bed. My parents didn't care, they adored him. Amy and Angus, trapped indoors by the rain one afternoon, had watched the musical *Oliver*. Bill Sykes' dog had similar markings. Spike was the chosen name!

My father had envisaged donning his wellies, grabbing a walking stick and striding across the fields with Spike in tow. What he hadn't known was that little puppies only need short walks for at least twelve months so Spike and Dad rarely ventured beyond the gates.

FINANCIAL INDEPENDENCE

I embraced computerisation in all its forms. I had long ago gravitated to using databases for my clients, updating the systems as they came onstream. I rarely got a letter from Jake now as he communicated by email more often than not to Amy rather than me. She was a natural geek. The advent of mobile phones had released me from my self-imposed house arrest. Dad missed not helping out but he really struggled with the systems I had put in place.

My next chore was to reduce the size of the off-site messaging client base. I had over sixty registered, paying me a weekly retainer. Under pressure, I had been unable to give the time to really connect with these clients. I had databases full of details of their business connections, friends, families, people to be avoided and so on. I knew the agents for the actors, the booking managers for the musicians, making sure their contact details were up to date. I knew their holiday dates, when they were unavailable but very little about their lives. Most of them paid on time but I was fed up with chasing the freelance computer programmer I had taken on the year before, for payment. His brain didn't run to paying my bill. He was also demanding.

Hadley was still with me even though he should have retired. The 80s recession had severely impacted on his pension savings. With Dad's help we went through customer by customer to weed out the undesirables.

First-off we checked Jennie's numerous introductions. We mustn't offend these contacts. Initially around ten, the list had grown to over twenty. We pulled up each name and Dad filled me in on the background information whilst I added it onto the database. I was not entirely convinced that all this personal knowledge would improve my service. I was wrong. It would change my life.

We Googled and checked Wikipedia for the more famous. We even discovered that two of them had married and were both paying me a retainer. Angie and I went to the cinema or theatre at least once a week as Amy and Angus no longer needed baby-sitting. I never told her the names of my clients but she must have realised who they were. We had seen almost every film for at least three of them. She was horrified at some of the ghastly sci-fi films she was dragged to.

Eventually we decided to remove fifteen people mostly on the basis that they were unpleasant or they were poor payers.

Having decided to reduce my clients and feeling much more positive about my work-life balance, in theory, I shouldn't have agreed to take on anybody new. Some chance. That evening, Jennie emailed me about an actor she had completed a film with recently. Confidentially, she told me his personal life was a mess and he needed some order in his professional communications. He was known as probably the nicest actor in the business. She had loved working with him. His name was Paul Walker (mental note to Zoe and Angie – more films to see). When filming he became totally absorbed in his character. He hated distractions (sounds like Prop). Lunchtimes he would pick up his mobile and despair at the number of messages. She described what I did for her when she was on set or out of easy contact and suggested he should speak to me.

I switched on the computer and typed in Paul Walker, actor. Up popped his picture alongside a very full list of his films. He was thirty-five, born in Essex but his family had moved to London. He had three sisters. He was married with three children. I clicked through the pictures to get a better look. Most of the them showed him smiling and laughing. His wife was amazingly beautiful. They looked like a charmed pair. His list of film credits was astonishing (I had seen several). He seemed to have worked non-stop since leaving RADA. I wondered if he had known Frances. No, she had probably left by the time he started.

Most evenings Amy and I spent out in the garden during the summer months. If it was warm, Graham popped around with wine. He and Amy had planted flowers perfect for attracting insects. They seemed to avoid the plants and headed straight for me. I was covered in bites from head to toe. Graham was trying to persuade me to take up bee keeping. I would have to hide in the house to avoid being stung. Amy knew I would eventually capitulate.

With a father who was a well-known environmentalist it was inevitable Amy would have inherited not only his genes but his interests. They exchanged emails all the time. I scanned in her reports and sent them off to him. His involvement in her life, even living so far away, was consistent. After Prop's legacy I had attempted to stop him sending the money. His reply was abrupt.

'If you don't need the money then put it away for Amy', So I did.

I didn't hear from Paul Walker but I did from Jake. His university was collaborating with a company based on the new Research Park being built on the outskirts of Norwich. He would be in the UK for two weeks and then fly up to Edinburgh. On earlier visits he had stayed in the main house but wondered if he could base himself with us instead? If not, he would book a hotel.

Amy would never have forgiven me if I had refused. He would actually be around for her birthday in October, the first in fifteen years.

If my clients noticed a change in the atmosphere, they never commented. I had more time for them. Efficiency alone does not make a good business. I had been too preoccupied to understand that. More knowledge helped me respond differently. Mary Duncan loathed pressure so I warned callers she would take a while to respond. Andrew Radley's wife had breast cancer and he was trying to do his job whilst supporting her. He was not coping well so I persuaded him to tell his employer. He was scared of losing his sales job. They understood and halved his workload.

I became good friends with Sam Rothwell's mother. He was an elusive artist and she spent half her life chasing him. He worked at night and slept all day. As soon as he surfaced for his messages, I would ring her.

I befriended the hassled secretaries of pushy agents who were chasing my clients for answers to scripts they had been sent. I explained Robin could not play his cello at three different events on one night. I was starting to actually enjoy the job. I understood why Dad missed helping out.

AMY RENAMES THE COTTAGE

With the onset of puberty, Amy developed an inordinate interest in my love life or to be precise, the lack of any sort of action in that area. I was not the type to go clubbing and the only males I knew were family, married, gay or unattainable in Australia. I could hardly turn up to her school to chat up her male teachers. At the cinema, the only member of the opposite sex I came across was the spotty young boy behind the counter.

'I can't believe that you have not been out with anybody since Dad. That was fifteen years ago. There must be somebody else for you to love', she muttered when we were sitting in front of the fire on the first cold evening.

'He is a hard act to follow. I haven't come across anybody I like as much as Jake'.

'But he is out of reach, Mum. Maybe you should go on a dating website'.

I sat there envisaging my profile. "Zoe, thirty-six year old single-mum. Two amazing sexual encounters, the last, fifteen years ago. Graduate with first class Honours degree (unused). Small business owner. Hobbies: Indifferent gardener, book-worm, avid cinema goer. No sporting activities".

Not a lot to offer. I could hardly tell my daughter about the overpowering physical reaction I had to both Yves and Jake. I had been spoiled and now I couldn't settle for second-best.

I hate the winter months. It was dark and it wasn't even six o'clock. I supposed I should get some supper. The phone rang and Amy answered it.

'Hello, this is Recluse Cottage'. She said loudly.

I grabbed the phone out of her hand. I apologised to the caller. My daughter was playing a prank. The caller laughed.

'Are you Zoe Chapman?' he asked.

'Yes'.

'My name is Paul Walker, your sister gave me your number some months ago'.

'Oh yes, Jennie emailed me. She thought I might be able to help out'.

'We worked together on a film. She is a very kind person and a brilliant actress. I hope I get to work with her again one day'.

'That is good to hear. She seems to like you too. Have you decided I might be of some use?'

'How much did Jennie tell you?'

'Not a lot, just that you found it difficult to deal with all the messages on your mobile phone when you were filming'.

His voice was very distinctive, not quite like Richard Burton, but you could imagine him being a narrator on a documentary. Very clear, quite deep, smooth, not quite as soft as David Attenborough.

I described what I did for Jennie. 'Is that what you need?'

'Spot-on. If it works it will be perfect. At the moment I only really need help when I am filming. I can organise myself when I am at home. What would you need from me?'

'Lists of your contacts and what they do, who you want me to prioritise, people you want to avoid. All Jennie did was to put a message on her phone giving my number. They should ring not text. It helps if I know your movements too, particularly if you are out of the country'. I gradually build-up a database for each client.

'Do you have many actors?'

'Yes, musicians, artists, writers and recently quite a few IT programmers. A whole range. My father is a composer/musician, Mum is an artist, Jennie, you know, her twin Frances, works on the technical side of the film business. Lizzie is a creative group head and my brother is an accountant! They have all introduced clients to me over the years'.

'Interesting family. All my sisters are married with families. Jennie says you have a daughter'.

'Yes, Amy. She is 15. My life took a different path from my more successful siblings. I became pregnant at university'. Why was I telling this man my story?

'But you must be happy to have Amy. I love my children. They are still quite young. Where did you go to university?'

'Cambridge. Amy was born 5 months after I graduated. I think I was more excited by her birth than getting my degree'.

'Is her father still around?'

'Yes, but lives in Australia with his other family'.

'That must be hard'.

He was so easy to talk to. Like a father confessor. I would be describing my lack of love-life soon.

'I am out of the country until December. When I get back, I will contact you again. Is that okay?'

'I will wait to hear from you'.

'Bye Zoe, great to talk to you'.

After he hung up Amy appeared. She had been sitting on the stairs listening.

'Who was that?'

'An actor friend of Jennie's, Paul Walker'.

She wandered off to Google him. I could hear her yelping down the stairs. 'Mum, he is gorgeous, not as good as Dad, but pretty close'.

'He is married to a beautiful actress, with beautiful children and probably a home designed by some famous architect. Out of my league'. I replied.

MEMORABLE BIRTHDAY

I was late collecting Jake from the airport. He had flown in from Schipol. Just once I would like to collect somebody from the airport without having to navigate temporary traffic lights causing major delays. Amy was on tenterhooks anticipating having her Dad in the same house as us for two weeks. I was on tenterhooks for very different reasons most of them physical. Having Jake in very close proximity for two weeks would be a strain.

He had already arrived and was at the entrance. My stomach felt as if I had a bunch of butterflies swimming around. Would my reaction to Jake ever change or would I be sitting in my old people's home trying to suppress my longing on one of his visits? Catching sight of me in the short-stay parking he waved, picked up his bags and came across. I had opened the boot and he stored his bags and computer.

His hands now freed he whisked me up in his arms and kissed me.

'You are looking very well, Zoe, have you put on some weight? You always were too skinny. It suits you'.

'I am wearing a puffa jacket, Jake', I retorted. 'We must get back because your daughter will be wondering where we are'.

'She knows I have landed because I rang home'.

'If you put me down on the ground I can start the car'.

'Okay, if you insist'. He dropped me down and I staggered to the car. I wasn't sure my legs would keep me upright. Wrenching open the driver's door I flopped down on the seat.

It was strange turning into the driveway. Jake had visited once to meet Prop but this was now our home. Amy was standing at the open door letting all the heat out and Jake barely had time to unwind himself and get out of the car, before she piled into his arms. Opening the boot, I picked up the computer and his shoulder bag. The larger case looked heavier so I left that to him.

His time with us was often of limited duration as he passed through. Now, we had him for two weeks and we would celebrate Amy's birthday together. It was a school day. Amy's party with the family would be on the Saturday. Mum had a house full.

'Can I email Clare to say I have arrived?' He asked as he pulled off his coat.

'Of course, use my computer. I don't have a password'.

Supper finished, we all sat in the lounge. Amy had loaded the log burner and it was roaring away. It had been hot in Sydney when Jake left so miserable wet East Anglia was a jolt. A year had passed since his last, very brief, visit to us after his conference in France. He said so much was happening in his field but Europe and Canada were in the forefront of environmental action. Australia was disastrous. They were in complete denial about the warming planet.

The warmth of the fire was making him sleepy. I could

see he was struggling to keep awake. Amy and I stopped asking him questions and before long his eyes closed. He was in Prop's wing chair his long legs stretched out towards the fire. You would have thought we were playing happy families. Domestic bliss!

I had a chance to look at him properly. His hair was slightly grey above his ears, the crinkly laugh lines around his eyes were more pronounced but otherwise there was little change. Amy whispered that she was going to take a shower. I was left to stare at the man I couldn't stop loving. As if he was aware of my gaze, he stirred but didn't wake up.

I washed up and made some coffee. He woke up as I came back in the room.

'Sorry, the fire made me sleepy'.

'You have flown several thousand miles to be here. I am not surprised. While Amy is upstairs let me tell you the plans. We have organised a party on Saturday for her. Most of the family will be around, some of her friends as well, but she wants to spend her actual day with us. I know you will be going to meetings but can you arrange to be home early?'

'Of course. They have arranged a hire car so you won't need to chauffeur me'.

'Would you like some coffee, or will it keep you awake?'

'I'm not sure anything will stop me from sleeping tonight. I have no meetings until the afternoon'.

Amy reappeared with her hair wrapped up in a towel turban. She was wearing her pyjamas and a bathrobe. Jake sat up and pulled her on to his lap.

'Our baby daughter' he laughed. His use of 'our' brought

a lump to my throat. I drank some coffee to wash it down. Just for two weeks they would both be mine.

Amy went off to dry her hair. Jake stood, picking up his coffee cup and sat down next to me on the sofa. Close but not touching. He took my hand. We sat in silence.

'Do you miss England?'

'Funnily enough, I do. Australia can be very hot at times. It saps your energy. You spend your days in air-conditioned offices and when you walk out the heat slaps you in the face'.

'Have you ever considered coming back?'

'Frequently but Clare would hate living here. She is Aussie through and through. The boys are keen to travel before they start university but they are young still. I am sure they will change their minds. Unsurprisingly, they do everything together'.

'Mum and Robert are talking about a visit next year. Do you think Amy would want to come again?'

Amy came back in just as Jake said this and her face was a picture. I think he had his answer.

'It would be the same length trip as last time'. He yawned "I think I must go to bed'. He kissed my palm, he still had hold of my hand and got up.

I cleared up and put the dishes in the machine. By the time I went up both of the loves of my life were fast asleep.

Next morning, I went to wake up Amy for school only to find her bed empty. Jake's door was ajar. Peering in, I saw two heads on the pillows. Amy opened her eyes and smiled. She slipped out of bed.

Angie was doing the school run and Amy hated not being ready. She was downstairs in her uniform. I had made porridge. She covered the surface with seeds, walnuts and raisins and milk to cool it down. She went up to clean her teeth as Jake came down. He was still sleepy but turned to open the front door when Angie knocked. What she made of his tousled state I am not sure. Amy rushed past putting on her coat, gave him a smacking kiss, and ran to the car.

'Bye Mum, bye Dad, see you later'. She waved.

It saddened me to think that she would only have her parents living together for two weeks of her fifteen years. Jake noticed and put his arm around me.

'I know how you feel. I wish I could change things for Amy but I can't. This is the best I can do. Let's make it very special for her'.

The garage delivered the hire car later that morning and Jake went off. He was definitely feeling more human. My morning was busy. Before he left Jake stood looking at Prop's painting hanging in my office.

'He meant a lot to you both didn't he?'

'I miss him every day. Along with Mum and Dad, he filled our lives. He was another grandpa for Amy. He helped me deal with my breakdown after you wrote to say you were getting married. I think only he knew the depths of my despair and depression'.

Jake turned to face me, shock registering his concern.

'You had a breakdown? Mum never told me'.

'My parents asked her not to mention it'. I got up and walked over. His sheer presence made the room seem small.

153

I just rested my head on his chest then looked up.

'It was so long ago now. I had a great deal of help. I had counselling for years. After Prop died, I was depressed but over the years I have learnt how to deal with it. Depression is always there but you live with it. Prop knew that too. He was my rock'.

Jake stroked my hair.

'I have never been there for you, have I? All I have done is inflict pain. It was not what I planned. To be so cruel'. He lent back against my desk pulling me towards him.

'I convinced myself that I had been straight all along with you to assuage my guilt, but I hadn't I know. I was fooling myself. Dad said I would one day have to accept what I had done and live with the guilt. He was right. My father loved you very much. Will you ever forgive me?'

I pulled back and put my hands on his face. His eyes were full of tears.

'I forgave you the day of your father's funeral'. I took both his hands in mine. 'I want these two weeks to be perfect for Amy but also for us. We have to take what little time we have and make it special. Look forward not back. Your wife and boys are in Australia and that is where you belong'.

He brushed his tears away and turned to get his coat and pulled out a handkerchief and blew his nose.

For the next two weeks the mornings followed the same pattern with Amy waking up beside her Dad. He actually dropped her off at school on his way to the research park.

It was always difficult buying Amy presents as she was not materialistic. Her Christmas list usually asked us to sponsor a goat in Ethiopia or buy trees for Africa. You couldn't go wrong with a book, that was always popular. This year my parents had bought her clothes. Not pretty dresses. She had asked for waterproofs for her field trip next year.

We agreed we would not open any presents or cards until the afternoon. I went into the spare room to wake them up and ventured beyond the doorway, just this once. I kissed them both. Jake moved and I laid down beside him with his arm along my back. Amy stirred and saw us lying together on the bed. Jake put his other around Amy and held us close.

'Happy birthday my dearest girl', he said. 'I remember the day you were born as if it was yesterday, not fifteen years ago'. She snuggled into his shoulder. This was as close to having her family together as she would get. She mumbled something and tears came to her eyes.

'What is it Amy?' Jake asked.

'I wish Prop was here to see us. He always told me that, even though you didn't live together, you both loved me very much'.

'What he said is true, Amy', Jake replied. I was too choked up to say anything.

'I must get up and shower or you will be late for school', he said.

Why, when you want an easy morning so you can get on with baking a cake does the phone never stop? By midday I had covered half the kitchen, my keyboard and the phone in cake dough or icing. By two o'clock I had managed to produce a lopsided cake. Amy wouldn't mind, she knew I couldn't match my mother's culinary skills. Graham called round with Amy's present. He had been storing it hidden away in his shed. It was a bee-hive. I had finally capitulated!

We would have to wait to the spring to set it up and add the bees.

Jake's present was in a small box on the bookcase.

I heard the car drive up and opened the door. It felt so domestic, me greeting my ex-lover and daughter home from work and school. This was all a bit make believe happy families anyway.

'Have you had a good day you two?'

I was pretending to be the good housewife welcoming the family home. It wasn't working as they both gave me a funny look.

'Let's have some tea and open up your cards and presents on the kitchen table'.

Graham and I had attempted to wrap up the bee-hive but our efforts were pretty awful. You could tell straight away what it was. Amy screamed with delight and ripped off the paper.

'I love it Mum'.

'Well when I get stung you will have to promise to get me to hospital quickly. Here is Graham's card. He designed and printed it himself.' It showed bees buzzing around the hive. 'His present is going to be the bees'.

Jake handed over his parcel. Beautifully gift wrapped it was a mobile phone. 'Now you can let Mum know when you are going to be late from school so she isn't hanging around'. When I said he was collecting Amy from school I had told her not to hang around until everybody had left! Jake had overheard and asked if she did it regularly?

'Well when Amy gets talking to her mates she forgets that I

am waiting at the gates'.

'So now you can ring her'.

We lit the candles on my wonky cake and Amy blew them out, whilst we sang *Happy Birthday*.

After supper we relaxed in the lounge. Jake had Amy screaming with laughter when he described my behaviour the evening of her birth. He mimicked me screaming at him, blaming him for the pain, then five minutes later when the contraction had stopped covering him in kisses, then pushing him away and telling him to go home when the next pain came. All the time digging my nails into his hands. If he hadn't been so big the baby would have been a reasonable size and not taken so long to be born. It was all his fault, you are too big, too big. He said my language had been far too obscene for him to repeat to a young girl of fifteen. I rocked with laughter.

His face changed again and he looked down at his hands. 'When they put you in my arms, I thought my heart would burst'.

Amy, who was seated on the floor in front of us, just put her arms around his legs. He pulled her up on to his lap and whispered, 'you were a very big baby though, Zoe was right'.

'This has been the best birthday in my life'. She turned to me 'I know how difficult this is for you, having Dad around for only a few days a year most of the time. I also know how sad you are when he goes, but I love you so much for doing this for me'.

It was getting late. Time for the temporary family to go to bed. I was glad Amy had her day with her father but I was exhausted. The emotion was draining. I kissed them goodnight and left them chatting in front of the fire. I heard

Amy come up shortly afterwards.

Saturday dawned and we drove over to my parents. The area in front of the house was packed with cars. The guest of honour was extremely excited. Jake hung back slightly not really sure of his welcome. The last time all of my family had all seen him was after Amy's birth. Frances and Jennie took him in hand getting him a drink and introducing him to Lizzie's new man. I saw Angie talking to him a little later. Our family get togethers are pretty boisterous and this was no exception. Amy was moving from one group to another being handed presents and cards. She went off with Angus, some of her cousins and school friends, into the lounge. The rest of us piled into the kitchen filling our glasses making a tremendous noise.

Jennie and Jake came up. 'I gather Paul Walker got round to contacting you', she shouted over the babble. Jake looked up, 'the actor?'

'Yes, have you heard of him?'

'He is very popular, down under. The boys love his franchise films'.

'I have just done an audition with him for a film next year and he said he had spoken to you'.

'He is going to come and see me in the New Year'. I replied.

Mum was encouraging everybody to eat. The dining table was sagging under the weight of food. If we didn't start filling our plates soon it would collapse. Sitting underneath, Spike was waiting for that to happen.

Dad had turned the second lounge into a music room with sofas spread around between the instruments. Music was blaring out and some of the youngsters were laughing at their parents gyrating to the Rolling Stones. After lunch, Dad was dragged to the piano for the usual sing-along. This was a well-worn tradition. Even Amy knew all the words to *We are the Champions*. An hour of belting out familiar songs and then it was time for Amy to cut her cake. We crowded into the main lounge. People were crammed in every corner.

Mum's cake was a decided improvement on my wonky effort. Amy blew out the candles to a chorus of Happy Birthday. I was standing in front of Jake with his hands on my shoulders. Dad was snapping all the groups with his camera.

Amy thanked everybody for coming. She looked around and her glance encompassed all of us in its warmth. She had written a witty, fun speech. She had kept it secret. From time to time Jake squeezed my shoulders.

'This birthday has been the best. The absolute best. I love being part of this family'. She looked over at me and Jake and smiled. I wondered what she was about to say. I looked up at Jake whose eyes were fixed on his daughter. His face said it all.

'For as long as I could remember, I have wanted to spend my special day with both my parents, to be a family for once', she was crying. 'Yesterday I got that wish'. She walked over and we were both enveloped in Jake's arms. The guests were cheering. Dad was busy snapping again. Spike was equally busy cleaning the plates lying around. Mum relieved the emotional atmosphere by offering tea or coffee and the groups started chatting again.

It was dark by the time people left. Dad was directing the exodus and we were kissing goodbye and waving from the front door. Finally, it was just the family lounging around on the sofas. They were all staying over, doubling up in the bedrooms with the children. The flat had been renovated and refurnished. The new tenant wasn't due for a few weeks so Charlie's family were sleeping there.

I was driving, so had avoided alcohol, drinking fruit juice, but I felt drunk. Mum was slumped in a chair when Amy went up and whispered something in her ear.

'I had completely forgotten, I will go and get it'. She rushed out and came back with a gift-wrapped box. It was about 18 inches square. She handed it over to Amy who came and squeezed herself between me and Jake. She put it in Jake's hands and kissed him. 'This is my present to you' she grinned.

He removed the wrapping paper, decorated with rare plants, and peered in. Tucked inside was a small painting of Amy standing in a field of sunflowers. Dad had taken a photo last year when they were out walking and Amy had asked Mum to transfer it to canvas for her. Jake lifted it out of the box and displayed it to the rest of us. He was swallowing hard, trying to hold his emotions in check, but failed. He handed the picture to me and pulled Amy to him. I could see the tears glistening in his eyes.

Mum came over and took the picture to circulate it around. She tapped Jake on the shoulder. He looked up.

'I hope you like it?' He took her hand.

'It is perfect, a treasure, thank you Sarah'.

'I will never forget your help when Eric was ill. When Amy told me what she wanted I was only too pleased to make it happen'.

Frances' boys were scrapping in the hall and she decided it was time to get them into bed. Mum looked happy but exhausted. I offered to start clearing up but Jennie and Lizzie told me to take my family home. It sounded so strange. They were both mine, if only for a very short time.

Amy kissed everybody about twenty times before we could leave. They all lined up in the hall and we hugged and said our farewells. They hoped Jake would have a good journey back to Australia and that it wouldn't be so long until they saw him again.

Thanking Mum and Dad we left. Sitting quietly in the back of the car on the short journey home, Amy took a deep breath which sounded more like a sob. Jake turned round to look at her. Quite a difficult operation in my tiny car for a big man.

'What is it?'

'Nothing really, I just wish Prop had been with us'.

The remaining few days followed the same pattern. I would get up, make coffee, and take the tray into Jake's bedroom and wake them up. All three of us would sit on the bed drinking, talking about the day's plans. After breakfast I waved them off, I showered, got dressed and my day began. Two days before his flight to Edinburgh, Jake's colleagues were taking him out for a meal, so he wouldn't be home until late.

The other nights were spent talking, filling in the missing parts of our lives. Sometimes Amy joined us after she had done her homework, other times she left us alone.

If Jake was in contact with Clare and the boys, he did so when he was away from the house.

On the last day Jake was dropping off Amy at school and then driving to the airport. He had arranged to hand over the hire-car there. We had said our goodbyes the night before carefully wrapping Amy's picture in bubble wrap and tucked into one of his jumpers. I stood at the door whilst Amy put her school bags in the car. Jake picked me up and hugged me. His farewell kiss was fierce, full of longing. He put me down and practically ran to the car. He drove off with Amy waving me goodbye.

The phone rang and my day began.

WE JOIN A FAN CLUB

In the January following Jake's visit for Amy's birthday, Paul had rung to fix up and come over. He arrived in a snow storm bringing boxes full of his contacts. We had arranged that he would leave them with me so I could create a database and then I would courier them back to him.

By the time he arrived Angie and I had streamed most of his films and we were keen to join his fan club. His range of acting was vast. Each film or TV series he starred in was different. Knowing him better now, I realise he chose his parts carefully. Many of his fellow actors had got bogged down in block-buster franchises and found it difficult to break into more varied roles. He obviously controlled his career.

School was shut so Amy was home. She had spent hours looking through his Instagram pictures and Google shots when I told her he was coming over. She rarely showed any interest in my clients even though many of them appeared on the silver screen.

'Mum, he is so good looking', she had reported. 'Can't wait to meet him. Jennie says he is her favourite actor to work with. He always takes care of his co-stars. Frances told me he is really popular with the technicians, getting to know them all'. She had worked on a Romantic Comedy with Paul a few years ago. 'He brings in baskets of fruit and wine and bottles of beer at the end of the week'.

'You seem to be doing a lot of research'.

'He has worked almost non-stop since he left RADA and is now almost an A-lister. He must earn lots of money'.

I think this interest coincided with her developing enthusiasm for the opposite sex. Angus was still very much around but so were other boys. An earlier actor client, who now had his own office set up, had been just as good looking and almost as successful as Paul, but she had shown no interest. I handed over to his new secretary but when he rang to say goodbye we had been talking about our interest in Scottish history and had discovered that we shared Scottish great grandparents!

Amy opened the door and took one of the boxes Paul was holding, plonked it down in the library and pushed past me to help him with the next. He was carrying a bottle of wine and chocolates too.

'Hello, I am Zoe and this is my daughter Amy. School is shut so we have her company. I am surprised you made it as the snow seems quite deep'.

'Well even though they are not very environmentally friendly, 4x4's are good in the snow'. He laughed. Amy looked pleased. He cared about the environment too. This was getting better and better.

'Your house is lovely and warm'.

'We have an AGA and it keeps the house at a perfect temperature. Let's put the boxes in the office and then we can have some coffee or do you prefer tea?'

'Always coffee. Plenty of caffeine on set. How is Jennie by the way?'

'Resting at the moment'.

He started pulling off his coat with Amy's overzealous help. He was smiling. He had a lovely smile. Amy was right, he was very good-looking. About six foot tall but much slimmer build than Jake, he had dark brown eyes and wavy brown hair. He had the shadow of a beard which seemed quite popular at the time.

Amy had already got out the mugs and had plunged the plunger. 'Do you have milk?' She asked.

'Yes please Amy, but only a small amount'. The way he pronounced Amy was almost a caress.

The snow continued to fall and Paul was not going home that day. He stayed over and left later the next day. By the time he went, we felt we had known him for years. We were definitely going to join his fan club! Angie was devastated not to have met him. She was quite cross.

We had spent the afternoon sorting out the Who's Who of Paul's life. I wrote notes in my little black book which amused him. I explained I used it to record important events.

'So, I am important enough to go in your little black book, am I?' he laughed

'Most of my clients have some record. It is not a diary though'.

He had a way of rummaging through his hair and it was sticking up in the air. I was tempted to pat it down but pressed my hand down tightly in my lap to stop myself.

He looked at Jake's graduation photo on the bookshelf.

'Is he a relative?'

'Zoe's Dad, he lives in Australia.'.

'Are you divorced? Sorry, I am being rude asking all these questions'.

'No, we never married. He lives with his wife and children in Sydney. We were at college together'.

'Jennie has talked a lot about your family. I feel like I know them all. I have met Frances too, of course. They seem like a talented bunch. I think I bought one of your mother's landscapes for Mum a few years back and your father put together a soundtrack for one of my films. Of course, we never meet so many of the people who edit and finish the films after we have wrapped. At the premiere it was obvious how much the score matched the story'.

'That is kind of you to say so'.

Jake had left his pyjamas behind. They had been in the wash. I lent them to Paul. I found a spare toothbrush and showed him the room. Amy had slipped upstairs and made his bed up. We had eaten defrosted pizza, drunk the wine and finished off most of the chocolates.

In the morning he brushed past me on the way to the bathroom. It was disturbing to see another man in my house dressed in my ex-lover's pyjamas. Even with his rumpled hair he looked great.

I had asked him if he needed to tell anybody he was staying over. He blinked and looked away. 'No there won't be anybody expecting me tonight'.

Graham appeared as Paul got into his car the next morning. The snow had stopped and it was bright sun. I introduced them and he drove off.

Graham kissed my cheek. 'Wow he was a beauty. Where did you pick him up?'

I slapped his face gently and said he was very naughty. Paul was a new client.

'Has he got a garden I can re-design?' He laughed and ran back in.

AMY FLIES OFF AGAIN

Elspeth broke her hip so the visit to Australia was postponed. It was nearly three years before Amy saw Jake again. His overseas trips had been to South America and Vietnam so there had been no opportunity to divert to the UK. We received regular emails so we didn't feel forgotten.

I was really enjoying my job. I had become an intrinsic part of my clients' lives. I spent time getting to know them. I recognised their moods and, at times, became a sort-of telephonic agony aunt. Not that my own life experience was of much use but they always found a sympathetic ear. I chatted to their families or friends, I knew their children's birthdays and I fended off unwanted contacts.

The month that Amy was away, Varena came to stay. She was taking up a post in Geneva and had taken some holiday before starting. She drove down from the palatial pile in Yorkshire. We had been friends for nearly eighteen years. We were still very in tune with each other's thinking.

One morning over breakfast, she commented that I was laughing more. We had been with Graham the previous evening and had got absolutely plastered. He was so deliciously camp. He had been describing a visit to a gay club in Islington on one of his trips. He demonstrated the weird dance moves to perfection and I had laughed so much

I nearly wet myself.

'Well last night was pretty hysterical'. The phone rang so we went in to the office. She looked at Prop's painting then picked up a photo on the bookshelf. After I finished the call, she brought it over to the desk. Some weeks after Amy's party, Dad dropped off a batch of photos he had printed. He had enlarged two and framed them. Varena was holding the only picture I have ever had of Jake and me. We had been laughing at Amy's witty speech and I was looking up at him. His hand was resting on my waist. I cried when Dad showed it to me. The other was a more orchestrated picture of Amy, me and Jake but it still caught our happiness.

'That picture is amazing, your father is a brilliant photographer'. She handed me the picture and then looked more closely at the group photo. 'She is nearly as tall as Jake. I am glad she is still slim'. Even at fifteen Amy had been close to six foot but where Jake's body was broad and muscular she was wiry and athletic. Her face was animated, always smiling. She had thick shoulder-length chestnut hair. Her eyes, like Jake's, were deep blue. She had been late to puberty and her breasts were still developing.

'I think she is going to be very beautiful with maturity'. Varena put the pictures back on the shelf.

Looking out of the window she commented on the garden. 'Have you become a garden goddess now? It looks amazing'.

'Well, Prop started it off and I felt the need to keep it going. Graham and I work a lot together in the summer. When Amy isn't running or studying she is out there with us'.

'I wish I had met your Prop. Do you miss him?'

'Not as much now. He is here with me all the time. I am not into religion nor was he, as you know, but I feel his spirit sometimes. It is difficult to describe but there are days when I feel he is guiding me along'.

For a few months after Jake's visit, I had felt the onset of depression and had gone back to counselling.

Later, after an evening out with Angie at the theatre, Varena asked if there were any men in my life?

'Plenty on the end of the phone but I just haven't found anyone who can match up to Jake'.

'Are you in danger of idolising him?'

'The problem is that our times together are so rare that I can't imagine what he is like as a father or husband. We are always on our best behaviour not wanting to ruin the brief times we spend with each other. Maybe I would feel different if we were married and living together'.

'What about you, have you anyone permanent?' I asked.

'No, and I like it that way. It doesn't impact on my job. What does Amy plan to study at university?'

I laughed, 'guess'.

'Environmental science, of course. I should have known'.

Jake had become the youngest professor at the university two months ago. He was heading up a vast new division specialising in bio-diversity. He told us in a Skype session. We had graduated from emails to face-to-face contact. It was lovely to watch Amy and Jake chatting away about their shared interests. He mostly rang us from work. Amy would make notes in between the calls and would bombard him with questions.

Varena left to catch her flight to Geneva. As I came back

into the house, the phone rang. It was Amy. She and Elspeth had just landed in Edinburgh back from their month in Australia. She sounded subdued but I thought she might have been jetlagged.

'Ring me from the house when you have had a chance to relax. Glad you arrived safely. I have just said goodbye to Varena. I will tell all when you get back. We have had a brilliant time'.

'I will do, speak later', and she rang off.

It was a busy rest of the day and it was nearly seven o'clock when she eventually called.

'Hello darling, are you feeling better now?'

'Yes, we had a nap this afternoon. Granny is still in bed but Uncle Robert is cooking dinner'. She sounded very quiet and not as happy as I would have expected after spending the month with her father. It was not just being jet-lagged, something was wrong.

'What is the matter?'

'Clare has been diagnosed with breast cancer. Oh Mum, it was awful. We heard it was positive the day before we left to fly home. They are so upset. Dad is trying to be brave for them all but he came out to the annex after they had gone to bed and cried his heart out. Granny was amazing. I was completely useless. I didn't know what to say'.

I seemed to have lost my voice. I took a sip of my coffee. 'She is young so maybe they have discovered it in time. The treatment these days is so much better. We will talk more when you get home. I will speak to granny tomorrow. Are you on the late afternoon flight still?'

'Yes'.

I rang off. How was it possible that somebody so young, vital and healthy should be devastated by this deadly disease? She wasn't even forty. Her boys were only sixteen. Poor Jake. He was so happy at his promotion full of ideas and now this blow. My heart ached for him. I wanted to console him but what could I do, thousands of miles away.

Elspeth rang after they had put Amy on the plane. She told me they had been shocked at how thin Clare had become when they arrived. Apart from saying she was having tests, they had done their best to give the visitors a happy time. For Clare's sake they had kept up the pretence. Jake felt it was good for Andrew and Richard to spend time with Amy. It had been Clare who looked after them as Jake was preoccupied with the business of setting up his new division. To take the pressure off Clare, Robert had booked some tours. They had visited Ayers Rock and historical aboriginal sites. Jake had spent the last week with them.

Amy and I had emailed Jake to let him know she was home safe and desperately tried to find suitable words to show how much we loved him and how sad we were for Clare but it couldn't convey the shock we both felt.

For the next few months communication with Australia was sparse. Our Skype calls had diminished and I knew this upset Amy. Even though she understood that Jake was worried about Clare she still missed his regular calls. She was busy studying and would have liked to discuss some of her work with Jake. I could see how sad she was but could do nothing to resolve the matter. I could hardly ring Jake and say how upset his daughter was because he had stopped ringing her. He had enough to cope with and it wouldn't have been fair. Amy was being let down again.

October was birthday month. It would be Amy's eighteenth and I would be thirty-nine. We were having a joint party but neither of us really felt like celebrating. The celebration would actually be on my birthday. It felt wrong but Mum said it was a milestone for Amy and should be commemorated, so we decided to have just a large family dinner. Looking around the table at my family, I felt so blessed. We may have had the usual arguments over the years but we were a tightly-knit unit.

Jennie was sat next to Charlie's wife, her beautiful face glowing. At forty-three she was five months pregnant with her first child. Her fertility clock had been ticking so after her last film she had decided to take a break. She and Stephen had bought a big Edwardian villa in Richmond and he now had his own practice. They had converted a large downstairs room into his surgery. Lizzie sat between Frances' two boys. Dad was trying to keep the peace between Charlie's girls. Angie and Angus sat next to Amy and Charlie and I were seated either side of Mum.

Stephen and James brought in the turkey and placed the carving dish in front of Dad for him to carve. After all he was the head of the house. Immediately the table burst into laughter. They weren't to know that Dad was useless at carving. He looked around in desperation and his eyes settled on dear Charlie. With his precise nature he made the perfect carver. We all got exactly the same amounts as we passed the plates around and started to tuck in.

Amy and I thought we would be too sad to celebrate but the day was lovely. Driving home later that night we were silent. It was a clear moonlit night and frosty so I drove very carefully. We had left early in the morning before the post wanting to help Mum with the preparations. As we drove in, the lights of the car picked up a porch full of flowers.

I think I must have mentioned my birthday to some of my customers. When we opened the door the floor was littered with cards. Amy was picking up the flower displays. One was enormous. Hearing our car Graham rushed out with a tree in a pot. He came in and helped us find vases. We even had to resort to using the milk jugs. He promised he would drop in a few of his vases, the next day. We stood the rest in the utility room sink.

'You went off so early I didn't have the chance to catch you'. he said as he handed over the magnolia tree. 'It will need a sheltered spot'. He advised.

'I have only just got back myself and was coming round to put the flowers in the house out of the frost. The temperature has only just dropped so I don't think they will be damaged'.

Over coffee I opened the cards. There were a lot. Amy had collected the family presents and cards and she now put them out on the shelves in the library. We laughed at the comments and drank our coffee. Graham had kept a note of the senders of the bunches of flowers so I would be able to give them my thanks. The large bouquet was from Paul Walker. I would read his note later. Amy had checked the emails. There was nothing from Australia. Communication with Jake had dropped off and I know Amy was upset that he had forgotten her eighteenth .

It had been a long day and we were tired. Graham said he would drop in the vases in the morning and left us. I turned off the lights taking Paul's card to read in bed.

It was actually a letter. He must have sent it to the florist to attach.

Hi Zoe,

Happy Birthday. Bet you have had a good day with your family.

Hope you like the flowers. As you know I am filming in Ireland and would have liked to give you something more personal but it has been so hectic.

I am so glad Jennie gave me your details. You have made my life so much more ordered, and, believe me, I needed that. I think you do far more than you expected and I hope I haven't taken advantage. These last eighteen months, as you know, have been very difficult for me. Your kind support has been invaluable.

When I talk to my friends, family, agent and anybody else you deal with, they all praise you. Not only are you efficient but you are friendly and kind. Mum loves her chats with you.

Warm wishes

Paul xx

NEWS FROM DOWN UNDER

The day after our joint party, Amy was still fast asleep when Graham came in with some more vases for Paul's flowers. I asked him to have breakfast with us. Amy came down.

After he left, she went up to have a shower and I sat down at the computer. Opening up my emails there were even more birthday wishes but then I noticed one from Jake. Relieved he hadn't completely forgotten Amy's birthday I opened it up. He was sorry he had missed her day but Clare had had a mastectomy and he and the twins had been at the hospital for the last few days. Unfortunately, the scan showed that the cancer had spread and she would need radical chemotherapy.

After breakfast we emailed him saying how shocked we were at his news.. We tried desperately to sound positive hoping that Clare would benefit from her treatment.

I felt so guilty that whilst we were celebrating such a tragedy was unfolding on the other side of the world.

He sent a brief reply thanking us but we didn't hear from him for several weeks. When he did respond by Skype he was in the office. He said Clare was determined that his work should not be interrupted by her illness. He admitted the pressure was gruelling but also helped him to keep his worries about Clare's health at bay. He said not to be upset if he wasn't in contact quite so much. His face was drawn, his eyes ringed with exhaustion. When he hung up, we both broke into tears.

LOOMING EXAMS

Amy was revising for her exams and we spent much of the winter in the kitchen. It snowed non-stop. When it wasn't snowing, it was raining. Contact with Jake was very limited. Each time we spoke on Skype he seemed sadder and more care worn. Clare was not responding to treatment as well as they had hoped.

Amy had applied to Cambridge but had to achieve top marks to obtain her place next September. She was revising all hours of the day and night. My duty was to keep her supplied with hot drinks and food. The kitchen table was strewn with books and notes.

On the day Amy's A level exams started, Jake sent her an email wishing her luck (not that she needed it) telling her she was going to do well. Amy's eyes were wet. Clare's illness had left a pall over the winter months. I was looking forward to the spring.

Amy got her place at Cambridge. In September Dad and I drove her down in his Jeep. I told her about my arrival in Dad's friend's psychedelic Volkswagen camper van, meeting Varena. She was in modern halls but after we unpacked, I took her down to show them both Prop's office. It still looked the same from the outside. I imagine nothing much would change as I am sure those old buildings must be listed.

We had lunch at the café down by the river. It was much smarter. I made Amy laugh describing me sticking my bottom in her Dad's face and then pouring chocolate into his lap.

My visit was bitter sweet. I couldn't believe it was nearly nineteen years ago that I had left. What had I done with my life? Was Amy to be my only achievement? I was nearly forty. I felt ancient.

I cried on Dad's shoulder going home.

I could feel my depression lurking but I was also busy with my clients. Angie and I were still going to the cinema and theatre. We had also joined an Amateur Dramatic Society and a Rock Choir. Angus was at the University of East Anglia but had decided to live in.

Whilst Graham and I were putting the garden to bed for the winter he asked me what I would really like to do? I had to think. Before Prop left me his bequest, I had always had to watch the pennies.

'I would like to visit some European cities'.

'Well let's book some trips'.

'You would go with me?'

'Yes'.

Amy had settled in at college. She had no difficulty in fitting in with the social scene and was having a great time. She was coming home to celebrate my fortieth birthday. It was going to be a quieter affair than her eighteenth. The day started with Graham and I having breakfast opening cards and reading emails. Paul had sent a bottle of perfume he had had made up thinking it would suit me. Graham thought it would suit him too! We were all going to Mum and Dad's for lunch. There had been silence from Australia for some time. I expect Jake was in touch with Amy at college. I must ask her.

Amy was stopping over for the night. I got up early the next morning and I opened up my computer to check my messages and emails. There was one from Jake. I was pleased he hadn't forgotten my milestone birthday but sad he had missed Amy's.

Minutes later I was banging on the shower door for Amy, tears streaming down my face.

'God Mum what is the matter?'

'Clare is dead. She died yesterday'.

Whilst we had been laughing and enjoying our celebration Clare had died in Jake's arms. I had never spoken to her however I was unbelievably devasted at her death, her life cut so short. It was too cruel.

The phone rang and I went in to the bedroom to answer it. Amy went off to dry her hair. She was crying too. It was Elspeth.

'Have you heard the news?'

'Yes, I have just opened his email'.

'My poor son and those boys. I can't stop weeping. I feel almost worse than when Archie died. At least he had a good life but she was so young. Robert and I are flying out as soon as we can get a flight. He will need help with Richard and Andrew. They loved her so much'.

'If I write a letter to Jake and courier it to you, will you take it with you, please?' I asked. 'Emails are so impersonal'.

'Of course, we won't be leaving for a couple of days at least. I think I will probably stay over for a while so I am packing more clothes. How is Amy? She seemed very fond of Clare?'

'Pretty upset, she is in her room, maybe she will ring you later'.

I went to find Amy. She was on her bed her eyes red with crying. 'I am going to email Dad but I want to write a letter from both of us and courier it to Elspeth to take out. She and Robert are trying to get a flight now. She thinks that she will stay on longer to help out with the twins'.

'I think I will wait until you have written your letter and then I will write my own to Dad and the boys'.

So, I sat down to write my first ever letter to Jake. We had exchanged emails for years but out of concern for Clare's feelings, I had never written a letter to him.

Dearest Jake,

I never expected to be writing to you in such tragic circumstances. I didn't know Clare, for obvious reasons, but she deserved many more years of happiness with you and your boys.

It can't have been easy for her to accept Amy. Not many wives would want anything to do with their husband's love child, but she made her feel so welcome. Amy always described Clare as a really good, kind person. She clearly was your soulmate.

I can feel your pain but I can do nothing to relieve you of your grief. I feel impotent. I know how much you loved her.

What more can I say except that you are in my heart always and I kiss your brow from afar. Amy is writing a separate letter to you, Richard and Andrew.

Take care of yourself and them. It is the worst time in their life to lose a parent. I am sure Elspeth will support you all.

With all my love

Zoe

Amy gave me her letter. It was short but so loving. As she explained no words can really express what is felt in the heart.

We organised the courier to go to Edinburgh.

We replied to Jake's email saying we were devastated by the news and how sorry we were, adding that we had written to him. His mother was carrying them on her journey towards her bereaved family.

Death makes you feel your own mortality, especially if that person is young. I needed to be with my own family. I rang Mum and asked if Amy and I could come over the next day.

'Of course, you know we love seeing you'. She sounded surprised. It had only been a few hours since we had been together.

'Jake's wife died yesterday'.

'What'! she exclaimed, 'but she had only just been diagnosed when Amy was over there. How unbelievably sad for Jake and his boys. Just dreadful'. I could hear Dad in the background asking what had happened and my mother's muffled explanation.

'We will see you in a short while'.

Driving over with Amy, I couldn't rid myself of the thought at how awful it would have been if Mum had died when I was just sixteen. I needed to see her, give her love. I needed her reassurance and I was forty years old. How unbelievably sad for those two young men to lose their beloved mother.

Robert attended the funeral and then had to get back to work. Elspeth stayed on. He rang me a few days after he got back.

'Hello Zoe, its Robert'. Apart from occasional calls he made to Amy I had rarely spoken to him but he was a good son and brother. He reminded me of his Dad.

'You are back. Did you leave Elspeth there?'

'Yes, she is desperately needed. They are all three of them in the most dreadful despair. It was so quick they hadn't had time to prepare. She had pneumonia and her body couldn't fight it'.

'That is so terrible. I am glad Elspeth is there but she is hardly young herself and it will be a strain'.

'She has found a purpose. She will be the strong one, Zoe. She took over as soon as she arrived. I have never, ever seen my brother at a loss about anything. It shocked me to the core. We gave him your letters. The twins took Amy's off to their room but Jake opened your's straight away. He was shaking so badly by the end that we had to hold on to him'.

'Jake told us that he had treated you so unkindly but that you had sent him this wonderful letter. He said you were so full of love. He handed it over for us to read. I hope you don't mind that we read it Zoe?'

'No, of course not, but I didn't want it to upset him. I wanted to console him'.

'I noticed it by his bed when I took his coffee up the next morning. I think it did help him. He was much calmer and had started to pull himself together. He had to get a grip for his boys' sake. Richard and Andrew loved Amy's letter too'.

Robert explained that at the funeral the church was packed with Clare's friends and work colleagues. She had been a popular member of staff, returning to work once the boys were at school.

'As I left Jake asked me to thank you for your letter. He said you will have to forgive him if he isn't in contact for a while. He hoped you would understand'.

Elspeth sent us short emails keeping us up to date with her news. The twins with their natural buoyancy were starting to recover but she was worried about Jake. He had thrown himself into setting up his new department and was unreachable.

She was sorry that Jake refused to contact me. She thought he felt he would be betraying Clare's memory by getting in touch. She had tried to reason with him but without success.

FURY

By the time Amy came home from her first year, Graham and I had visited Paris, Prague, Amsterdam and Barcelona. Our winter exploits would take in Vienna and a trip to Auschwitz. We only spent a few days away as I needed to keep up with my work. When I told Paul what I planned he sounded delighted.

I had been assisting Paul for nearly four years. It had been a very busy time. He had been nominated for an Oscar and won a Golden Globe. The original plan was for me to be on duty when he was filming but as his domestic life had started to fall apart, I became more and more involved.

Quite early on he had told me that his wife Chloe, also an actress, (I hadn't seen any of her films) was jealous of his consistent career. Every time his agent sent a script over for his consideration she would sulk. When they had married, her career had been running in parallel to his, but parts had dried up. Without work she got pregnant. They now had three children. To avoid upsetting her, he arranged for his agent to send scripts to me and I would courier them on to him depending on where he was. They were never to be sent to the house.

Paul loved his wife very much and he adored his kids. I couldn't imagine him being unfaithful even though there must have been plenty of opportunity with his co-stars. Jennie told me they all adored him but he was totally loyal. He had loads of friends both female and male. They often rang me to find out where he was and what he was up to. I became quite friendly with them too but always on the phone. He enjoyed working with women, especially female directors. Emma Harley, who had directed a rom-com with him, had stayed friendly. She called him one of the girls. He had been such fun to work with. He just fitted in but his wife didn't see it that way. He was regularly accused of having affairs with his co-stars.

Jennie once said she couldn't get her head around such a beautiful woman being so insecure. He couldn't have loved her more. In public they seemed like the perfect pair but in private the marriage was disintegrating.

Amy spent time in the Orkneys on a field trip during her summer break but we had a few weeks together before she went back for her second year. She was troubled. I couldn't put my finger on it but from years of listening to my clients on the phone I was able to pick up the changes in their moods. It had served me well. She loved that Graham and I were having a good time on our travels and had asked lots of questions.

'I think it is time you told me what is worrying you', I said.

'There are a lot of changes going on at college at the moment'.

'I changed my course tutor to Prop so if you are not happy with your course let's talk about it'.

'Oh, it's not about the course, that is great'.

'Then what is it?'

She turned to face me with tears in her eyes. I wondered if she was having boyfriend problems.

'We have a new Professor starting this term'.

'I am sure that won't be difficult'.

'Yes, it will. It's Dad'.

My hands flew to my face and I had to sit on the bed as my legs just gave way.

'How long have you known about this?'

'Granny told me back in May. He and the twins are going to be living in Cambridge. He was offered the job to expand the bio-diversity unit at the college'.

Jake back at Cambridge and he had not cared enough to tell me. He had left it to his daughter. What a coward. My upset turned to fury.

'How dare he leave it to you to tell me, how dare he?' I screamed at Amy who pulled back in fear. I have never raised my voice to her and she looked as if I had hit her.

'Mum, don't shoot the messenger. I have lost sleep since I knew what was happening'.

Elspeth had transferred her contact to Amy at college but now I realised why. Even she was afraid to tell me. I felt betrayed.

Dad offered to take Amy back to college for the new term. He knew I couldn't be anywhere near the city. Poor Amy she was caught between the devil and the deep blue sea. It wasn't fair.

After she had left, I googled Jake's name and leafed through his biography and read the local Cambridge papers about the brilliant new professor returning from Australia to head up this new division in The Department of Earth Sciences. There was an up to date picture. He had aged, his hair had more grey and he was thinner. Reading through I realised how little I had actually known about his scholarly life. Always on the fringe never at the centre.

My anger saved me. That, and Paul's mental deterioration. Suddenly somebody needed me.

His wife was filming a BBC science fiction series in the volcanic Canaries and had the children and a nanny with her. Paul had wrapped his film early and, missing his children, had decided to fly out, arriving late in the evening. He had booked in to the hotel and walked along to knock gently on the suite door. It was opened by the nanny. She looked horrified. It was gone 10 o'clock and she was baby-sitting. He had asked if his wife was in. The nanny said she was out with the other actors.

'Tell Chloe that I will see her in the morning, I have a room along the corridor'.

Something woke Paul around five in the morning. Looking out of the window he saw his wife get out of a car. The driver walked round and kissed her. They spoke for some time and then kissed some more. He drove off and she stood waving at him and walked into the hotel. Her clothes were dishevelled.

Paul got dressed, called the reception and ordered a taxi to take him back to the Airport. There was no direct flight to London so he flew to Madrid and then to Heathrow. He rang me from there.

I answered the phone.

'Hello Zoe'.

'Paul how can I help?'

'Can I come and stay at your house? I need somewhere to hide for a few days'.

'What on earth has happened? Of course, you can come here'.

'I am at Heathrow. I am going home to pick up some clothes and the car and will come on'.

He lived in Richmond not far from Jennie. His journey would take a while and would give me time to make up a bed and go for some food.

He arrived five hours later. I couldn't think what the problem was and had ruled out several possible reasons.

He parked up and I went out to meet him. I opened his door and realised that his face was streaked with tears. I pulled him out and took him indoors. I had made some fresh coffee and gave him a cup.

'Have you eaten?'

'Not since last night. I am not sure I could manage any food the way I feel'. He couldn't look at me, he kept staring into his cup.

I sat down beside him and took his hand. 'You need to eat something. I can make you a sandwich'.

'Okay', he nodded.

He ate in silence, gulping down the coffee. He had stopped crying but was almost catatonic. He wasn't aware of what was going on. At one point he asked where he was and why

I was there. He was in deep shock. He had started shivering although the kitchen was warm. I ran out to his car and got his bags in.

'My dear you need to go to bed. We can talk in the morning. I will make you a hot water bottle and bring it up'.

Lifting the smaller of his bags I led him upstairs into the spare bedroom. He sat on the window seat watching me.

He was like a child letting me undress him. I unbuttoned his shirt, laid it on the chair and then pulled his tee-shirt over his head noticing a small tattoo on his shoulder. I was speaking softly like you do to a frightened child. He stood up and turned round with his back to me and I pulled his shorts down. He stepped out and I lifted his feet one at a time into his pyjama bottoms. I was seriously worried about his mental state. Pulling back the sheets he slumped on the bed and I pulled the duvet around him. He was still shivering.

'I am just going to get the hot water bottle to warm you up Paul'. He gazed vacantly back at me and nodded. 'I will be back'.

I made sure the bottle was not too hot. By the time I returned, Paul was lying on his side. He seemed slightly more lucid. I lifted the duvet and put the bottle near his feet. They were frozen. I turned the light off so only the glow from the hall was visible. I stroked his head and told him he was safe now. He sighed. I sat with him until he slept. I was stiff from kneeling beside the bed. When I came up to bed later he was whimpering in his sleep.

He must have woken in the night as I noticed the bathroom door was open. He slept through until three o'clock the next day. I looked in on him from time to time to make sure all was well.

I was sat at my desk typing when he put his head around the door. His hair was sticking up in spikes. I jumped up and took his hand.

'How are you feeling?'

'Not really sure, honestly. I was wondering if I could have a shower. I stink'.

'Of course, let me get you some towels. Would you like a coffee?'

'Yes please'. He turned to go upstairs but stopped at the bottom step.

'I knew I could trust you Zoe, thank you'.

Showered and dressed he looked much better. The colour had returned to his cheeks. He sat down at the kitchen table and told me what had happened. He knew he couldn't go back home and I was the first person he thought of. His mobile phone was flat so we charged it up. His message box was full of calls from Chloe.

He stayed with me for nearly four weeks. Only his agent, his family and close friends knew he was at my house. He alternated from despair to fury and back again. There were days of complete silence. When he was feeling well enough, Graham came in and they played chess. We found an old set of Prop's in Amy's room. He didn't seem to mind that I continued with my work and fitted in around my day. Sometimes he cooked a meal.

One day, my parents drove over with Spike. Paul had a dog but she spent most of the time with his sister who looked after her when he was filming. He was missing his children and his dog. Spike had grown into a lovely creature. White with brown markings. Dad was convinced he had spaniel in him.

Paul went off with Dad and Spike for a walk. Mum and I sat in the lounge.

'He seems a really nice man'.

'He tries very hard not to get in my way during the day and we have worked out a way of living together. It is very strange having a man around. The most I have ever lived with a man since college is two weeks with Jake'.

'Have you heard from him at all?'

'Not a word. He has been back since June according to Google. Amy has not mentioned him once and Elspeth never rings me now. I think she is too ashamed'.

'Are you still angry?'

'Yes, he is driving a wedge between me and my daughter. I hate him for that'.

'Would it help if I rang Elspeth myself?'

'No, but thanks for offering. If Amy continues to be estranged, I will have to talk to him. But just at the moment I am too worried about Paul. He is still very frail and he has to start filming soon. They have delayed the start by two weeks already. He has instructed a solicitor who has suggested mediation as the quickest way to getting a divorce but I cannot see him coping with that in his current state. His agent, who is very fond of Paul, is worried that he will just give away everything to Chloe. He is, I gather, worth well over ten million.'

'Wow, there is big money in the business. Jennie spent nearly two million on their house in Richmond'.

Dad and Paul came back in demanding coffee so we stopped at that point. They left soon after.

'I enjoyed the walk with Eric. You are very lucky with your parents. Jennie spoke so fondly about them too. I think it is time I got back to work. I have loved feeling safe here with you but I can't keep running. I hope you don't mind but your Dad told me about your breakdown after Jake got married. Do you think you can talk to me about that time? How you got over it?'

'If I am absolutely honest I have never got over it. I have learned to live with my disappointment. Jake has coloured my existence for so long. I have spent my time waiting for him and life has passed me by, so I am not sure my experience will be much good for you'.

After supper we put on the log fire in the lounge and Paul sat in Prop's wing chair. It brought back memories of Jake.

I told Paul my life story that night from Yves on to Jake and then the time in between. I held nothing back. I told him everything. Of the nights when Jake and I made love so often I could barely walk the next day. In the telling I realised how sexual the relationship had been. Had there really been any love on Jake's side? I was beginning to believe I had made that up in my mind or maybe he just said it to keep me happy.

He sat quietly, occasionally asking a question, but mostly he just listened. It was like going to confession.

'Eric told me that Jake had taken up a professorship at Cambridge and not told you and Amy is studying in his faculty too'.

'Yes, she knew he had been appointed in June and concealed it from me until she went back in September. He stopped emailing me long before his wife Clare passed away. She died on my fortieth birthday. I had written to him and he sent a message back with his brother thanking me for the letter and he would get in touch later. He never did. From then until now only Amy and his mother knew of his plans. I think he had told her long before June that he was returning to the UK. Now he has his daughter and his boys all together and he is driving a wedge between me and my Amy. He is making me hate him'.

Paul came to sit on the sofa beside me and put his arm around me. We just sat like that for some time and then he took his arm away. 'I think it is time we went to bed'. I nodded and turned to put the light out. I cleared up the coffee cups and walked upstairs going into the bathroom to clean my teeth. Paul had already gone up. I took off my clothes and got into bed. A few minutes later Paul slipped into the room and came over to the bed.

I laughed, 'You did mean we should go to bed'. He ducked under the covers and stripped off his pyjama bottoms then he turned to me and removed my nightdress. It had been nearly 20 years since I had a man touch my body. How was I going to react?

He stroked my breasts, kissed my nipples, my mouth, my face, all the time using his hands to rouse me. I was hesitant, trying to remember long forgotten passion. Slowly I was starting to respond, my hands were exploring his body, running my fingers through his hair. His were stroking the insides of my thigh. I moved to open my legs and I felt him tease my clitoris. I stroked his engorged penis and guided it into my vagina. He moved on top of me looking down with a smile and then penetrated me. I spread my legs around his body pressing him further inside. With infinite gentleness he brought me to a climax. I gasped. How had I lived this long without this unbelievable physical joy. Once he knew I had climaxed he let go his control and his sperm pumped into my demanding womb.

I couldn't stop smiling. He lay beside me stroking my face and kissing me gently. I had waited half my life for this but he loved another woman and she had betrayed him. I was his solace, his escape from his pain. If I helped him move on then it was worth it. There was no future but the now had been perfect.

I wanted him inside me again and he knew it. I stroked his penis until it stiffened. Kissing me hard he pulled me on top of him. I guided him in and felt myself arch with the joy. I started to move slowly looking down at his beautiful face moving my body up and down to his rhythm. He was holding my breasts and moving his mouth from nipple to nipple. I felt my body climax and this time we reached it together his penis throbbing with his release.

Laughing with sheer joy I collapsed onto him and rolled off.

'That was amazing', I whispered.

'I am glad you enjoyed it. I wanted to give you something back. You have taken good care of me these last few weeks and I wanted to show my appreciation'.

He tucked me up in his arms and we fell asleep. When I woke up he was looking at me.

'How long have you been awake?'

'For a while. I am so used to being early on set. I rarely sleep beyond six'.

I ruffled his hair then moved my hands down his back getting hold of his buttocks and pulling him towards me.

'Oh it's like that is it, you want more sex?' He grinned.

'Well I have waited nineteen years'.

We showered together and I went down to get the breakfast. Paul came down a few minutes later.

'I am going to ring my agent and solicitor this morning. I need to sort out flights too'. Working for him over the years I knew how conscientious he was, extremely dedicated, not the typical A-lister. His agent, when I rang him to say Paul was with me, needing time to recover, had been certain the studio would be co-operative. They had delayed the start of filming by a month.

'I must do some shopping for food'. Waiting for Paul to come down, I had had a reality check. I needed the morning-after pill. I had no idea if it was only available on prescription. I would call in at the pharmacy after my shop. I wasn't going to run the risk of another pregnancy.

The pharmacist assured me I could get the pill (it actually worked for up to three days after sex) online. I was not sure if last night was a one-off. I needed some condoms too.

I ordered a pill from my mobile before I returned home. Paul was fully occupied on the phone most of the morning. It was great to hear him so purposeful even though it meant him leaving. I had got used to having a man around, especially one as delightful as Paul.

He stuck his head into the office and waited until I finished my call.

'So do we now have a plan?' I asked.

'Sort of, yes. I will stay here until after your birthday'. I had completely forgotten it was coming up. I had nearly missed

Amy's with my preoccupation over Paul's mental health. It had been a bad few days. I had ordered some books she wanted and sent off a card. When I rang to wish her a happy day, the conversation was desultory. Our lines were still crossed. I did not mention Paul was in the house.

Friday, three days away. He said we should go out for a meal, we had been cooped up in the house for too long. I reminded him of Amy's nickname for the house. He laughed 'Oh yes, my first conversation with your daughter'.

We never went out for the meal. I was worried that he should not be seen out with another woman, especially one who couldn't keep her hands off him. If he was recognised, it would not help in his divorce proceedings. As a substitute, we ordered an Indian takeaway! We invited Graham to join in our lavish celebration of my birthday.

Business calls, that day, were interrupted with non-stop Happy Birthday being sung by my family, their children and Uncle Tom Cobbley and all. It wasn't until late in the afternoon that I realised I had not heard from Amy. She had sent a card with a book token.

I took her call as we sat in the lounge drinking beer. Graham and Paul were playing chess.

'Hello Mum, sorry I haven't rung before but it has been hectic. Have you had a good day?'

'Yes I have. I am going over to Mum and Dad's at the weekend. Graham has shared a take-away with u...' I stopped and corrected myself. 'Me'. I had nearly said us.

'What have you been doing to make life so busy', I asked innocently trying to lift the conversation?

There was a silence. 'I have been with Dad and the twins, it is one year ago today since Clare died'.

My face must have registered my confusion. Paul and Graham were looking at me.

'Oh, I had forgotten'.

'How could you have forgotten Mum'! She exclaimed. I wondered if my birthday would forever be linked to a death in Australia.

'Were you able to help? How are they coping?'

'It was a bad day and I am pretty shattered. I will ring you again at the weekend. I am feeling rather emotional'. She wished me happy birthday again and rang off.

I put the phone down too upset to speak. Was I going to keep paying the price of Clare's death? Was I losing my only child too?

Graham got up and said he was going to make some coffee. Paul came and sat by me taking my hand.

'What was that about?'

'I don't think I told you that Jake's wife Clare, died of cancer on my fortieth last year. Amy has been consoling Jake and her half-brothers'. I felt mean being so upset.

Graham came back with the coffee and we tried to bring back the warm atmosphere of the evening but it had evaporated. One call from Amy had dispelled it.

Finishing his coffee, Graham stood up and yawned. 'It is time for bed'. He lent over and kissed my cheek. 'Happy Birthday, dear. Don't let Amy's call upset you. I think she is probably as mixed up as she could be'.

Pecking Paul on both cheeks he went off calling out that Paul should not leave tomorrow without a fond farewell.

It turned out that I wasn't a one-night stand. The previous two nights had been equally as energetic. I had laughed when Paul drew out a condom. I opened my drawer pulled out another and said 'Snap'.

I had explained I was not in a rush to become a mother again no matter how much sex we indulged in.

On the last night Paul wiped away my tears and just held me until I slept.

He was off to London to collect his dog from his sister. He would be staying with his parents until he flew to Los Angeles. I altered his schedule on the computer pushing back his return by two weeks. It would be closer to Christmas. He had organised mediation meetings with Chloe in January before returning to the States to complete the series. She had agreed that he could take the children to his parents for Boxing Day and the following week. He made no commitment to returning to see me. I would start taking his calls on the day he flew. He said he would be in touch and tell me what was happening.

He was true to his word. He rang at least twice a week even from the States.

The house felt dreadfully empty after Paul had left. He had gone next door to say goodbye to Graham and was rewarded with two smacking kisses on each cheek.

Laughing he hugged and kissed me goodbye several times. 'Thank you Zoe for these weeks. You must talk to Amy, she needs to be able to speak to you openly about her relationship with Jake no matter how much it hurts you. Take your courage into your hands and start the conversation with her. I doubt any contact with Jake would be beneficial. I expect he is still pretty upset. Don't rush it'.

SECRETS

Amy didn't ring on the Saturday but turned up at the house on Sunday. She had caught the train and then arranged a taxi.

I had stripped Paul's bed even though he hadn't slept in it for the last few days and was ironing when I heard a car pull away and then a key in the latch. Amy called out and I said I was in the kitchen.

'I am so sorry Mum for ruining your birthday. It was really cruel of me'. She took the iron out of my hand and placed my palm against her face. She turned and kissed it. I patted her hair with my other hand.

'I heard a car, did you get a lift from somebody?'

'No, I came by train to Norwich and then caught a taxi'.

'That must have been expensive'.

She remained silent for a while. 'Dad gave me the money for the journey'.

I waited for an explanation.

After she had finished her call to me she had spent until the early hours of the morning sobbing. She felt so guilty, spoiling my special day. Not having slept, she looked dreadful and had passed Jake on the way to her lecture the next morning. She explained that nobody knew he was her father. They had agreed this. She was a friend of his sons. It made life easier for her. He had taken one look at her and called her out 'Ah, Miss Chapman, glad I have caught you, can you spare me a few minutes please?'

'You look terrible Amy' he commented as soon as he had closed the door.

'Well I have done something I am ashamed of. I hurt Mum badly last night when I rang to wish her happy birthday'.

'Of course, I had forgotten. It is the same day'.

'Mum had forgotten that Clare died last year too and I criticized her for celebrating her day'.

'Oh lord, Amy I am sorry. You need to make things right. It is not Mum's fault. You should go and see her'.

'I said I am not sure I can make things right. Mum is convinced that you are taking me away from her, that now you have all your children together. You may not have Clare, but at least your family is complete. Why have you never communicated with her? She has asked so little of you over the years. She always wanted me to get to know you'.

'I can't contact Zoe. Clare has only been gone a year. What do you think Richard and Andrew would feel if I did?'

'Maybe you should have told her that. It would have saved so much pain. She would have understood. She always does where you are concerned. I have been stuck in the middle keeping secrets, my conversations always wary of upsetting either you or her. It has been very difficult and I am exhausted'.

If Amy had come an hour later I would have been on my way to my parents' house for lunch. We would have missed each other. She told me all this as we drove over. She had spent Saturday running. It was her way of reducing stress.

'You need to stop worrying about mentioning Jake and his family from now on. I understand. I have hated the collapse of our friendship. You used to be so open and suddenly you were keeping secrets. It is time we started again'.

'I know. Now tell me what you have been up to these last few weeks?'

What had I just said about secrets? Oh dear. We had agreed with Graham that we wouldn't mention Paul's stay.

'It has been busy, lots of client work and Graham and I have been planning our trip to Austria'.

'When do you go?'

'The beginning of November for five days'.

'Five whole days off, Mum. What a luxury'!

By the time we got to my parents our easy friendly relationship had been restored. Whilst Amy was upstairs collecting some books to take back I had rung Mum to say Amy was coming to lunch but asked her not to mention Paul's visit.

I drove her back to Cambridge that night.

Whilst Paul was in America the gossip papers displayed a large picture of Chloe wrapped up in a man's arms leaving a restaurant. The heading was "Is Paul Walker's marriage on the rocks"? Poor Paul, I knew he would hate this. He disliked the press and avoided them as much as possible.

When he rang, he was apoplectic. 'Couldn't she wait until we get the divorce?' His fury told me that she still had a hold on him. I think he would have been indifferent had he got over the breakdown.

Filming overran and it was Christmas Eve before he flew in. I had a brief call from the airport to say he had landed.

In the end the next time we met up was at Jennie's wedding the following March. Amy had taken a day off from college and we collected her from Kings Cross. Dad had driven us up. The new tenant was looking after Spike.

The ceremony was at Caxton Hall but the reception was at the St Ermins Hotel.

Paul had already arrived. He was talking to actor friends. He smiled and waved but didn't come over. Amy nudged me. 'Call him over Mum. I want to tell my friends at college who I met at Jennie's wedding'.

'I am sure he will make his way round to us'. I knew Paul would take his time as he moved from group to group. The registrar arrived and asked us all to sit down. Jennie, Stephen and Lisa came in.

We walked on foot to the hotel after the ceremony. Dad was holding Lisa's hand and we were chatting when Paul appeared at my elbow. He touched it lightly and squeezed. Amy was ecstatic. She started talking ten to the dozen and he took her arm and walked along with her. Her face was a picture. She would have lots to tell her mates.

He turned back to me and took my arm. Amy and I walked along holding on to him. At the hotel each member of the family had been allotted to a table. I saw Charlie making sure everybody was in the correct seat. Nothing changes! Paul was not on my table.

Dad's speech was hilarious, made even funnier by Lisa trying to take the microphone out of his hand.

When the dancing began Paul walked over and asked Amy to dance. Dad was instructed to take a photo. Jennie had come to sit with me.

'Paul has told me about his stay with you'.

'How much did he tell you?'

'Enough to know that he has become a good friend' she winked.

'I am not sure it will lead anywhere. He still loves Chloe'.

'Well Zoe, you can be quite patient' she giggled.

'Wicked'. I retorted. 'By the way Amy doesn't know of his visit'. The dance finished and he came and sat down. Stephen walked over with Lisa and he and Jennie started dancing. Amy had wandered off and Mum took Lisa.

'Can I come down to see you?'

'Do you need to ask?'

'You won't need to add it to your schedule', he laughed. Dad's mate was doing the disco and most of the music would have been heard regularly at home. Paul and I danced to the strains of 'Nights in White Satin'.

It was time to go. We were dropping off Amy on the way back. Having kissed Amy on the cheek he gave me a quick peck on the lips. 'See you soon', he whispered. Amy gave me a strange look but said nothing.

ON AND OFF RELATIONSHIPS

Our time together followed a pattern. Paul would appear as often as he could between contracts but he was away for a lot of the time. He had bought a flat and shared this with one of his nephews. It was close to Chloe's house. His divorce was now official. She had got the house and a large amount of alimony. When home, he spent as often as he could with the children. His life was hectic. I knew, I kept his schedule. I wondered if this was deliberate. Work was proving his saviour.

This didn't leave much time for me though. I seemed destined to be hanging around for my lovers. I was no nearer to knowing what he actually felt about me. It is difficult to compete with a beautiful actress. At least Paul kept in touch, unlike Jake. Graham and I continued our visits to European capitals. My years of study were not completely useless. He loved hearing all the background stories. On one trip, he said I should write a book.

Freed of restraint, Amy spoke a lot about her times spent with her half-brothers and, of course, Jake. Richard was going to Birmingham to study civil engineering and Andrew to Nottingham to train as a doctor. Life was moving on.

I borrowed Dad's Jeep to take Amy back for her final year. I had stopped being afraid to return. Before going home, I went on a pilgrimage to Prop's rooms. I was stood looking up at the windows thinking of that dear man who had changed my life so much when I heard my name.

'Zoe?'

There, stood with two other cloaked Dons, was Jake. He excused himself and came over.

'Have you dropped Amy off?'

'Yes, I was just remembering my time spent in Prop's office. I still miss him, he changed my life. Amy and I loved him so much'.

My eyes were watering. I wasn't sure whether it was sadness about Prop or the shock at seeing how changed he was.

He was only a few weeks older than me but he could have been mistaken for fifty. His eyes were dull and ringed with dark shadows. His face was lined, deep grooves running from his mouth and without his tan his skin looked grey and drawn. He was still as tall but his body had lost some of its bulk. I couldn't imagine him in a gym. My snarling, laughing, rowing lover was now so sad.

I reached up and rested my hand against his cheek. I didn't know what to say.

He put his hand over mine for just a second. He took a deep breath.

'Are you rushing off or can we talk?'

'Where do you suggest?'

'How about our café? I will need to let my secretary know I will be offsite. If you go ahead and get a table I will catch you up'.

I needed a chance to get myself together. My shock had rendered me almost speechless. Now I knew why Amy had been so protective of him. Clare's death had ripped the life out of him. We walked across the bridge in silence. He turned off into the block ahead of us.

'I won't be long'.

I was seated near the river's edge. I had ordered a sandwich but told the waitress to hold it until Jake arrived. I had no idea what he would drink even.

He made his way between the tables his mouth a hard line. He had become so severe.

'I was remembering the day we met here', he said.

'It was a long, long time ago', I replied.

'But it was unforgettable in every way. It led to so much. It gave us Amy'. The waitress came up and asked if we were ready to order. I said I had chosen a sandwich but wasn't sure what he drank these days.

'Just a coffee, please'.

'Me too'.

Neither of us knew how to start. The gulf between us was so great. The only link between us was Amy. The safe subject would be Amy.

As if he read my mind Jake said , 'Amy has been amazing since we returned. She has helped the boys tremendously'.

'And you, has she helped you?'

'As much as she could, yes'.

'Zoe, I am so sorry I didn't get in touch and let you know

what was happening'.

'Amy told me you said that you felt any contact with me would betray Clare'.

'That is part of it but I was a coward, Zoe. I knew what I should do but was frightened to take that step. I was frightened of the effect on my boys. Amy made it clear to me after she came to see you, that you deserved to be treated differently'.

'That was almost a year ago Jake. If I hadn't been outside Prop's office today would you have contacted me? We have to stop our daughter being the go-between Jake, it isn't fair. You need to consider her wellbeing too'.

'I know, maybe seeing you today was meant to happen'.

'I am not asking for a relationship. I just want what is best for our daughter. It is not betraying Clare's memory to want to make sure Amy gets the most out of her parents being able to talk to each other'.

'You are right'.

The waitress brought the food and our coffees. We seemed to have cleared the air.

'What are you doing these days?' He asked.

'Probably more than last time we were together at Amy's birthday. Graham and I are making short trips around Europe. We go every three months or so. I have this wonderful undemanding boyfriend'.

He laughed. It was good to see his eyes crinkle with amusement.

'Angie and I joined an amateur dramatic society and a rock

choir. We still go to the theatre and cinema'.

'Amy told me about Jennie's wedding. She showed me the picture your Dad took of her dancing with Paul Walker. Everybody at college knows about it. Do you still work for him?'

I felt a bit guilty but said 'Yes. He is very busy. He is hardly in the country'.

'Amy said he had got divorced, so there was hope for her, but she did admit when Richard challenged her, that he was a bit too old for her'.

'She insisted my Dad take the photo. Paul was ordered to stand in several different poses so his face was really clear'.

Jake looked at his watch. 'I am sorry I must get back, I have a meeting at two'.

He went over to pay. He took my arm and steered me out on to the pavement.

'Are we good now?' He asked.

'Yes, I think so, but how do we take this forward? Are we still going to be strangers again or are we going to try and be friends for Amy's sake?'

'I will ring you'.

'Do you promise?'

'Yes'.

My car was parked near the café so I reached up and kissed him.

'Goodbye my dear'. I whispered.

He bent and kissed me again and walked off. I hope none of his students were in the area.

The phone was ringing as I drove up. I knew it was Amy, she always rang on the landline for some reason. I rushed in and picked up the phone.

'Mum, Dad gave me a note to say you had met him near Prop's old rooms and had gone to the café by the river. Does this mean you are talking now?'

'I really hope so. I must say Amy I was shocked at how changed he was'.

'I couldn't tell you without feeling uncomfortable about it. He has aged. I do my best to cheer him up but with Richard and Andrew gone off now, he is lonely. I have taken to running in the evening in the streets with lighting and drop off at his house when I have finished. We have a drink and a chat and then I run back. I hope nobody thinks I am having an affair with my Prof'.

'Well he kissed me goodbye, so he is going to be seen as a Romeo now'!

'Did he really, oh that is great. He has been so closed off. I know it worries the twins. I miss them too but I have so much going on'.

'Do you attend his lectures? Does it feel weird to be taught by your father?'

'Not often, but they are brilliant. I really admire him. His knowledge is second to none'.

'Got to go now or I will miss supper. Bye Mum, love you'.

On my forty-second birthday I got my second ever card from Jake, my first was after Amy's fifteenth birthday when we celebrated with Graham and Amy. I was surprised that Paul had not sent one. He had been doing night shoots and I had a pile of messages for him. I would need to speak to his agent tomorrow to find out if he knew why he was out of touch. I was slightly worried. He always rang when filming. He was in Southern Ireland doing a costume drama.

Angie, Graham and I were finishing off a bottle of wine when the phone rang. I was actually slightly drunk. It was Amy for the second time that day. She had already been in touch first thing before lectures. Maybe she felt she needed to make up for last year.

'Hello Amy, is something wrong or have you forgotten you rang me this morning?'

'No silly, Dad wants to wish you happy birthday. We have just eaten'. She put Jake on the phone.

'Happy birthday, did you get my card?'

I giggled 'yes, I have now got two for my memory box'.

'Are you pissed?' He asked. That sounded like the Jake of old.

'Completely, Angie and Graham are here celebrating with me but I seem to have drunk the most. Angie is driving so she kindly let me drink hers. Graham hasn't far to go and I think I can manage the stairs'.

'Amy didn't tell me you had become an alcoholic.' He laughed. I so loved to hear him laugh.

'She is too loyal, but now my secret is out'.

'Well we better let you go and get some strong coffee'. He handed back to Amy who asked when I had taken to drink.

'Just this evening darling. Kisses to you both. Bye'.

Angie and Graham were listening to the exchange in astonishment.

'Was that really Jake?' Angie queried.

'The very person', I replied. They looked at each other and laughed.

'How many years since you last spoke to him?' Graham asked.

'Well actually it was the day I took Amy back to uni. I bumped into him outside Prop's old office'.

They chorused together, 'and you didn't think to tell us?'

'I wasn't sure he would keep his promise to ring me so I didn't say anything about it. He even sent me a card'. I tottered drunkenly over to the large display of cards and tried to find it. I needed my glasses, damn, where were they. I found them and pulled out Jake's card. They kept looking at each other wondering what it all meant. I didn't know what it all meant either, I was just happy for Amy's sake. It must be great not to have warring parents. Not that we had actually been warring.

They agreed it was time for me to go to bed and sleep off the drink. Angie had just driven off when a car turned into the drive.

'What has she forgotten now?' I asked. In the dark it wasn't clear who was driving the car but it wasn't Angie and it wasn't her car. Graham watched the driver get out and then went to the front door. He didn't come back. Instead, I felt a cold pair of hands touch my face and I nearly shot off the sofa. I looked up to see Paul beaming down at me. He bent down and I pulled him over the back of the sofa screaming with laughter.

'Why didn't you tell me you were coming?'

'I nearly didn't make it. My flight from Dublin to Stansted was delayed and the car hire office was closing down. I had to plead on my knees with them to give me a car'.

I was kissing and laughing and trying to pull his clothes off. He had a scarf and a thick coat on and I couldn't see to undo the buttons. I was frantic, I had missed him so much.

'Happy Birthday'.

'You are the best present so far. I have missed you. Since you came into my life the vibrator doesn't seem to have the same attraction'.

'Oh, I am glad I compare favourably with a vibrator', he laughed. 'Stop trying to get my clothes off and let us go to bed'.

'I thought you would never ask'.

He went back out into the car and pulled out his bags, slammed the door and ran back into the house.

He was home with me for two weeks before he went up to London to see his children. In that time we made up for the months he had been away. He read three scripts and rejected two as boring.

'You know Zoe I think you need a dog', he said one day as we cuddled up in bed, exhausted from a particularly zealous session.

'What generated that thought?'

'Well if I am going to visit more often, I would like us to go out for walks and take the dog with us'.

Suddenly I clicked. He wanted me to look after his dog.

'Are you bribing me with the chance of seeing you more, by asking me to look after your dog?'

He started stroking my stomach.

'Oh no you don't my lad. You can't reduce me to a quivering wreck so I can't think straight'. I slapped his hand away but he started on my breast instead. 'If I don't say yes then you will go on torturing me. Is that it?'

'Exactly. You take such good care of me and you know how much I love her'.

'But what if she wrecks Graham's perfect garden?'

'She is very well behaved, I trained her myself'.

'And that is a recommendation'.

'Well I have trained you, haven't I? Look how much I have taught you and how well behaved you are. I am your master'.

'You are a pest, Paul Walker. You know that don't you. You think you can bat your eye lashes and I will do just what you want. You turn on all your charm and I give in, don't I?'

'Does that mean you are agreeing to look after her?'

'Ok but you must promise not to leave me alone for so long. It has been dreadful. Mind you if I have your dog, I won't know if it is me or the dog you are coming to see'.

'I don't have marvellous sex with the dog' he was grinning.

'I should hope not'.

Four days later Paul drove up to town to see his children and returned with Lilly. I am not well up on dog breeds but I am assured she is a Dandy Dinmont by the various dog walkers I meet on our treks around the village. I fell in love with her as soon as I saw her. She has not met Spike but I know they will be pals.

I was feeling flat after Paul left. He has a way of filling the house with his personality. I had not broached the subject of my meeting with Jake but he had commented on Jake's card. I decided to come clean. He was pleased we had patched things up for Amy's sake.

For a week I didn't change the sheets so I could smell the subtle perfume he wore. It was specially made up for him in London. One of the benefits of being very rich, I suppose. He had also left a jumper in the lounge and I cuddled up to it at night on the sofa. How pathetic.

I looked at his schedule wondering where in the world he was. New York meeting a producer, then on to Los Angeles. He would be back at the beginning of December.

When Dad brought Spike over to meet Lilly I asked him if they could have her for the four days Graham and I were going to be in Rome. They were getting on well, with Lilly following Spike around. I knew Dad would say yes. He had been going through his prints and had found one of us dancing at Jennie's wedding. He thought I would like it.

There are hundreds of lovely pictures of Paul on the internet but this was my very own picture. One that nobody else would have. He was looking down at me and we were laughing. The weekend after our trip to Rome, Jake rang. He wondered if I would like to have lunch at his house with Amy.

'I would love to but I need to bring the dog I am looking after'.

'What have you added dog-sitting to your range of talents? Will we need to feed it too?'

'Very funny. I only do it for special clients who pay me well. It is Paul Walker's dog, Lilly'.

I felt oddly nervous loading Lilly in the car securing her safety clip before we set out for Cambridge. I was glad Amy would be around.

On Sunday, you could actually park near Jake's house. It was just outside the restricted zone. It was a terraced four storey building, early Victorian I think. Amy flung herself out of the house to meet Lilly who barked loudly to be let out. I grabbed her lead before she ran off. Paul wouldn't speak to me ever again if I lost her.

'Mum she is lovely. Has she met Spike?'

'Yes, a few weeks ago. They followed each other all round the house which is good because Mum and Dad did dog-sitting for the dog-sitter when Graham and I went off to Rome. Don't think Paul would appreciate his precious dog being chewed by Spike'.

Jake was in the kitchen cooking with an apron on. He was stirring the soup. I went up to him on tiptoe and kissed him on the cheek. He looked down and smiled. I can never get over how tall he is. I always seemed to be craning my neck to look at him when we were young. That is why he picked me up so often. What on earth made me think of that?

Amy opened the back door into a small, neat, walled, garden with a stone patio. Lilly and Amy raced out.

'Maybe I should have had a dog when Amy was growing up. She loves animals so'.

'I expect you had rather a lot of differing responsibilities. A dog would have complicated things'.

'You are right but a cat wouldn't have been much trouble. Mum and Dad have five now'.

'I suppose you won't drink – there is some juice in the fridge. My lovely assistant has deserted us'.

I opened the fridge and found some glasses after opening a few cupboards.

'Are you drinking wine?'

'Yes there is an open bottle over there'. He nodded to the dresser.

'Lunch is nearly ready'.

'Can I do anything to help? You seem very much at home in front of the cooker. Suppose it makes a change from lecturing'.

'Well I needed to get up to speed pretty quickly when Mum left to go home'.

'Of course, how is she? I don't hear from Elspeth now Amy is at college'.

'I seem to need to apologise. I obviously put both Amy and Mum in impossible positions. I stretched their loyalty'.

'Grief can do that to you. You stop seeing what is going on around you most of the time and other people start making decisions for you. They start building up a protective wall without you realising it'.

'It was selfish of me though'.

Amy and Lilly came back in with a whoosh of cold air

'It's too cold out there. Amy shut the door behind her. 'Have you two had the chance to talk? I can't stay out there much longer'. She put her arms around Jake and pressed her face in his back. I loved seeing them together. I felt weepy so I gulped down some fruit juice.

By the time we left a complete thaw had set in. I told them stories of Graham and my trips all over Europe. How Graham had nearly fainted when somebody called him my husband. I was pleased to see Jake relaxed and laughing. He had been sad too long.

When he had helped me put my coat on, I turned to face him. Amy was sorting Lilly in the car.

'You know Clare would not have wanted you to be sad, don't you? She would want you and the boys to be happy'.

'I think I am getting there slowly. Our daughter has certainly helped. She takes after you Zoe. She is very loving and kind'.

He bent down, picked me up and kissed me goodbye properly.

INTO THE LIMELIGHT

Paul kept his promise. When he was in the UK he did his best to be with me, and Lilly, of course. He even travelled up for our family Boxing Day party.

Amy had asked me if she could travel back to Cambridge to spend Boxing Day with Jake, Richard and Andrew. We had Christmas lunch with Graham and then I drove her back to Jake's house. I didn't go in.

I had told Amy, Paul was in the area for Christmas and I had invited him to come over and see Jennie. He arrived at gone midnight. He had only managed to see his children on Christmas morning. I knew this caused him stress. Chloe wouldn't dare move the new boyfriend in but Paul knew he was at the house more often than his own. She was aware of the conditions set out in the divorce settlement and wouldn't dare have him living with her. She would not risk reducing her alimony.

My siblings all knew Paul and I were now an item but I didn't want Amy to upset her relationship balance with Jake by having to conceal that I had a partner. I had gone for lunch again shortly before the twins came home for Christmas.

It was over a year since Paul came to me to hide. His work schedule had kept us apart for much of that time. He had never said he loved me but he tried his best never to let me down. I think he knew how damaged I had been by Jake. Graham had asked me, if Paul went off, would I regret the relationship? It took a while for me to answer.

'No, I have realised you need to take risks. I have spent so many years closeted away. Even if it is a short-lived relationship it has been wonderful. I still think he loves Chloe which makes it hard for me. I seem to have made it a habit of being second-fiddle don't I?'

We had two weeks in January before Paul went to Los Angeles and Hawaii. Filming was planned for about three months. This was the longest he had been away and I was dreading it. Amy was frantically revising but still found time to meet up for our monthly lunches with Jake. In March, Lilly and I arrived to find she wasn't there. Jake was looking much better. He had taken up cycling and was going to the gym again.

'Amy has got some extra study groups this weekend'. He said as Lilly and I padded through to the kitchen.

'I had forgotten how awful this period was. What had we failed to cover? Do you remember Varena decided she had missed out a whole section and went ballistic trying to read and understand about some weird tribe in Ethiopia?'

'Do you still see her?'

'Yes, about once or twice a year. She emails me a lot. She is based in Geneva now'.

'Have you told her about us?'

'Yes, she is not too impressed, frankly'. I didn't say that she was worried about me having two men who didn't seem to want to commit to me in my life at the same time. She thought I was playing with fire.

'I am not surprised, she has cause to worry, my record is not good', he smiled ruefully.

We spent the day reminiscing about our time at Cambridge. Amy would have found it very boring.

'Have you come across any of your fellow alumni here?' I asked.

'We had quite a few in Australia. I handed over to a later graduate'.

'Are you happy here?' I queried.

'Very, it is an exciting time for bio-diversity and we have a lot of funding. To be honest, if Clare had agreed, I would have come home a long time ago. This is where the real environmental research is happening. As well as UEA'.

'So, you made the right choice. Do Andrew and Richard agree?'

'Yes, I think so. I wasn't sure at first. They were pretty cut up at Clare's death but Mum said I needed to take them away from the house. There were too many memories'.

I was late leaving. The time had flown past. Lilly was looking at me wanting her food.

I stood up and picked up my bag. Jake walked to the door whilst I collected my coat. I put on Lilly's lead. As before Jake picked me up and kissed me. I came up for air. My response had been immediate.

'Jake are you sure you want to do this?'

'I am not sure what I want Zoe but I just felt the need to kiss you'.

'If you don't put me down now, we might do something we both regret. We have only just started talking again'.

He put me down on the ground gently letting his hand stroke my hair. I fled to the car. What is the matter with me, I thought. You can't let this happen again.

Returning home from Jake's house, I let Lilly wander around the garden for a wee and then went into the house. The landline was ringing insistently. Shutting the door to stop Lilly going out again. I rushed to get it.

'Zoe its Paul. I have been trying to get in touch. Is your mobile off?'

I had turned down the ringer tone when I arrived at Jake's.

'Sorry the ringer tone was off. I have been out with friends'.

'Anybody I know?'

'No' I lied. He didn't actually know Jake, he just knew of him.

'What is so important you have your knickers in a twist about, Paul?' I was feeling guilty and I was taking it out on him. How could I do that?

'I think it is time you came to a premiere with me'.

'What, me walk along a red carpet with you. You are joking aren't you?'

'You will be doing your job. You are my support worker aren't you?'

'I don't think that is in my job description'.

'Well it is now. Put April 28th in your diary. You are back from Bruges by then, aren't you?'

'Yes'.

'Well there is no excuse'.

'I wouldn't know what to wear. Paul what is this all about?'

'I have just found out that Chloe is attending the premiere of my film and I bet the new man will be in tow. I will strangle the woman who organised the guest list. Is she stupid? I don't want to be standing on my own without somebody on my arm'.

'Can't one of your multitude of female friends who I speak to, help? I will ring round if you want me to'.

'But I want you'. This was a new development. 'I have asked Mary to get in touch with you to help find a dress. She will look after everything. All you have to do is turn up'. Mary was Paul's stylist. She was brilliant, he looked good in casual clothes or evening dress. She made it look like he was laid back about clothes.

I didn't want to let him down but I felt I would be a poor substitute for his elegant ex-wife.

'Ok then I agree'.

'You are a darling, did you get my package?' To help me walk Lilly in the winter, he had asked Mary to find a Barbour coat and boots.

'Yes, they are lovely and warm. Far too good for me to mess up in the mud'.

'I have got to go now, I will be in touch, take care'. He hung up leaving me totally flabbergasted. How he felt I could be made to look anything other than completely out of place walking on a red carpet, God only knew.

Mary rang the next day asking me for measurements. She held on while Graham, giggling fit to burst, measured my bust, inner leg, waist, hips and everything in between. I had emailed her my picture which I had scanned off one of Dad's photos. She then asked what colour I felt best in. I remembered my midnight blue dress and pumps I wore for Jennie's play at the Barbican.

'Midnight blue'.

'Good choice. I will sort something out'.

'How do you do all this from afar?' I asked.

'With somebody like Paul, he is rarely around so I have got used to it. Mind you I know all his measurements'. Not quite all his measurements I thought. I knew one she didn't have!

She sent me photos of the clothes she had chosen. Apart from one which was too fussy they were just right for somebody who wasn't wanting to expose their entire body to the population. She had found pumps with a slight heel. The dress I chose was three quarter length. No chance I would trip over. It had short sleeves with a reasonable neckline. She said my bust was just right and should be slightly exposed. It was nipped in at the waist. Next day the outfit arrived and I tried it on. It fitted like a glove. I was transformed.

Mary rang to see if everything had arrived. She said I should get Graham to take a photo on the mobile and send it to her. Graham was loving all this. It was decided to keep my hair down.

All that was needed was a small clutch bag. She said it helped you to avoid waving your hands to hide that you are nervous. Even the most experienced red carpet walkers get nerves.

'Please stop Paul from putting his hands in his pockets. Make him keep hold of yours. He hates premieres and is an absolute pain. We will send a car to bring you up to London and take you to his flat. I will find a bag and send it with the makeup lady and hair artist who will meet you there. We will keep the makeup to a minimum. Just enough to highlight your eyes. Those are Paul's instruction by the way. He doesn't want you to look like a diva'. I didn't think he would need to worry about that. I had no such pretensions.

'Thank you, Mary, you have been so terrific'.

'Paul pays me a fortune to keep him looking good. Don't worry'.

I was beginning to understand how little I knew about Paul's life.

This entire operation had taken just over a week. There were four days to go. Paul had rung to say he would be at the flat the night before but not get in until late. I asked him if he wanted me to bring Lilly up with me.

'Yes, I can drive you both back the next day'.

'Can you stay?'

'Yes for about a week or so'.

As the days went by, I got more and more agitated. I rang Jennie who was an old hand at these things. 'Just stay close even when he is being interviewed. Keep hold of his hand. He absolutely hates premieres even though he comes over as loving the attention. He is the perfect actor. If Chloe is there she will attempt to hog the limelight. She always does. She is a walking clothes horse and loves to show off. Do you know if he has seen the finished film?'

'I don't know'.

'It is helpful to know what the final cut has been. When you are filming you do it in parts. The editing is the most important bit and then it is the addition of the soundtrack. They all go into completing the film'.

The night before, Graham helped me put the dress and shoes into their bags. I even had new underwear. I had a small overnight case as we would sleep at Paul's that night. The Mercedes arrived at my little house early next morning and the chauffeur got out. He looked askance as I brought Lilly out with her rug and safety clip.

'Is the dog coming?'

'Yes, she is Mr Walker's dog and is perfectly behaved'. I answered snootily. Two can play at that game. He carefully put the clothes bags and case in the immaculate boot. Graham checked everything was there, blew me a kiss and disappeared to shut up my house. I laid Lilly on her rug and clipped her in and walked around to the other door which he held open for me. I sat stroking her. It was beneath his dignity to speak to me or maybe he was forbidden to.

I actually slept most of the way. Being nervous does that to me. It seemed just minutes since we had left home. We drew up at a recently renovated mansion block in Richmond. Lilly jumped up ears alert. Paul must be around and sure enough he came out just as we got out of the car. He directed the Chauffeur to put the bags in the flat on the right. Lilly was beside herself and wouldn't stop barking until he picked her up. Laughing, he kissed me and pulled us towards the flat. I remembered Lilly's blanket and went back to get it.

Paul thanked the Chauffeur and handed him a twenty pound note. Once the door closed, he rushed over and swept me around in a circle with Lilly standing on her hind legs to get at him. He covered my face with kisses.

'God I have missed you Zoe. I have got the coffee on in the kitchen'. He pulled me through to a state-of-the-art luxury kitchen. The whole flat had been tastefully decorated.

'We have several hours before anybody arrives'. He almost leered at me.

'You are sex mad'.

'Well I have been away for nearly three months with no sex'.

Coffee finished, we made our way to his bedroom. I hung up the clothes alongside his which had been delivered. Lilly had settled down on the carpet by the window.

'Where is your nephew?'

'At work, so don't worry he won't interrupt us'.

After months of deprivation our first contact always had a hint of desperation. There was no time for gentleness. Our need of each other was too great.

Lying back on his pillow I had a chance to have a real look at him. He was extremely tired. His eyes were dull. Seeing my concern, he put his hand up and pushed my hair from my face. 'I will be alright later. I couldn't sleep last night after I arrived. It was rather too long a haul from Los Angeles. We had to stop off in Houston because the plane had engine trouble and we were filming right up to the eleventh hour'.

'Why don't you sleep now. We have a few more hours. I can see what food is in'.

'Oh, there is plenty of food. I think I will just sleep. Do you mind?'

'I might just walk Lilly around the block'.

'Don't forget the poo bags. They are in the hall cupboard on the shelf'.

I put Lilly's lead on and let myself out of the flat picking up the keys from the lock. It was one o'clock. We had a few hours before Paul needed to get up and shower. He loved his showers just letting the water run over him with his face held up to the head.

Lilly and I let ourselves back in an hour later. The flat was deathly silent. I kept her on the lead because I thought she would run in and wake Paul up. He was still fast asleep. I went in to the kitchen and made coffee and gave Lilly some food. I decided I would have a shower myself. There was another en-suite in the neighbouring bedroom. Hoping I wouldn't wake him up I showered and wrapped myself up in a bathrobe hanging on the back of the door.

I let him sleep for another hour then made a fresh pot of coffee and took a cup in. He was lying on his side with his hair all tousled. He looked innocent. I felt my heart pound. I realised I needed to accept that I was falling in love with him. He stirred. I touched him gently. He reached out and pulled me on to the bed. I was still slightly damp.

'I feel more human. I can smell coffee, have you made a pot?'

'There is a cup on the side table'. He sat up and lent back on the bedhead. I gave him the cup. 'What time is it?'

'Three thirty. You have half an hour before your gang arrives'.

'I had better get up and have a shower. Can you make me a sandwich?' He flung his legs off the bed and headed for the

229

shower. I covered up the bed and plumped up the cushions.

He appeared in the kitchen just as I finished a chicken sandwich. He was dressed in his shorts. 'Your sandwich is there with some fruit'.

He sat on the stool and pushed up my robe stroking my bottom. 'I am looking forward to seeing your dress. Mary says it is just perfect'.

'Graham sent her a picture from his phone when I tried it on'.

'Has Amy started her exams yet?'

'Yes, she has had the first one. Jake says she is a star pupil. All her tutors are betting on her getting a First'.

'Do they know she is his daughter?'

'After she gets her results they are going to let people know'.

'Have you seen him?'

'Yes a few times'.

The bell rang and Paul went to open the door. He was still in his shorts but that didn't seem to faze the people who came in. They busied around setting up their apparatus.

The hair stylist asked what time we had to be at the cinema. Paul checked. 5.45. We would need to leave by 4.50 at the latest. They sat me down and got going on my hair. By the time they had finished it was gleaming. Paul was going for the unruly look. His hair had grown on set and there was no time to re-style it. Then it was the make-up. Just a light dusting on my face to stop me perspiring under the lights and then some work on my eyes. The effect was subtle.

A different me emerged. Even Paul had his face dusted. The dark shadows under his eyes were erased. Mary arrived to dress us.

Now for the clothes. She had gone for the casual look for Paul. Open pale blue silk shirt and a grey silk fringed scarf. His jacket had a mandarin collar and was black. It was slightly longer than usual. There were no pockets for Paul to put his hands in, Mary laughed. Paul tapped her hand with a pat.

Then it was my turn. Mary sent me off to put on my tights, bra and pants and then ordered me back to put on the dress. She zipped me up looking all round to make sure it was hanging properly and blew out her cheeks.

'That means she is happy' Paul said. 'Let me look now'. I slipped on my pumps and then turned to face him. His smile told me everything. I looked good. He bent over and kissed me.

'Right we need to get a move on you two. Here is your clutch bag Zoe. Keep hold of Paul's hand. If you get cold just think in a few minutes you will be under arc lighting. That is how the ladies are almost nude in the winter without being covered in goose bumps'. Mary reassured me.

I put the house keys and a handkerchief in the bag. Paul handed over a credit card for me to hold. He kissed Lilly and told her to behave, took my hand and we ran to the car.

He yelled his thanks to the team who were packing up when his nephew arrived back from work. 'See you later, we have got keys. Can you take Lilly out before you go to bed?'

We were only five minutes late. Paul took a deep breath and got out of the door being opened by the commissionaire. He turned to take my hand and help me out squeezing it to reassure me. I smiled. He looked momentarily grim then turned and put on his smile walking confidently up the carpet holding my hand. We made our way through the microphones and interviewers, his screaming fan club, with me following holding on tightly to his hand with a fixed smile. 'Don't forget, Zoe you need to smile' I could hear Mum and Rosy in my head. Paul walked me over to the three ladies who ran his fan club giving them all a kiss and saying he would see them later. He introduced me. Gwyneth said it was nice to meet the voice at the end of the phone. He was insistent that they got tickets to any UK film premieres. They were also invited to the party afterwards so we agreed to talk then.

After several minutes of talking to reporters we were ushered into the main entrance to have our photos taken. I started to walk away so they could catch Paul on his own when he put his arm around me and pulled me to him. He smiled that beautiful smile of his and I wanted to melt. He stood looking at me for a few minutes and then I felt him stiffen. I looked around and saw up ahead, his wife Chloe, with her new man. She looked magnificent but I noticed her smile didn't reach her eyes. Observing her partner, I wondered why anybody would prefer him to Paul. The director of the film came over with his wife. Paul introduced me. 'David, Sheila, this is Zoe'.

'First time on the red carpet?' She asked.

'Yes, it is a bit daunting, all those flashing lights and people shouting at Paul wanting interviews'.

'Paul handles it well even though he hates it'. She said. She lent in to me 'We are all going in together so Paul can get past his ex-wife'. They moved either side of us and Paul tucked my hand in his arm. The four of us brushed past without appearing to notice them.

In the auditorium away from the noise outside I felt Paul's body relax. I had been so preoccupied with supporting him and not making a fool of myself, I hadn't noticed the many famous actors attending the premiere. It was definitely a gaggle of stars. We were among friends. They came over and chatted. We had agreed I would be introduced as his assistant. I think he had asked Sheila to look after me.

The photo sessions started. On one side the ladies' dresses were being snapped and against another wall the members of the cast. Paul was standing beside a tall woman with a swan-like neck dressed in a deep green velvet gown. Her hair was long, dark chestnut. She had a gentle face which was astonishingly beautiful. I couldn't take my eyes off her.

Sheila tapped my shoulder. 'Come and meet Paul's girls'. I knew all about his girls. He had starred in films with them and remained great friends. Jennie was one. I had spoken to all of them over the years. They were always ringing trying to discover his whereabouts. If he was in the UK he would meet up and have lunch. I occasionally took a call from the States as many of them were based there. If Paul was going to be in Los Angeles or New York he would ask me to ring and let them know.

We walked over to a group of women clearly enjoying themselves catching up with the news. They moved aside to let us join. Sheila introduced me. 'This is Zoe, Paul's assistant'.

'Zoe', came back a chorus. 'How great to meet you'. One by one they moved over and chatted to me. They were charming, animated and friendly. I could see why Chloe got jealous and why Paul was so fond of them.

She was in a group making a lot of noise. It sounded like the braying you get in the House of Commons. Suddenly I heard my name ring out above the noise.

'Zoe, is that our little Zoe? What are you doing here?' Everybody turned to look at me and the next minute I saw two of Dad's very, very famous rocker mates waving at me. Charlie and Pete rushed over to me and swung me off my feet. In the commotion I saw Chloe glare at me then turn back.

'What are you doing here? How is your daughter and Eric, Sarah and the family?' They flung questions at me like bullets.

'I work for Paul Walker'.

'Are you still living in East Anglia or have you moved to London? Can we take you out to lunch?'

'I am still based in East Anglia. Going back tomorrow'. Hurriedly I filled them in with family news and said they should come up and see us. Dad would be delighted. He was loving being the country gent. The photo sessions were coming to an end and guests were being ushered into the auditorium. Paul appeared at my shoulder. I introduced him. We were just starting to talk but were asked to move on politely. We agreed to chat at the after-party.

Taking our seats Paul whispered 'Everything OK. Has Sheila looked after you?'

'Oh yes, she has been so kind. She introduced me to your girls'.

'I bet that was fun'. He grinned. We sat down and the lights were dimmed. He took my hand.

The film had been in post-production for nearly two years. It had wrapped a couple of years after I had started working for Paul. It was a historical love story about John of Gaunt and Katherine Swynford. Years ago, I had read a book by a writer whose name I had forgotten. I had even persuaded Dad to divert to Lincoln Cathedral to see Katherine's bier on a trip up to Yorkshire.

It was my favourite story for a long time. John of Gaunt was the son of King Edward III, Katherine Swynford was his mistress. She first met him when she was seventeen and he was twenty-five. She was the daughter of a lowly Queen's herald. She and her sister were orphans under the care of Edward III's wife. I loved the story of love and loss. He upset the nobility by marrying her after the death of his second wife. They had several sons and a daughter when she was his mistress. They were legitimised by the Pope after he married Katherine. Through John and Katherine's family, the visible products of their love for each other - the Beauforts - their descendants had sat on the Scottish and English thrones.

Sitting beside Paul, holding his hand, I disappeared into the film. I was unaware of anything except the film and Paul. The cast read like a Who's Who of the acting world. Between them and the director they had created a wonderful film.

I watched Paul age from twenty-five to his mid-fifties. He changed from a vibrant go-getter to an old man, worn out by the country's politics, never achieving his goals. Paul was John of Gaunt. His co-star Rebecca Von-Rycken, who played Katherine, was just as I had imagined she would have been, calm, beautiful and loving. Never losing her faith during the difficult years they were apart, bringing up his children. They were a perfect blend. The casting team had done a brilliant job. Now I understood what they meant about chemistry.

I realised that Paul really knew his trade. He took his acting life very seriously. He was the ultimate professional. I felt tears well up when I thought of him. I was glad that he shared what little life he could, with me. I was so moved by him. I wanted to let him know. I turned my tear-streaked face and looked at him. He put up his hand to wipe them away and smiled.

The audience erupted in cheers as the film ended. It was a triumph.

Tension over, the party following, was raucous. Alcohol flowing freely, dress jackets undone, uncomfortable high-heeled shoes being cast off. It was tremendous fun. Paul asked me to find his fan club ladies and make sure they were looked after. He needed to speak to a chosen few. I saw them in the corner and I made my way over to them picking up Charlie and Pete on the way. Gwyneth, who was in her fifties, recognised them and looked flustered. She would explain later who they were to the younger fans.

'Have you got drinks and food?' I asked. Charlie these ladies run Paul's fan club. They are brilliant'.

Pete laughed, 'All our fans are living in old aged people's homes'. They all screamed with laughter. They pulled up chairs and sat down. I loved the banter with these two. I had known them since I was a toddler. Assured that the ladies were in good hands, I looked around for Paul. I could see him with a group of his mates. I went over to the refreshments. I was ravenous. Grabbing a plate of food and a glass of juice, I was walking back to sit down with the gang who were falling about laughing at Pete's jokes when I realised I was in the proximity of Chloe and a group of actors. I was going to have to navigate around them.

I felt my elbow being held and an arm around my waist. Paul lent forward. 'You are a bit too close to the enemy camp. Come on I want to introduce you to Rebecca'. He took my glass and we about-turned towards a more friendly welcome.

People were lounging around in chairs and I put the food down on a table. 'Rebecca, this is Zoe, my assistant'. She stood up and held out her hand. 'Hello, pleased to meet you'. Turning to the man by her side. 'This is my husband Rolf. Do come and sit down. That food looks good. I think I will send Rolf over to get some'. Paul pulled out a chair and I sat down.

'If you will excuse me, Rebecca I need to go over and talk to my fan club ladies, will you keep Zoe entertained for a while?' She nodded. He wandered off somehow managing to avoid Chloe's group on the way. I saw him sitting down in the middle of the ladies laughing with Pete and Charlie. Their jokes are pretty raunchy so I hope they weren't being too obscene.

'How long have you worked with Paul?' Rebecca asked. 'I am sure he is good to work for. I loved filming with him, he is an amazing actor, so serious about his profession'.

'About five years now shortly before he started this film. Congratulations. You became Katherine. I read the book years ago. I think the film was based on it but with obvious changes. You played her just as I had imagined'.

'Well, I knew nothing much about the history. I am Danish, but I did a lot of research after I had been offered the part. She certainly made an impact, didn't she?'

'Yes, I am a bit of a history buff. I did a degree in European History at Cambridge'.

'So, you will probably be more aware of Danish history than me too', she laughed.

Rolf came back with the food and we munched away. Paul arrived too with a loaded plate and a large glass of wine.

'Are they okay?' I asked. He slurped an enormous mouthful of wine before he responded. 'I needed that. They are having a ball'.

We explained to Rebecca and Rolf about my Dad's connections with the music business which was how I knew Pete and Charlie. I found it difficult to work out her age. She could have been thirty or forty. Rolf was late forties, I think. Not their generation of rock stars. I imagined they would be into something more refined. They were so polite. Rolf was German and his English wasn't great so I chatted in German. Paul looked on with a slight smile on his face.

It was getting late. Paul had arranged for the fan club to spend the night at a hotel and a car had arrived to take them off. Kissing and waving Paul goodbye they departed. They were paralytic and stumbled against each other. Pete and Charlie came over to say goodbye too.

'Pity you aren't staying over, Zoe, but tell Dad we will be up to see him soon'.

I got both cheeks covered in smacking kisses and they flew off.

A man was hovering behind Paul and lent over to give him a message.

'It seems our lift home is here. Better say a quick goodbye'. He kissed Rebecca, shook Rolf's hand and dragged me off to the groups still around. I thanked Sheila for looking after me. Holding my hand we moved through. Kisses everywhere. I got kissed too by people I had never met. Plans were made to meet up. Eventually we found ourselves at the car.

Snuggled up in bed later I told him what a brilliant actor he was and that I loved him. He pulled me to him and kissed me. He didn't say he loved me.

I GO TO MY FIRST GRADUATION

Filming in Los Angeles had been very challenging. Physically and mentally. Paul was exhausted. He always gave 110%. For the first week home he slept most of the time. We walked Lilly and I fended off calls. He was silent a lot of the time, listening to music or reading a book. I had found my tattered copy of Katherine. Graham came in and they played chess. At night he was often asleep before I got into bed. We had not made love since he first returned.

My visit to Cambridge for lunch with Amy and Jake was looming and I was scared to mention it. Had I made a mistake telling him of my love? Was I just providing him with a base to hide away?

'Do you mind if I go off and see my parents?' I asked.

'No, I have got to make some calls. I will take Lilly for a walk this afternoon'.

I have been so lucky. My family, especially my parents and Prop too, have been around to talk to if I had a problem. I needed my Mum's advice badly.

I was asked about the premiere. Mum had seen a photo of me walking hand in hand with Paul on the red carpet. Charlie and Pete had rung Dad. Amy knew I was going up to be Paul's 'date'.

'So, it wasn't so bad then?' She asked.

'By the end I was thoroughly enjoying myself and the film moved me to tears. You must see it when it comes round. I was so impressed by Paul's talent'.

'Then what is the matter now?' She could always read me like a book.

'I think I have made a big mistake'.

'How?'

'I told him I loved him and since that night there has been a cooling off in our relationship. He is exhausted but I am beginning to think I have read more into things than I should have. I know he likes me but I am wondering if that is all?'

'What did he say when you told him?'

'Nothing. I suspect that he is still very much in love with Chloe. If you could see her Mum, she is so beautiful. I can't compete. I am sure he isn't ready to move on and my stupid declaration has worried him. He thinks I am pushing him into commitment. I have so little experience with men and what I did have has gone seriously wrong'.

'How long is he staying with you this time?'

'I am not sure, I would need to look at his schedule. He is filming a series in the UK though'.

My mobile phone rang. It was Paul.

'Hello Zoe, look I am going to take a trip to London for a couple of days and I need to go off pretty soon. When will you be back?'

'We are just going to eat so not for a while'.

'I need to go. I will pack some things and drive to the flat. I will take Lilly with me. I will ring you tonight to let you know when I will be back. Take care'.

'That was Paul, he is off to London, taking Lilly with him. I think he is running away. Oh, Mum what have I done? It is Jake all over again'. I burst into tears and she hugged me to her.

'Poor Zoe, you give so much love to everyone and get treated so badly. I don't know what to say'.

By the time I left, I was resigned to returning to an empty cottage. I knew in my heart that he would have taken all his belongings. I was right. Even Lilly's blanket and bowl had gone.

He did ring that night. He had left because he knew he had used me to escape and was ashamed. It had been unfair and needed to stop. He admitted he was still in love with Chloe and seeing her at the premiere with the new man had shown he was not over her. He cared deeply for me but had no idea what the future would bring which was why he had decided that he should leave. My admission that I loved him had shocked him into realising how wrong his behaviour had been.

I couldn't speak so I just put the phone down.

I was destined to live alone. I knew in my heart that Amy would probably move to London for work or even stay in Cambridge. 'Recluse Cottage' would need to work its magic again. I had survived this long and I would recover, I knew, but also it would be a struggle. I would need to find the courage to move on. I was in despair.

FRIENDSHIP RENEWED

By the time I lunched with Jake and Amy I had achieved a measure of calm. We discussed the exam Amy had taken, she had two more to go. She actually enjoyed the first exam. Jake and I had become relaxed around each other. Amy asked where Lilly was?

'Paul is not filming so she is with him. I quite miss her' (and him, but I wasn't going to admit that to Amy).

'Mum is planning an end of exams lunch for you Amy. Can we agree a date so it doesn't clash with your college celebrations?' (At least Amy would get the chance to go to the Prom.) 'She has invited you too Jake, and your boys, if they are back'.

'I would love to see them again'. Jake replied.

'Right, when Amy gives me the possible dates we will see how many of the family can be there. Why don't you come over to me for lunch sometime in May. I can return the compliment of all these meals'.

'Dad and I went to see Paul's film the other day'.

'What did you think? I know history is not exactly your thing'.

'We loved it. That actress is so beautiful, isn't she Dad?'

Jake nodded.

'I met her and Rolf her husband at the premiere. He is German and his English was poor so we were able to chat away in German. At least no longer doing translations hasn't impacted on my conversational skills. What did you think of Paul's performance?'

'He was amazing. Do you think he might be in the running for an Oscar?' Amy asked.

'I don't know enough about that but I can tell you the audience erupted into cheers at the end. The director, Derek, who was sat with us, couldn't stop smiling. His wife, Sheila, looked after me. I think Paul asked her to watch out for me'.

'How is he?' Asked Amy.

'I don't know. I don't work for him when he is not filming'.

'I must go as I have promised to water Graham's greenhouse. He is staying with his new boyfriend'.

The post exam party was just right. Most of the family were there except Jennie. Lisa had a temperature so they stayed away. It was lovely to see Jake, Richard and Andy relaxed among my dear family. Angie and Angus came over too. Angus was going to stay on and do a PhD at UEA. It was a warm day for early June so we had lunch outside.

Angie came up. 'Are we going to see Paul's film? It is on in Norwich. I am sure you would like to see it again'. I had not told Angie of his departure. She probably assumed he was filming.

'Yes, it is good enough to see many times. Let's go this week'. This would be a challenge.

Two days later I was in a crowded cinema watching Paul's dear face. I lost myself in the film. Angie was totally silent, apart from saying what a good pair they made. We cried about the film. I was crying too at the loss of this lovely man. He had never been anything but kind and I hoped he was finding some peace.

'Wow Zoe, what an experience. Paul is such a good actor. The film is brilliant'.

'I found the book the film was based on for Paul to read. Would you like to borrow it?'

'Yes please, I will collect it on the way home when I drop you off'.

'Seeing it for the second time I noticed so much more. I think I will get the DVD when it comes out'. I didn't feel it necessary to tell Angie that I would look at it to remind myself I had been in his life for a short time. The nights were the worst. I longed for his body near me. I spent hours looking at Instagram and Twitter, Googling him regularly to see if there was anything I could find out. I did wonder when my feelings would subside.

I bought an outfit for Amy's graduation. Most of Amy's friends now knew she was Jake's daughter. Jake had told his fellow Dons. We were going to attend together. Richard and Andrew were coming too. An exception had been made with the number of guests. When the day arrived, I knew the outfit I had bought would be too hot. I had nothing else other than the dress I wore to the premiere. It was simple and not at all dressy. I pulled it out of its wrapping and pressed it to my face. Memories flooded back. It had been a wonderful evening. Mary had sent me pictures of our walk down the red-carpet hand in hand. I put them away in my bedroom drawer. I felt like kissing his face. I laughed, remembering Amy kissing Jake's photograph. At least Amy now had Jake in her life.

We were meeting up at the house and then on to the ceremony. I arrived an hour before we needed to leave. I had only spoken to the twins briefly at Amy's lunch. Richard (he of the bent earlobe) opened the door and let me in. He was almost as tall as Jake but looked just like Clare. He shook my hand politely and said 'Hello, come on in, we are in the kitchen'. I did not know if Jake had told them of our regular lunches so I let him lead the way.

Andrew came charging down the stairs and greeted me. Both of them had slight Australian accents.

Jake called out, 'Andy are you dressed?'

'Nearly Dad', and he flew back upstairs.

Jake came to the kitchen door. 'Come on in Zoe'. He kissed my cheek and then pulled up a chair. 'I have got coffee on'.

'I can't drink too much or I will need the loo', I laughed. Richard smiled back. Amy had told me he is the more reserved.

'Did I tell you about the time Varena and I got delayed going up to Jennie's first show at the Barbican?'

'What happened?' Richard enquired.

'It was my sister Jennie's graduation performance. King Lear. Our journey was a total disaster, delays, cancelled trains. We arrived within five minutes of curtain up and my mother refused to let us go to the ladies'. I told him that I had sat through the play's first half terrified I would have an accident. We had drunk a lot of coffee on the train as we sat fuming at the delay.

'Fortunately, it wasn't a comedy'! I added.

Andy reappeared and plonked himself down grabbing a biscuit and his coffee.

'We love having Amy as our sister, you do know that don't you'. Jake was getting his gown and cap. 'She has been so great with Dad since we went to college. He looks better doesn't he?'

'Yes, I was shocked when we met each other in Cambridge. He loved your Mum so much. She made Amy so welcome on her visits. I am sorry she isn't with you anymore'. I put my hand out and patted his. He turned it over and held on. I saw a glimmer of wetness in his eyes. He was going to make a good doctor, I thought.

Jake reappeared catching sight of me holding Andy's hand. 'We need to get going or we will be late for Amy's day'. Opening the door, he ushered us out leaning down 'You look beautiful, that colour is perfect'.

Walking along next to Jake with Richard on the other side I was so glad that Jake and I were friendly again. I was so pleased to see the love they had for him. I am not small but I felt dwarfed. I was running to keep up until Jake slowed the pace.

The graduates were all seated with their caps on and their gowns. I sat down with Jake next to me, Andy the other side, Richard sat next to Jake on his right. Amy was stood up searching for us. As my companions were at least a head taller than everybody else she found us quickly waving madly and blowing kisses. She probably couldn't see me but we all waved back. The batch of graduates this afternoon were around five hundred. The ceremonies would be going on for quite a time.

Normally Jake would be on the podium but as a parent he remained in the audience. When they called out Amy Chapman's name I felt like I was choking with emotion. Jake looked down and took my hand. Of course, she had got a First. We now had three Firsts in our family. The handover of the scrolls is very quick and the clapping limited to a short time. It was a great moment for each of the parents but it had to be got through or the ceremony would go on forever. The students filed out before the parents. Amy was waiting for us as we came out.

She was in my arms, crying, then she turned to Jake and he held us both. Richard and Andy held back but she pulled us all into a group hug. Jake had his family. She went off to have the graduate photos taken. When she came back, we were approached by another photographer, offering to take family groups. I now have copies on my bookcase. Jake and Amy, Jake, me and Amy, me and Amy and then all five of us.

It was time for the students to sling their mortar boards in the air. I have a picture of that too, along with her graduation photo. My world felt complete for a short while. That day will live with me forever. All the hurt was forgotten. We were all going forward, me too.

Jake offered to bring some of Amy's belongings that she didn't need back home. He and Andy came over and put her boxes in her room. I fed them lunch. Amy was staying at Jake's as she had an interview in Cambridge. I showed Andy around the garden. We had moved the hive over to Graham as I seemed to get stung even wearing protective clothing.

'This is beautiful. Did you do all this yourself?'

'Oh no, Graham next door is a garden designer. He and Prop did it when he retired'.

'Prop?'

'Has Amy not told you about our dear Prop. He was my professor at Cambridge but when she was a baby Amy couldn't say Prof. It came out as Prop and the name stuck. Our whole family called him Prop. He lived here almost until he died when we moved him to my parents' house. He died surrounded by those he loved. I think of him all the time when I am in the garden. My mother painted his picture. I have it in my office'.

'Did she paint the one of Amy in the field of sunflowers?'

'Yes, she took it from a photo my father had taken'.

'Dad loves that painting, he loves Amy. She is very special to him'.

I faced him 'Do you mind about that?'

'Not at all and I am glad you are all back in his life. Mum wouldn't have wanted him to be sad but, I can tell you, that first few months after she died, we really thought we had lost him. He threw himself into work. He didn't sleep. It was awful. I am glad Grandma was there'.

'What changed?'

'He got a letter asking him to apply for the Cambridge post. It was his way out. I think he had started to hate Australia to be honest'.

'Are you planning to study psychiatry Andy? I think you will make an excellent psychiatrist'.

Graham came round and I introduced him to Andy. They went off to look at the hive and I went back in. Jake was sprawled in Prop's wingchair dozing. Memories of that last visit came flooding back. Evenings spent by the fire sometimes with Amy but more often than not, she had left us alone.

'I was remembering those weeks I spent here', he said looking up.

'I thought you were asleep? I didn't mean to wake you. They were very important times for Amy'.

'You have done well with her. She moves me so. You don't begrudge me my family do you Zoe?'

'I did when you failed to get in touch but not now. I like your young men too. Andy is going to make a good doctor. Richard is shy but I hope he doesn't resent me being in your life again?'

'They both said that they thought Amy's Mum was great'.

'Can I make some coffee? I think I need to wake up before I drive back?' He stood up and I followed him out into the kitchen. He opened the cupboard looking for the mugs. 'You have changed things round. Where are they kept now?'

'Over there near the kettle'. I didn't want to tell him Paul had moved them around.

Andy rushed in. 'You haven't got stung have you?'

'No but it was close' he replied.

'Graham has been showing Andy, Amy's beehive'.

'I remember that birthday present, she was screeching with excitement. Nothing changes, she is as noisy as ever'. He grinned, downed his coffee. 'Come on Andy we must go'. A quick kiss from Jake and a cuddle from Andy and they were gone.

We met up a lot over the summer on the weekends because Amy had started a job as a trainee editor on a Geographical magazine published in Cambridge. It was good experience but I doubted it would keep her interested for long. She lived at Jake's. They mostly came to me as the summer crowds made parking difficult. As a senior professor, Jake had a parking space at the College so he kept his car there. He cycled to work mostly. He was working on a paper with some colleagues, for presentation to a conference in Canada, so his summer was busy.

Graham had been nagging me to start my book. I kept saying I was thinking about it but, he was right, I needed something intellectual to challenge me. I just couldn't find a subject which excited me. I spent evenings researching on the internet. I diverted from time to time to look for Paul. One picture popped up showing him with his children messing around in a boat. This was on Instagram.

I had taken on more clients to replace the large retainer that Paul had paid me but I found myself struggling to keep up my enthusiasm.

Jake had finished his submission and rang up to ask me out for a celebration. We ended up at a small restaurant overlooking the Broads. The food was mostly fish, and delicious. We had been surrounded for most of the year by his family and I hadn't really been alone with him very often since I bumped into him in Cambridge.

I felt shy. It was almost as if I had lost my chaperone. Now I could misbehave but didn't know what to do. I chuckled to myself.

'What are you laughing at?'

I told him what I had thought. He was looking more like

the younger Jake as he had let his hair grow slightly. He had worked in the sun and was tanned and his eyes had recovered their brightness. I know he loved having the children with him. He had told me they squabbled a lot of the time. After we had eaten, we sat on a bench by the Broad. Small lights marked out a pathway. It was probably the last warm night of the summer.

'Have you thought about us at all?'

'How do you mean?'

'Well at this moment, I have a strong desire to kiss you but I don't quite know how you will respond'.

'I have always enjoyed kissing you so I can't see that I would object'.

'I just wanted to work out if you see our friendship as platonic?'

'What has always worried me about our time together was the violence of the sexual attraction we felt. I think it was destructive really'.

'You may be right. But we feel differently now. Don't we?'

I could only just see his face but I took it in both hands and kissed him pulling him towards me.

'Take me home Jake'.

He rang to tell Amy that he had drunk rather a lot of wine and couldn't drive home. He would stop over at my place. Amy knew I rarely drank much so I expect she thought I would drive.

We finally made love for the first time. Most of our relationship had been purely sexual. This time it was different. There was joy and kindness. After so many years apart it was tinged with sadness too. Jake had warned me he was out of practice and I would need to be patient with him.

In the morning lying in bed with my head on his chest and my leg flung over him he asked 'Do you think it is time we got married?'

I had waited for almost half my life to hear this but now I was totally confused. I needed to be honest with him.

'I have to tell you something. For the last year or so, Paul and I have been having an affair. Apart from my family, Varena, Angie and Graham, nobody else knows, not even Amy. When he found out his wife was having an affair he came here and hid away for a month. He was in a very bad place. As he recovered, we started sleeping together. I thought I meant something to him even though I knew he still loved his wife. He was out of the country filming until the night before the premiere. He asked me to attend so I thought maybe I was starting to play a bigger part in his life. That night I told him I loved him, I still do. He didn't respond'.

'He brought me back to the cottage. He was exhausted with filming so he spent a lot of the time asleep. When he was awake he barely spoke, when we walked Lilly it was in silence. In the end he went out alone. After a week of this I was a nervous wreck. I felt used'.

Jake pulled me closer and stroked my hair kissing the top of my head.

'Oh, my poor love', he whispered.

'I had to see my parents. We were about to eat lunch when he rang. He said he had to go to London on business. He would take Lilly. He would ring me that night'.

'When I got home it was as I had expected. He had packed his bags and taken the dog's bed, bowls and food'.

'Did he ring?'

'To be fair he did. He said he was ashamed. He had abused my hospitality and taken advantage. He had been shocked by my admission of love. He was sorry. I have not heard from him since'.

'So you aren't working for him now?'

'No, I rarely worked for him when he wasn't filming. It was only when he was on location but I Googled him and saw that he was working on a series in Northumberland so it was obvious he had ended the contract. He was away for long periods of time but he always came back here when he could. I thought he cared. He flew back from Ireland to be here for my birthday last year'.

'I think he does care but not as much as you do'.

'What makes you think that?'

'Just a hunch really. If he hadn't, he wouldn't have felt any guilt at his behaviour'.

It was surreal. Here I was talking to the longest love of my life and he was consoling me for being in love with somebody else. The thought made me laugh.

'What made you laugh?'

I moved on top of him putting my legs either side. 'Just the thought that you were consoling me for the loss of Paul'!

I took hold of his penis and stroked it. He responded immediately. I bent and kissed his face. He lifted me up and lowered me slowly onto him. I was moving up and down when he picked me up and turned me over on my back. I flung my legs around him plunging him deep into my body. He held himself away and looked into my eyes, lowering his head, he kissed my face, all the time bringing me to my orgasm. When it came I let out a gasp and I could feel him throbbing, desperate to ejaculate. He let out his breath, relaxed and moved over wrapping me in his arms.

We slept some more and when I woke up Jake had showered.

'Come on lazy-bones, I have cooked some breakfast'.

Sat at the table he said, 'I can see you will need time before you give me an answer'.

'I won't make a commitment until I am sure I have made the right decision. I don't want any lies between us Jake'.

As he left, I stopped him and he picked me up for a kiss. 'Thank you for giving me so much pleasure' I whispered.

PATIENCE PAYS OFF

Graham popped round. He had seen Jake leave.

'Am I to take it that you have had a good night?' He leered.

I put on a fresh pot of coffee. Graham was my gay father confessor.

'I have had my first-ever offer of marriage. Here I am nearly 43 years old and never once have I been asked. What a sad case'.

'What did you say?'

I told him everything. 'I love Jake, I will always love him, but I can't commit until I know I am free of Paul and just right now I certainly am not'.

'What did he say?'

'He consoled me. It was bizarre to be using him as a confidante. I suppose nobody knows me better than him. We have so much shared history, not just Amy'.

'How have you left it?'

'We are going to continue to meet up. I couldn't bear not to continue our friendship'.

'I take it you had some light relief?'

'Yes, but it won't happen again, as wonderful as it was, because I can't use him like Paul used me. We have to deal honestly. In the meantime, I have Varena here for a week and we need to plan our next trip, then we have the Choir and the Amateur Dramatics. I will be fully occupied. On top of that I need to get a new mobile phone'.

Varena had been home for her grandfather's funeral and was on her way back to Switzerland, leaving from Norwich. We picked up where we left off and ordered a take-away and consumed several beers.

'What have you been up to? I saw your photograph with Paul on the red-carpet. How is he by the way?' Varena had briefly met Paul on one of his short visits. She was the only other person outside my immediate family, Angie and Graham who knew about our liaison.

'A lot has happened since then but you should be the first to know, after Graham, that Jake has asked me to marry him'.

'What, is this turning into a love triangle?'

'Not really, Paul has gone'.

She jumped off her seat and put her arms around me. 'What has been going on in my absence? Tell me'.

I related the whole sorry tale. I also told her about Amy's graduation. I showed her my photos. I welled up remembering the day.

'Jake's family are all so tall but only Amy looks like him. I suppose the twins take after their mother', she said.

'Yes'.

'The pictures are beautiful. Is that the dress you wore for the premiere?'

'Yes, it was a hot day and the outfit I bought was too thick so I pulled it out of the back of the wardrobe. I have got to know Richard and Andy well too. It is lovely to see Jake's family together'.

'I saw the film when I was in Yorkshire. My mother cried for most of the second half, especially when she left him after the riots. I must say that the two of them were brilliant. In fact, the whole supporting cast were great. Do you think they might get nominated for an Oscar?'

'I am no judge. I dug out my copy of the book the script was taken from and read it again. I lent it to Paul too'.

'Do you think he has gone back to try and patch up the marriage?'

'I think that is a lost cause, personally. I Google him regularly but everything is so stage-managed. He doesn't use social media. He puts the odd picture on Instagram. You can't find out what is going on in their personal lives to be honest. He hates being public property'.

Jake had been teaching Amy to drive. He had laughed saying he wasn't sure what was more challenging, being with me at her birth or the lessons with Amy. He had run the whole gamut of abuse, I think.

'You are very patient, my dear'.

'So are you'.

Amy passed her test first time and she and Jake were driving down to see Varena before she left. They arrived just before lunch. Varena opened the door to Jake. Their last encounter before Amy's birth had been brutal so they were both slightly wary of each other. Never one to hold back, she pulled him towards her, kissed him and whispered 'I am so sorry about your wife Jake. It must have been traumatic'. Jake was taken aback but recovered.

'Thank you Varena. Can we start being friends again?'

'Well if Zoe and you are now best mates then how can I hold back?'

Amy was thrilled that she could drive. 'I can come and see you more now Mum. The trains on a Sunday are awful. I do miss seeing you'.

'I presume you intend borrowing Dad's car then?'

Amy got bored listening to us reminiscing about our time at college and trying to cram twenty-two years of catch up over lunch. When we had finished eating, she went off to meet Graham's new love and see how her bees were. Varena and Jake went outside and got out some chairs while I made the coffee. I could hear her asking Jake how things had been since Clare died. I realised he needed to remember her in good ways and I had avoided this. I felt guilty. They had ended up arch enemies because of me and here she was knowing exactly how to talk to him. I held back a while and let them continue chatting. I could hear them laughing too.

When I went out with the coffee Jake said 'We thought you had gone to have a lie down'.

'Ha, ha'.

Sitting in the garden with my two oldest friends, I felt so content. My daughter was happy, Jake was looking so much more like his old self. After they left, Varena made some tea and we sat in companionable silence.

'I think Jake is starting to remember the good times with Clare', Varena said.

'I really hope so. If you had seen him that day in Cambridge outside Prop's office, you would have been shocked. I am ashamed to say, I have not really had the courage to speak to him about Clare. What you did this afternoon has shown me I need to let him talk more'.

'He told me that Amy had kept them all together when they had returned to Cambridge. She seemed to know exactly what to do'.

'I was so angry that he had not told me they were back. I was scared I had lost Amy. Jake now had his family complete and I was outside looking in, hating him. I understand now what Amy was doing and I am so pleased by what she achieved. Her love and care helped them all'.

'She is like you in that respect. You give so much love and it makes me sad to think how lonely you must have been over the years. Jake told me that he really enjoys living with Amy especially now the twins are away. His work is challenging and it is good to relax at home with her in the evenings. You don't mind that?'

'No, I have prepared myself since Amy went to college. I knew she wouldn't come back here. If anything, I am surprised she is still in Cambridge but I suspect she feels she can't leave her Dad. She has spent so many years without him. I am lonely, but not alone. I have my family, Angie, Graham and now a part of Jake again'.

Varena is such a presence. Her departure left a gulf in the house. I decided I would ring around the family at the weekend and catch up with their news. I had bought the DVD of Paul's latest film. Angie had borrowed it and just given it back. I would relax and watch it in the evening.

Varena's approach to Clare's loss was to let Jake talk. I

suppose I was lucky Paul could be seen on the screen. I had resisted going down this road but maybe watching him would be cathartic. I would only find out if I turned the machine on. Curled up in Prop's old chair, I took a step towards living with my loss. In comparison to Jake's it was not so dramatic. Paul had not died. He was still a living human being not cold in the ground.

This was the third time I had seen the movie. Alone, away from the cinema, I found it was even more dramatic, intimate. I remembered sitting with my hand tucked into Paul's feeling him relax as he knew that it was going to be a success. It had been released in the States a few weeks later to rave reviews and was grossing enormous amounts of money. The Americans like our history more than we do. Maybe in the winter I will catch up on Netflix or Amazon with his earlier body of work. It would keep me occupied in the winter evenings. The dark nights were always problematic for me.

My ears were burning at the end of Saturday. I had spent hours catching up with the siblings. I saw Mum and Dad most weeks so I wasn't completely out of the loop but it was good to hear their voices. Jennie had just finished filming in Northumberland and Stephen was childminding. He said she would be back later that day and he would get her to ring on Sunday. Stephen now looked after Jennie's engagements.

Putting the phone down, I remembered seeing on the gossip media that Paul was back working on a series for TV in Northumberland. Surely there wouldn't be two sets of film crews working up there. I suspect she had wanted to protect me by not telling me they would be filming together. I have got to stop my family taking pity on me. I wanted to stop being "poor Zoe".

I was beginning to understand how difficult it must have been for Jake. It was as if the death of a loved one makes them disappear, as if they had never existed, except in their minds.

Jennie rang on the Sunday.

'Hello Jennie, how was Northumberland?'

'Wet and starting to get cold. I am glad it was only two episodes'.

'Were you filming with Paul? I saw a report somewhere'.

'Yes, he is the lead character in a crime series'.

'That is a new angle. I don't think I have seen him in any murder mysteries'.

'It is a pretty dark production'.

'So not much fun on screen'.

'No, we had to make up for it in the evenings. I know most of the crew and acting gang so it was great fun'.

Obviously, Paul was recovering from his marital drama. Taking a deep breath, I asked, 'How is he?'

'As he usually is when on set. Totally committed. Always on time, never causing a fuss and looking after the team'.

'And in the evenings?'

'He came out with us but I think he was playing a part there too'.

'How do you mean?'

'Look, I have known him for fifteen years and he doesn't offload his private life on us. If he wants to talk he will, but this time he wasn't right. When not centre stage his face was sad and his laugh seemed slightly false. He did ask me how you were. I kept to the basics. I said you and Jake had patched things up. Amy graduating, Jake, you and the twins at the ceremony, Amy now living with him. Great pictures of you all together. I don't know why I said that, I think it was a bit of a dig really. He didn't behave well to you and I wanted to let him know I did not approve'.

'Is he back with Chloe?'

'Definitely not. He is looking to buy a house but hasn't found one so far. He has commissioned some woman to find him one. He said he wanted a proper home. I know he is seeing his children much more. We stayed on for the wrap party but I expect he will be on his way back to London'.

We gossiped some more and then she hung up. I was pleased I had spoken about Paul. I think there is a time when the hurt gets buried and you start to regain your equilibrium.

THE BUSES ALL COME AT ONCE

It was no good, I had to replace my dodgy mobile. I had been putting it off. Our village has a very good bus service and I rarely used the car in town. The parking was awful. I think the young woman in the store was glad to see the back of me. I had chosen one phone, then seen another and gone back to the original choice. Her eyes were glazing over at my questions. I expect she was wondering if she would get a coffee break before tea time. It was two hours later when I hopped on the bus.

Rural buses are my favourite. They wind through all the little hamlets dropping people off and picking up new travellers. The gossip is delicious. Today I was sad because one of the regulars had lost her elderly dog and the whole busload was consoling her. I was upset that I no longer saw Lilly but at least she wasn't dead. I nearly missed my stop but my neighbour lent over and reminded me to get off.

'Oh yes, thank you so much. I was in a dream'. I was planning another trip but wasn't completely convinced Graham would come. He had this new man in his life who fitted his lifestyle much more than I did!

Prop's house was only just round the corner. Funny that, I still think of it as his, even after all this time. We had planted a largish hedge at the front for privacy and it was getting quite tall. I must get it trimmed, I said to myself. Turning into my drive I hadn't noticed the car parked alongside my little machine but I did hear the dog barking. My head shot up and the next minute Lilly came charging towards me.

Paul had let her out and was opening his door. I dropped my packages and picked her up. She licked me all over, great slurping licks. I was drenched. Strange that I should have been thinking about her just before. I was trying to gain time before I had to speak to Paul. He was leaning on the car, watching. His face was unreadable. Serious.

I would be drowning soon so I dropped Lilly and she ran back to Paul. I wiped my face, picked up my parcels and approached him.

'Hello, what are you doing here?' I was trying to keep my voice level to hide the fact that I was shaking.

'To see you'.

'Why, what have we got to say to each other?'

'Can we go inside? I have been trying to ring you all morning but your mobile was off. I tried Graham's house but his answerphone is on. I decided to take the chance you might be here'.

'He is away at the moment. My mobile is broken so I have just been into town to get a replacement. It hasn't been activated yet. They said it would take a few hours'.

It seemed stupid standing outside the house so I walked past. 'You had better come in'.

I was actually feeling cold. Not physically, but emotionally. He shut his car door and followed me and Lilly into the house. She ran around from room to room. I picked up the mail and put it on my desk. Paul followed me in. He looked around and saw the graduation photos on the bookcase. He walked over and studied them picking up the one of Jake, Amy and me.

'I expect you are really proud of Amy'.

'Yes I am. Jake calls that photo the three degrees'.

I turned and went to the kitchen and I filled a bowl of water for Lilly. She lapped it all up.

'We have been travelling since early today from Northumberland'.

'Shall I make us a drink? Do sit down'. He pulled up a chair. I put the kettle on the AGA and got down a cafetiere and some mugs. 'Are you still drinking black coffee?'

'I think I should have some milk today'. I handed him the jug of milk from the fridge.

I needed to be direct. Why was he here? Was there something more he wanted from me?

'What do you want Paul?' He took a sip from his cup and looked up. His eyes were infinitely sad. 'Is there something more you want from me?'

'You know Jennie and I have been filming in the North'.

I nodded. 'She rang me yesterday after she got back'.

'She told me that you and Jake were together again'.

'Well not exactly, but we are friends now and I see him regularly. After I delivered Amy back last year, I went to look at the building where Prop's rooms were and he was walking past with some colleagues. It was the saddest moment. He looked dreadful. We had some food and coffee at the café where we first met up. For Amy's sake we agreed to try and retrieve our friendship. I didn't tell you as I felt it would complicate things. He hadn't contacted me because he felt it would have betrayed Clare's memory and he didn't want to upset his boys'.

Lilly had curled up on my feet and was fast asleep. I looked down and then back at Paul waiting for him to continue. He seemed to be finding it difficult to speak.

'I have missed you'.

'Me, personally or my many services?' God, that was catty, I thought.

'Can we start again, Zoe? I know I messed up big-time and did everything wrong'.

'What does that mean in practice Paul?'

'I have postponed the start of my next contract. I want to be with you and try to make it up to you. I know I behaved dreadfully. When you told me you loved me that night after the premiere and I said nothing, that was unkind. I should have explained, not kept silent. I couldn't make a commitment to you knowing how mixed up I was. Chloe was still in my head. I didn't want to promise something I wasn't certain of fulfilling. After we got back here, I realised I had been selfish and not thought about my behaviour being misinterpreted. You offered me such security and I had taken advantage. I know that now. You deserved so much more but at that time I couldn't give you the answer you wanted'.

'So, you left without saying goodbye. At least Jake did that, he stayed until Amy was born. I collapsed at the airport the day he flew off. The problem here, Paul, is simple. I felt like used baggage after Jake left. I achieved peace and brought up Amy, then along you come and do the very same, but in a different way. Jake never lied to me ever, nor did he use me like you did. I am only just now starting to get my life back and bang, here you are again'. I had bottled this up for so long the venom poured out of me. All those nights of crying, loss and, most of all, rejection. I am not sure I liked this version of Zoe. People hurt me but I didn't retaliate. I felt exhausted by my fury.

His face was distraught. He took my verbal blows without speaking.

'Are you here because Jenny told you that Jake and I were now on better terms?'

He waited before he spoke, choosing his words carefully, looking me straight in the eye.

'Have I left it too late to tell you that I know I love you and want to marry you?' He flinched when I screamed back. 'I have waited half my life to have the man I love ask me to marry him and now, within the space of two weeks, I have two offers at the same time'.

'Jake has asked you to marry him?'

'Yes'.

'Have you accepted him?'

'No. When he asked me, I knew I had to be honest and tell him about us or what I thought mistakenly was us. I told him everything. How I had made the mistake of telling you I loved you, your lack of response and your departure a week later'.

'And did he still want to marry you?'

'Yes, but he also knows I am far from certain that I can commit to him whilst you are still in my head. We have never lied to each other'.

'Am I still there?'

'Do you think I go round telling all the men I know that I love them? When I say I love somebody it doesn't evaporate in three months. I have only loved two men in my whole life and loving them seems to have brought me so much pain. At least, now with Jake, that pain is going away. We were able to be together at Amy's graduation and there was such joy. Of course, you are in my head and my heart but I am not sure I am brave enough to risk more sorrow when you decide you got it wrong again'. He pushed his chair away and stood. I looked up, my face streaked with tears. He took out his handkerchief and wiped them away gently. He looked at his watch.

'Can I take you somewhere?'

'What now?'

'Yes, it isn't far'.

'I need to wash my make-up off my face'.

'I will get Lilly in the car while you do that. Bring a warm coat and your boots'.

Totally bemused I locked up and flung my boots and coat in the boot. He had a new large 4x4 and I had to climb up into the front seat.

We drove in silence for about ten minutes. On the edge of a small village we turned into some gates with a tiny lodge house and drove up a short drive. Ahead was a large building. It looked to be late Queen Anne or perhaps early

Georgian. It was white stucco but much of it had fallen off. Arriving at the front door I noticed a man standing in the porch with some papers. Paul got out and walked round to the rear and pulled out my coat and boots. He opened my door and I turned to get out. As I did so he stopped me and removed my shoes. He gently fitted my boots on and I jumped down. He helped me into my coat. His touch had sent a shiver through my body. He went to the back of the car (do you call a very large 4x4 a car? It is more like a tank) grabbed his boots, put them on, then let Lilly out.

Taking my hand, he walked over to where the man waited at the entrance to the house.

'Mr Walker, I am Robert Chase. How do you do?'

'Pleased to meet you'. He turned to me 'This is Zoe Chapman'. We shook hands and then followed the agent into the house. I suddenly remembered Jennie telling me that Paul was looking for a house. Was this it? What did it mean? My head was throbbing after all my fury. This was not good for my health.

'Helen Weir did explain that the house is in need of radical work?' The agent asked Paul. Looking around at the few rooms visible this property made the house Mum and Dad had renovated look positively palatial. There wasn't a room that didn't have split floorboards, plaster coming off, broken boarded up windows. The rooms were not large and the ceilings not as high as the later Victorian houses but they were perfectly formed with fireplaces in each one. At the rear was a Victorian extension housing the domestic rooms. There was a dairy and wash room off the main kitchen and, to the side, rooms which would have been the preside of the butler and housekeeper.

The main house had four large bedrooms, a dingy bathroom

and, down a set of stairs there were six smaller rooms. Presumably these were the servants' quarters. Another staircase at the end of the corridor led back down to the kitchen. I nearly tripped on a broken floorboard and Paul caught me. After that he kept hold of my hand.

Outside were several outbuildings. The garden was completely overgrown. I thought Graham would love to re-design this. We drove around the remaining part of the estate in the agent's car.

After the tour he gave Paul some very swish details. Paul took them and asked if he had the architect's plans and the builder's estimate for the work.

'Oh yes, sorry they are in the car. Let me get them'. Whilst he was away, I tugged at Paul's arm. 'Are you seriously considering buying this wreck?'

'Shush he is coming back. Wait until he has gone. By the way I don't want to give him the impression I am too keen'.

Paul looked at the papers the agent brought back. He ummed and aaghed, made faces and generally looked concerned at the information. I wondered if the agent knew he was an actor.

'Remind me of the price again?'

'With the farm and the other cottages, the total price is three million'. I bit my tongue before I could expostulate, choked and turned to blow my nose. £3 million was an awful lot of money.

'Thanks very much for showing us around, we will go off and have a good read, talk to a few professionals and come back to you'. The agent handed Paul his card and said if he could provide any further information to contact him.

I thought myself that he ought to know the name of a demolition expert.

'One thing, before you leave. The house isn't listed is it?' Paul asked.

'No. Right I will be off. I hope to speak to you soon'. He drove off slowly down the pitted drive past the gates that were lying on the floor.

Paul turned to put Lilly back in the car.

I sat on the front seat and he pulled off my boots putting my shoes back on. Flinging my coat and our boots into the back of the car he put his shoes on and got in. I made sure Lilly's safety clip was properly fixed and we sat looking at the house.

The atmosphere between us had changed. I had stopped being angry and he didn't look so unhappy but conversation was still strained. I looked at the agent's details and the other papers as we drove home. With all the renovations Paul would be spending nearly £4.5 million for his country pile.

We called into the village shop for some food for Lilly and then drove back to my house.

'I am really hungry Paul, I need to cook something quickly. Is a fry-up OK?' I wasn't expecting to be entertaining. 'I have eggs, bacon and maybe some mushrooms. I also have some cold new potatoes that could be fried'.

'Perfect'.

The weather had turned chilly in the last few days so I had brought in some logs. Paul got the woodburner going whilst I cooked. He spread the papers out on the kitchen table.

'The total package is an enormous amount of money'.

He went to his coat and pulled out a pair of spectacles and put them on as he sat down. 'How long have you had those?' I asked.

'I have always been slightly short-sighted but it has now got worse. I have to wear contact lenses on set'.

'They suit you'.

After we had finished eating we sat next to each other and peered at the plans.

'It seems an awful lot of money?' I queried.

'I don't intend to pay the asking price'.

'So, you are really serious about purchasing the place?'

'Yes. My accountant has told me I need to invest my money in some property. I have too much lying around that the tax man can get his hands on'.

'But £3million. Wow are you that rich?'

He smiled, he was looking more relaxed. 'If you know I am very rich will you marry me for my money?'

'Don't change the subject'.

'I have worked non-stop for nearly 20 years since I left drama school. I am an A-lister and could demand really high fees if I wanted to. I don't, but I could. I bought the house Chloe got in the settlement for cash. I have a small block of flats which I rent out at much lower rates to people who would struggle to get a mortgage or rent generally. That income alone pays the alimony. For the Gaunt film I took a lower salary and a share of the net takings. You probably know how well the film is doing'.

'I hadn't realised'.

'That is what I love about you Zoe. You are not materialistic. We ought to go in and put some more logs on the woodburner'.

When I came in with a pot of coffee he was lounging in Prop's chair, glasses on the end of his nose, using a calculator he had taken from the office, to work out some figures.

'But there is a farm attached to the property with animals, what would happen to them when you are filming. They will all be dead by the time you came back'.

'Silly girl, there is a farm manager living in one of the cottages'.

'So you will be a gentleman farmer'.

'I am no gentleman according to you. I have done a great deal of thinking since I left you. I spend my life in hotels and on planes. I am tired Zoe. I hardly saw my children in the early days. I was the husband providing for his family but I was not there for them. I think the reason Chloe hated the arrival of those scripts was as much about the fact I would be leaving as jealousy of my success. I want a place I can bring the children to. I want a home'.

He looked so sad I pulled up the stool and laid my head against his legs.

'You are really serious about this aren't you?'

'Yes, but here's the catch. It only works if you marry me'.

I pulled back.

'Paul that is unfair to put it all on my shoulders. That is as bad as Jake not realising he was using Amy all those months'.

'I love you Zoe and I know you love me and I also know that if you choose Jake, I will have to live with that, but the thought breaks my heart. I understand what he offers and I think I am a bigger risk. Given your past history I can see that he might be the better option, you have so much between you'.

'How long do I have to decide?'

'As long as it takes. I can hardly ask you to rush this given the fact that I have behaved so badly towards you'.

'But, the house'.

'I may still consider buying it. It will take at least 12 months of constant work. If you decide against marrying me, I have no doubt I will recoup the money when I sell it'.

He gathered up the papers and called Lilly. 'Now it is time I went back to London'.

'It is late. I will make up a bed and you can start off tomorrow'.

I slept very little that night. I tossed and turned. Eventually I gave up. Paul's door was open and I peeked in. He and Lilly were cuddled up together. It reminded me of the two copper heads of Jake and Amy when he visited from Australia for her fifteenth birthday. I smiled and went down to get some warm milk. I went in to the office. I needed to talk to Prop.

'Well Prop, what do you think of this? I am in a real pickle. Should I put together a spreadsheet of the pros and cons? No, you wouldn't approve of that. As you said, life rarely goes in straight lines but even you couldn't have imagined this. Who do I choose or do I choose neither of them? I love them both. If I choose one, I will hurt the other. I have lived with Jake. I know what he is like but Paul's time with me has been so intermittent and how do I know if we are compatible. Compatible? Strange that after twenty years Jake and I had become compatible. Is that what growing older does to you or is it that you accept the differences? What do I tell Paul when he wakes up?'

Sadly, Prop could give me no answers. I crept up to bed, but I did sleep.

Paul woke me with a mug of coffee. He said my mobile had been working overtime in the office. I had work to do. I quite liked being brought a drink in bed. I could get used to this. One plus for Paul, but Jake had done the same. This wasn't going to work.

I cooked scrambled eggs, fed Lilly and then went in to check all the messages. Paul was sat at the kitchen table making calls. An hour later I had done what was needed and went to see him. He should wear glasses all the time. They made him even more handsome. He was on the phone to his agent. I think of him as an actor but I realised listening that he was a pretty shrewd operator too. He finished the call and looked up.

'I know so little about your world Paul. I caught a glimpse at the premiere but I realised I was just a tiny cog in a very big wheel'.

'I don't make love to them. I did to you, that sets you at quite a distance'.

'If Chloe, who is very much part of your world, couldn't cope, then how do you expect me to survive?'

'You underate yourself. You have a brilliant mind. I wouldn't expect you to change your lifestyle for me. I want to change mine. If I didn't work again we would have a very good existence. If you asked me to I would give it up for you. You have already played a pretty large part in my life but I want you to be able to follow your own dreams. Not mine. You must have thought about what you want to do now Amy has gone'.

'Well yes, I have started researching the book Graham is bullying me into writing'.

'There you are'.

'I would imagine myself rather lonely living in a large house like the one you are looking at buying, especially if you are away for long periods'.

'What if you came with me some of the time? It is not as if we would have any children to look after. I get lonely among the crowds too. I want to love and be loved. I am naturally monogamous. My girls will tell you that. We get on and have fun but they knew I stayed faithful to Chloe, even when the marriage was falling apart'.

'You love being an actor and are brilliant. I couldn't ask you to stop doing what turns you on'.

'I have spent the last three years running from one film set to another and I haven't really had much of a life. My accountant says I am earning too much money', he laughed. 'The time I spent with you up here in the cottage renewed me. I love the country and almost hate the city. I want to farm, but more than anything I want to be with you'.

I stood behind him and rested my hands on his shoulders then ruffled his hair. My favourite activity. He turned round and looked up. I pulled off his glasses and kissed him. He moved his chair and sat me on his lap.

'I have got to go back to London to sign a contract at Leo's office. Can I come back later this week?'

'I am not sure I will have made a decision by then but yes, you can'.

Five minutes after he and Lilly left, Graham was knocking on the door. I let him in and he rushed into the kitchen put the kettle on the AGA and turned round expectantly.

'Well?'

'You will be pleased to know that my hitherto mundane boring life is now in turmoil'.

'How do you mean?'

'After twenty years I have now had an offer of marriage, twice over'.

'What, Jake and Paul'! he exclaimed. He danced over to the AGA and made himself a cup of tea and sat down. 'Tell Uncle Graham more'.

I described the day with Paul. Graham actually knew the house we had visited because he had lived in the village. It had belonged to an elderly couple whose son had been killed in the Korean war and they had just withered away. They had died several years ago intestate and the government executor was now selling it. I told him that the garden was totally overgrown and he practically drooled.

'Do you think Paul will buy it?'

'I am not sure. He wants my answer to his marriage offer I think. When I said that was too much pressure he said he would probably go ahead anyway, buy it and if I turn him down sell it on at a profit'.

'He is very rich you know'. Graham said.

'How do you know that?'

'There is a website which basically guesses actors' incomes. They base it on the rates they know top stars get paid. They are probably underestimates. I looked Paul up earlier this year'.

'How much?'

'Well over £15 million. He has worked non-stop doing three or four major films a year for nearly twenty years and the money they earn is astonishing. He is at the top of the game'.

'What, and I was worried about him spending £3million on this farm'! I exclaimed. Now I was going to have to deal with that too.

'I am not sure you are helping dear', I whispered. Timid little me trying to cope with the world Paul lives in. There wouldn't be a Sheila around every day. I was getting another headache.

I UPSET AMY

I was busy with clients for most of the time. We were rehearsing Educating Rita for the Amateur Dramatic Christmas show and I was playing Dr Bryant's partner Trish who was having an affair with his colleague Brian. Angie was playing Rita. She was really good. Paul called and left a message on my mobile saying he would be up later. I texted back telling him the key was under the mat. We would be in the village hall rehearsing.

Angie was in full flow when suddenly she stopped. There was Paul standing at the door listening. I am not sure how long he had been watching. This was hardly Hollywood style acting. The director turned round and, recognising Paul, walked over and asked him to come and sit down. Angie put her script on the table and walked to the front of the stage.

'How on earth can I do this with you sitting watching me Paul?'

'We all have to start somewhere' he laughed.

Fred, the local postman was playing Frank Bryant, but he hadn't arrived so Angie was rehearsing with his stand-in who left much to be desired and when he found out from the lady doing the prompting who Paul was, he completely dried up.

'Why don't I play Frank and give you some helpful hints, Angie'. He put on his glasses and then hopped onto the stage and was given the sheets. He took a while to read through then looked at Angie.

'Right Angie how about we do it this way?'

As I said, Angie was good playing Rita, but with Paul as Frank she was amazing. We were all standing around in silence. Paul helped her get the timing with the jokes and showed her some moves to add emphasis to what she was saying. They were very subtle. When they finished, everybody clapped and gathered round Paul, asking for help with their parts. I saw another side to him. He was a top actor but he was so generous and patient with his advice.

Angie came off stage and sat with me and Don, the director. He asked how we knew Paul. Angie looked panicky and turned to me. 'I work for him, taking his calls when he is on set. He was in the area and called to see me, but I had left him a note to say we were in the village hall. I help out quite a few actors other than Paul. He has worked many times with my sister'. There had been an assumption that I would be a good actress because I had a famous sister. They soon found out none of her talent had rubbed off on me!

'I have watched his career', said Don. 'As an amateur thespian, I like to look at acting techniques. He makes it all seem very easy but I can tell he has put in a lot of effort. My wife and I went to his Gaunt twice.'

Paul extricated himself and came over pulling up a chair. 'Angie you are very good, in fact better than some of my co-stars, have you had any training?'

'Not exactly but I did a lot of drama at school'.

We all went off down the pub. The local ceilidh was playing.

Graham was there with Anton his new partner. Paul was suitably welcomed and introduced. By the end of the evening we were all prancing around singing along with the band. There was hardly room to swing a cat but nobody cared. Angie's husband Brian came and collected her as she was completely paralytic – a mixture of alcohol and Paul's praise, I think.

The four of us walked home. It was pretty chilly so Paul gave me his jumper as he had a coat. It smelled of him. I had missed his smell. I burrowed my nose into the soft cashmere.

Lilly barked as we got home. I loved the way she got so excited when she greeted everybody. Going round in circles. Paul let her out for a wee then got his bags out of the car.

'You were very kind tonight, thank you' I said.

'Angie is good. I wasn't being generous. She has real talent'.

He went upstairs and plonked his bag in the back bedroom. 'Can I take a shower? I have been travelling all day'.

'Yes', I called up.

I was having a dilemma. Would I be complicating things if we had sex? That part of our life I knew was pretty good. It was the total unknown other areas that worried me.

I undressed and went into the bathroom and climbed in the shower with him. He looked really surprised. I don't think he expected any form of sexual contact and I loved him for not making that assumption. This was my decision. He wrapped his arms around me and I stroked his buttocks. I had forgotten how firm they were. We just let the water flow over us.

'Are you sure about this?' He asked.

I nodded and switched off the shower. We dried each other off. Lilly was already sitting on his bed. 'Leave her there or she will just get in the way. She has got used to sleeping with me. See how desperate I have become'.

We climbed into my bed.

'I haven't had sex for some while and I may not be much use to start off with', he said. His hands were stroking the inside of my leg and I felt his fingers move inside me. I arched up and he kissed me hard all the while stimulating me. When he could tell I was close to climaxing he pushed his penis in hard and I thrashed about pressing my legs around his body. I cried out and he released himself.

To me the sexual act is as much about love as physical enjoyment. If the two components come together then it is a very sensuous experience. I have gone years without sex but somehow my body never forgets. I woke early to find Paul's arm around me and his hand on my breast. He was curled into my back with one leg over mine. I could feel his genitals resting on my bottom. I moved slightly and he woke up. I turned and nuzzled up to him inhaling deeply. I ran my hands through his hair and then down his back and lifted his leg taking his penis in my hand and stroking it. He smiled sleepily.

'I think I should make some coffee to wake you up'. When I came back with the tray he was slightly more alert. He was still extremely tired from his punishing film schedule. Should I be demanding more sex I thought. We drank our coffee.

'You are insatiable Zoe Chapman'.

'Well I have a lot to catch up. I intend to make up for all

those years I only had my vibrator for company'.

'How many times a day will you be making demands of me? I need to fit it into my schedule'. He laughed. 'I have a new role - sex slave'.

I whipped my slave into action. Well to be precise it was insistent stroking. Without too much hesitation he responded.

Before breakfast he went off for a jog. He needed to get fit for his next film. He had found a gym in Norwich where he could train. He was lithe and wiry but still pretty muscular but he would need to build himself up for his next role. We had already spent a small fortune at the supermarket and the local butcher (he paid). He had an advisor for this too! Paul laughingly told me once he had to live on eggs and avocados to play a dying man in one of his films.

Half an hour later he hobbled into the house.

'What happened?'

'I pulled a muscle earlier this year on the set. Luckily it was towards the end of filming and I had physio help but I think I have damaged it again'.

'I will ring Stephen after breakfast to ask if he knows anybody locally who may be able to help'. I pulled out a pack of peas from the freezer and he sat at the kitchen table resting his leg on the chair holding it against the damaged muscle.

Working for Paul, I knew all the links in the chains that kept his life running smoothly, but I realised over the weeks he was with me, how little I knew about him.

What had I learnt so far? He loved sport, particularly football, and Formula 1 racing (he was friendly with several of the drivers). When he was in the UK he tried to get to some of the London football games with his mates (lots of these, some old school friends). He listened to a massive range of music singing along when driving in his car (he certainly wouldn't have a career as a singer). He disliked bland food. Flying was a means to an end but he didn't particularly enjoy the experience. He saw his mother (Eileen) and father (Tom) as much as he could and regularly rang his sisters. They were all slightly older than him but above all this, he adored his children, Phoebe, Becca and Tim. I had always known how much Lilly meant to him. Paul rarely lost his temper but when he did it was nearly always because of some injustice being meted out to the underdog. He supported quite a few charities. He was dreadful at DIY.

Stephen rang back with the details of a college friend of his who did sports physio. He worked a lot at Carrow Road. We got an appointment for the following Monday. He advised Paul not to do too much running until he had a chance to see him.

We settled into our daily routine. Me in my office and Paul in the kitchen with his papers all over the table. Oh, I have forgotten something else I have learned. Although tidy in most things (he hangs his clothes up carefully and his car is neat) he is extremely untidy when working on his paperwork. I listened to him wheeling and dealing when I wasn't making calls myself. I was just thinking it was time for more coffee when he came in with steaming mugs. Telepathy.

'Chloe has texted me about the kids. I think I will collect them and go over to see my parents. Are you okay with me going off this weekend?'

'You need to see them and I need to visit Amy and Jake.

Start of term for Jake is very hectic so I haven't seen them for a while'.

Amy rang several times during the first week Paul was at the cottage and she handed me over to Jake when she had finished. Paul would get up and leave the room to avoid any embarrassment. Jake and I had settled back into being comfortable with each other and had lots to talk about. He would chat about his work, colleagues and trips he was making on behalf of the college. With his distinguished good looks he was very photogenic and his expertise was well-known. BBC and Sky used him regularly as a contact when environmental disasters occurred around the world. He was the go-to man who could be relied on to provide answers. He, Amy, Andy and Angus, were planning a trekking trip to the Himalayas next year. They had decided not to invite me along! He would be in Delhi for a conference and the youngsters were flying out to join him.

Another thing I discovered about Paul. He liked travel. Not the journey, but the places to visit. Graham and Anton had become an item and our planned visit to Berlin looked like being a threesome. I was not sure about this.

'Why don't I join you? You won't feel so much like a gooseberry. When are you going?'

'For five days around my birthday'.

Paul looked pleased. 'Why are you smiling' I asked?

'In the hope that we might at least be talking again, I cleared my diary for your special day'. I remembered his arrival from Dublin last year. Graham didn't pop in quite so much now that Anton was around so I would need to go next door and see him.

'Why don't we get Maria to sort the flights and the hotel for us?' Maria worked at a travel agency and did all his flight and accommodation arrangements. I had spoken to her a lot.

'I am not sure Graham and Anton will be able to afford any hotel you stay in Paul'.

'I get really good deals and I am very popular in Berlin. I go for the film festival most years. A lot of the professionals are too grand to go to the less well-known ones'.

'Ok I will chat to Graham'.

Before we went on holiday I had to talk to Amy about Paul. She now knew that Jake had asked me to marry him. Jake also knew about Paul's offer. He had laughed hysterically, tears running down his face.

'Zoe, you do get yourself into scrapes. They say things come in threes. Who else will that be? Have you any more men in the background?'

'You may think it is funny but it is causing me a great deal of consternation. I had thought I would take time to get over him and then commit to you but his return has thrown everything up in the air. My emotions and thoughts are all jumbled up and I am now going to have to explain it all to Amy who has no idea that we even had a relationship, poor as it was. She thought it was work related. What I am certain of is that I need time to get to know him, the real him. We saw so little of each other. He was always working. You and I didn't fit, and you knew I would have hated climbing mountains like Clare, and it could be the same with Paul. There is a whole part of his life I have had no connection with. First off, I have spent my life watching the pennies. He is extremely rich and has a very different lifestyle'.

It never occurred to me how strange it would have looked to an outsider. Me, using Jake as an agony-aunt. It showed how far we had come after all this time. I was totally comfortable with him. I loved being with him and Amy.

In the end Amy resolved my dilemma but not in the way I had planned. When we sat out the back in the kitchen with Paul's music blaring out it was possible not to hear cars driving up. Even Lilly didn't react. I was sitting on Paul's lap in full view of the front door and Amy was standing looking at us. I hadn't heard the key in the door. I felt like a naughty schoolgirl and jumped up. She knew Jake had offered marriage and here I was sitting on another man's lap.

Lilly finally woke up and saw Amy, her paws slipping on the mosaic floor, in her rush to get to her.

Amy shut the door and came into the kitchen. I was standing clasping my hands not certain what to do.

'Hello Amy', Paul said. He looked straight at her. 'Good to see you again. I will leave you two to talk'. He stood up to get Lilly's lead. They went off.

'Does Dad know what is going on?' Amy screamed at me after they had left.

'Yes, he knows everything'.

'You didn't think, either of you, to tell me what was happening?' She made me feel dirty as if I was some sort of licentious slut.

'Paul has only been back with me for the last few weeks', I stammered.

'Back, what do you mean, back?' She could barely contain her fury.

To gain time, I filled the kettle and moved the papers to the end of the table.

'Sit down Amy and stop shouting at me. You know how it upsets me'. She was about to speak but thought better of it. I gave her a cup of tea.

I told her everything I had told Jake about my 'relationship' with Paul. By the time I had finished she seemed calmer but I still felt she could erupt at any time. I was choosing my words carefully.

She sat there, her tea getting cold, just looking at the table. When she looked up I could see her tears. My first instinct was to wipe them away but something held me back.

'You were able to tell Dad all this but not me, why?'

'If you remember, last year when Jake and the boys returned, we were barely on speaking terms'.

'How long has Dad known?'

'About a month. I told him about Paul after he had asked me to marry him. I needed time to get over him before I gave Dad an answer. I didn't expect Paul to come back into my life and then ask me to marry him too'.

'What'! She exclaimed.

'Yes, after twenty odd years on my own I have two marriage offers on the table'.

'So, you were with Paul at Aunt Jennie's wedding'.

'Yes, but we had agreed not to advertise that fact because he didn't want me to get hassle on social media'.

'Is he living here?'

'It has only been a few weeks. We realised we barely knew each other. Your father and I weren't right all those years ago. It has taken a long time for that to change. I worked for Paul and I knew his days were very busy and complicated but I need to know if we can live together. Currently the thought of the way he spends his life terrifies me'.

'The world Jennie, Frances and Paul inhabit is like another planet. It takes a very special person to cope with it. I am not sure I can. Paul thinks differently, but I have got used to my quiet existence. I have achieved a measure of peace. I am attracted sexually to Jake and Paul but marriage needs so much more than being good in bed'.

It felt wrong talking to my daughter about my sex life.

I had been standing with my back pressed to the AGA leaning against the rail with my hands clasped tightly looking at Amy, waiting for her response. She picked up her cup and came over. 'I think it is time we had a hot cup of tea'.

An hour later, Paul came through the back door. Through the glass he could see we were talking quietly. He put his head around the kitchen door.

'Is it okay to come back now?'

'I think you need to ask Amy?' I replied.

He looked at her and she got up and shook his hand. She was almost as tall.

'Are you and Mum good now?' He asked. 'I would hate to come between you. She loves you so much'.

'I know'. Her face was streaked with tears from crying. He pulled out a handkerchief and gently wiped away the smudged makeup.

Amy had been in Norwich interviewing a researcher at the Soil Institute but he had been taken ill so she had decided to take the chance to meet up with me. Maybe fate looked kindly on us that day. She sat talking to Paul whilst I took some calls. By the time I came back she was saying 'You won't hurt Mum will you? Dad caused so much pain but they are good friends now'.

'You are right to take Zoe's side and I respect you for it. I will try not to let you down Amy'.

'What are you doing for your birthday Amy?' I asked.

'Not sure, what are you doing for yours?'

'We are going with Graham and Anton to Berlin for five days. Paul has kindly agreed to come to stop me being a gooseberry with those two'.

'Has Dad met Paul? I think it would be interesting to have my birthday bash with your suitors, Mum'. She giggled.

'I am game', Paul replied laughing.

GETTING TO KNOW YOU

Two days before our flight to Germany I found myself at a small discreet restaurant in the old part of Norwich. Jake used it occasionally to entertain visitors. Sat either side of me were Paul and Jake with Amy sitting opposite, barely containing her amusement. Jake and Paul shook hands when we arrived then spent the rest of the evening laughing, mostly at my expense. Every cock-up I had ever made was faithfully reported. Amy added quite a few to the list. I had dreaded the event but the three of them bantered away determined to keep the tone light.

Sitting watching them all in the dim light I felt a warm glow. The three people I loved most in the world all sitting together. Amy admitted, as she left with Jake, that it was one of the best birthdays, but not number one. That was still her fifteenth birthday when Jake had flown in from Australia and stayed with us.

Outside the restaurant Jake picked me up and kissed me in his usual fashion. I am sure he will be doing that when we are in our dotage. I whispered my thanks. Putting me down and wrapping his arm around Amy he held out his hand to Paul. 'May the best man win'. He laughed. Amy kissed us all and ran off with him holding his hand.

Watching Jake and Amy together reminded me how often

she had wanted us to be a family. For most of Amy's life, Jake had been apart from us. At her fifteenth birthday I can remember almost word for word the emotional speech she had made about her dream of sharing her day with both her parents. I didn't need to see Dad's photo to know how much it would mean to Amy if I chose Jake. She would finally get her wish. This thought would not leave me. I had dreamt of Jake all those years. If I decided on Paul, I would be denying Amy her dearest wish.

Two days later the four of us landed at Berlin Schonefeld airport. Maria had arranged a minibus to collect us. We travelled Business Class. Graham and Anton were ecstatic. On the drive to the hotel, they pummelled me with questions. I had done a quick trawl through my books on the history of Berlin and its politics, so was up to speed with most of their demands. The driver spoke broken English so I talked to him in German. He seemed relieved. English visitors are known for only speaking one language.

The only hotel I knew was the world famous Hotel Adlon. Paul had stuck his nose up at that choice. He told Maria to book his usual boutique hotel. He was greeted like a long-lost friend as he walked in with the rest of us trailing behind. Not the usual obsequious tone adopted by hotel employees, but a really obvious pleasure at his return.

The furniture was modern. It looked Danish. Simple, clean cut lines but very comfortable. Gunther the owner came out to the reception area. 'Herr Walker it is so good to see you again. But it is not festival season?'

'Good to see you too', Paul replied. 'We are here for a brief holiday. He introduced us and we all shook hands'. I spoke to him in German.

He was taken aback. He replied in German, 'It is rare to

293

hear English people speak our language, if you don't mind me saying'.

Speaking in English he turned and took the keys from the porter. 'Let me take you to your rooms. I have arranged for some light refreshments'. We were on the first floor at the back of the hotel looking out on to a small immaculate garden. Graham and Anton were next door. The porter followed behind us with our bags. They all fitted on the trolley. We rarely took many clothes with us on our trips.

'See you in a couple of hours, you two', Paul said.

'Let me know if there is anything else I can do', he said closing the door.

The room was painted in grey tones, giving it a peaceful feel. The only splash of colour was a dark blue throw on the bed.

'I always have this room when I come here', Paul said. I had moved to the table and was already eating. There were all sorts of fresh fruits in the bowl for afters. Paul took off his shoes (he would be barefoot all the time if it was possible) and grabbed some food. His phone bleeped. It was a text message : Just completed the purchase it is all yours, the best of luck. Doug.

'You went ahead and bought that wreck?'

'Yes, I can see its possibilities'.

'If it isn't a rude question how much did your haggling bring the price down?'

'By a million' he said laughing.

'And how much did the architect reckon it would cost to renovate it. Correction, rebuild it?' I queried.

'About 1.2 million but that includes an enormous fee for Graham to design the garden', he laughed. He tapped a reply back to his solicitor and flung himself onto the bed.

'Come here, I want to celebrate my purchase'.

After three days walking around the sights of Berlin, Paul was convinced I had a future as a tourist guide. I cried uncontrollably at the Jewish Museum and the site of the Berlin Wall. I gave a full history lecture on the rise of National Socialism and the Second World War whilst they sat on a bench at Unter den Linden eating ice creams. At night it was still warm so we ate out at the restaurants Paul frequented. Graham and Anton would disappear after the meal and trawl the gay clubs. On my birthday we went to a Beethoven concert. On the last evening we returned to the floodlit Reichstag with its modern dome.

Sitting at a café drinking a last-minute beer, Graham leaned over to Paul. He indicated a group of four women who were casting furtive glances at Paul. One of them walked over and said in very poor English. 'Pardon, are you Herr Paul Walker?' Paul smiled and said 'Yes'. She turned to her friends and called out in German.

Paul asked what she said.

'Something like, it is him, come over'. I translated. 'I think you should invite them for a drink. We can move the tables together'.

I went over and spoke to them. They seemed delighted that I could speak German. They were out for the night and had noticed our group. They had spent a lot of time doubting it could be Paul, not here in Berlin, and so on. When I asked if they would like to join us they got up as one and said a loud, 'Ja'.

Paul had got the waiter to move a table near us and the four ladies came over surrounding him. He ordered drinks. I translated their questions, his replies. He flirted playfully making them feel special. He made their day by kissing them goodbye.

Paul had contacted the Von-Ryckens who had a flat in Berlin and we lunched with them on the final day. The minibus was collecting our bags, plus Graham and Anton, then calling in for me and Paul on the way to the airport.

The four of us stayed over at the flat then drove back to Norfolk. Lilly was being dog-sat by Mum and Dad.

Bob the Builder had retired but Dad gave Paul his son's phone number. Mum was deeply amused at my marital offers. She told me not to play fast and loose or they might both go off!

Bob junior called in to see Paul when we got back. Several gallons of coffee later, he reckoned he could do what Paul wanted. He would need an extra team and he knew several specialist craftsmen who had been laid off by a heritage builder who did all the work on the Cathedral. Poor management he said, touching his nose. Amazingly the survey had said that the structure was fundamentally sound.

They drove off to have a look round.

Paul's phone bleeped. He had left it behind. It was Eileen, his mother. She had made it clear to Paul that she was pleased I was back in his life. I don't think they had really liked Chloe.

'Hello Eileen, its Zoe. Paul has forgotten his phone. Can I help?'

'Zoe did you have a good trip to Berlin?'

'We were sad to come home. We walked our socks off. I had blisters. Paul is off seeing his new purchase with a builder. Can I take a message?'

'That is why I am ringing. Tom is really interested in this project and we wondered if we could pop up this weekend and have a look around?'

'He hasn't said he is away but I will get him to ring you. Maybe you could stop over for the night? Amy's room is free.'

'That idea is great. Nice to put a face to the voice after all this time. The premiere photos tended to hide you behind Paul'.

'It wasn't the photographers' fault. It was timid me hiding behind him. I have never done anything like that before'.

Paul walked in minutes later. 'Did I leave my mobile' he yelled. 'Are there any messages?'

I told him I had invited his parents up to stay so they could see his monstrosity of a house.

'It is not a monstrosity. You will love it when Bob junior has finished. He thinks it will take at least a year though. I met the farmer who is renting the fields. Seemed like a nice chap'.

'Paul you are off filming January. How are you going to cope with all the decisions when you are away?' I was getting worried that he might want me to do the management.

'I am going to get a project manager. You can let me know what is going on when we talk'.

'Is this all a great plot to get me back on the job, so to speak?'

'Well I rather think you might consider making polite conversation with one of your suitors'.

Between them Jake and Paul were teasing me the whole time. They found it hilarious that I was sitting on two offers of marriage. I didn't really mind being the butt of their jokes but I did warn them that if I got a better offer, I was off.

Unlike me, Paul's Dad was impressed with his purchase, congratulating his son on his choice. Not sure Eileen felt the same. Not the silent type normally, she did not say a word. I sympathised.

DECISION TIME

In November I went to another premiere. My billing this time was Zoe Chapman, Paul's girlfriend. I had been promoted. Chloe did not attend. I coped without support from the director's wife and I had my picture on Google!

The Christmas Amateur Dramatic show went down well. Paul had helped out when he was at home. The monstrosity now had an outfit of scaffolding and plastic. The roof was made waterproof not that there was much to protect inside. Paul's accountant was delighted with him. He was spending money like water keeping the tax man at bay. Graham was fully occupied in sorting out the grounds.

Christmas was complicated. Amy, Jake, Andy, Richard, Paul and I went to Mum and Dad's. Andy and Richard were also in the picture now. On Boxing Day Paul went off to his parents collecting his children, en route. He got back for New Year's Eve. We all went to celebrate with the Chapman siblings who had taken up residence at the family home. Now everybody knew what was going on. Jake and Paul kept saying they wanted to dance with their fiancée. I yelled back saying I was absolutely not their fiancée.

It reminded me of Wimbledon but I was such a different person now. With age had come confidence. I was getting used to Paul's world, his entourage, the people who made

Paul Walker function outside of his acting.

I knew it was time to make my decision. I had spent months playing out the possible options. I loved two men but I could only have one. In the end it was the past that made the choice clear. Amy was not even a year old when Jake had found somebody else to love. He was settled in Australia but he never gave me a chance to travel out to see if we could make things work. I believe he loved me but I would have been his second choice. My feelings for him far outweighed his for me at that time. Only Clare's death had brought me back into the picture.

Both Jake and Paul were ambitious but Paul had offered to give up his career for me if I asked him to. Jake did not. I would never have asked either of them not to follow their chosen paths but only Paul loved me enough to offer that sacrifice.

It was time to talk to Jake.

Trying to find a quiet space in my parents' house is a challenge. Jake and I found one on the stairs to the loftroom on the second floor. Putting his arm around me, 'I know what you are going to tell me Zoe. You have made your choice haven't you?'

I nodded and lent back against him. 'It is Paul isn't it?'

'Yes', I whispered.

'You have made the right decision Zoe. You would be safe with me. I am tried and tested, but you are ready to take risks, finally. I am sad but not surprised. You make a good pair and I know he loves you. Amy and I have watched the way he looks at you. Have you told him?'

'No, I wanted to talk to you first. I will always love you Jake and hope for Amy's sake we remain close to each other for the rest of our lives. I need your friendship'.

'New Year's resolution. New beginnings'.

We turned to go downstairs. He picked me up and kissed me. 'Go find your man Zoe'.

Paul was talking to Jennie and Frances. Shop talk! He looked up and pulled me on to his lap. 'Are you ready to be my fiancé Paul? I accept your offer of marriage, my love'.

'You are sure?'

'Oh yes, absolutely'. I ran my hands through his hair ruffling it up. I love his hair, his smell, his smile. I love him so completely. Jennie and Frances chorused, 'About time too'.

Jake had told Amy. She was searching for us and then pushed her way through the dancers. She bundled into me and Paul as we tried to stand up. We ended up in a pile on the floor on top of Paul who was laughing. 'I take it you are happy about this Amy?' Paul managed to gasp as he tried to get up off the floor.

The word had got round and the group on the ground got bigger as my exuberant family congratulated us. Through the crowd I could see Jake laughing. He blew me a kiss. Spike and Lilly were going berserk.

We got married in the late spring after Paul got back from the States. I flew out three times during the filming. I couldn't bear to be without him for so long. I had finally decided to close my off-site messaging business.

It is difficult to have a quiet wedding in the Chapman family. Charlie actually had two celebrations. Frances was the only one who succeeded in keeping her arrangements quiet. She and James secretly crept off to the Registry Office. Mum and Dad sulked for weeks.

Paul and I had no chance after that.

The marquee my parents erected in the garden was enormous and the cars were parked down the road right through the village. There were a lot of guests. I spent my time worrying about the cost. Paul was adamant that even though the wedding was at their house, my parents enjoy every minute. They were not to be involved in the organisation.

Guests were staying in every hotel within a 20 mile radius. Paul's ladies had to come, his fan club, actor friends, footy mates, Formula 1 drivers, his agent and entourage, family and, most important of all, his children. The Chapman family and friends made another huge batch of guests. Mary offered to help with our clothes but we decided to choose our own. She came as a guest instead.

Jake was Paul's best man. Amy was my bridesmaid. Dad walked me down the aisle then turned to the assembled crowd and said, 'At last'. The vicar tried to stop laughing but failed. The guests clapped. For our honeymoon we went to India.

We spent the rest of the year living between Recluse Cottage and the flat in London. When Paul was filming, I visited regularly. I wasn't going to let him be alone again. I had been promoted from his wife to his manager. I was now even more intimately involved in the Paul Walker empire.

'Recluse Cottage' is no more. It has been renamed by Amy to 'Gay Corner'. When we moved to the monstrosity, I rented it to a gay friend of Anton and Graham.

The renovation was a triumph over adversity. There were so many hurdles along the way. Six steps up, five back. The final result is testament to Paul's vision and tenacity. We have a beautiful home. Amy has renamed it to 'Paul's Folly'. The Postie knows it as Melton Grove. Graham's garden design is settling in. It will take a few years to mature. He is constantly visiting, rearranging the planting and tutting when I have been remiss and not done as instructed.

Lilly has been joined by Teddy. As you will guess from his name, he looks like a teddybear. He is of unknown parentage, a soft brown woolly sweetheart. We rescued him from the local animal sanctuary. Several cats have moved in too. A tortoiseshell stray gave birth in our kitchen. Phoebe, Becca and Tim adopted one kitten each, leaving another for me.

In spite of the breakdown of their parent's marriage they are delightful children. Chloe has done a good job. I first met them on my wedding day. They came with Paul's Mum, Dad, sisters and their families.

They stay with us as often as school terms allow. Like their Dad, they love the countryside. As you would expect, with such handsome parents, they are attractive children. Phoebe and Tim are like Paul, outgoing and fun-loving. Becca is studious and shy. Mum says she reminds her of a young me. We spend hours together on the library sofas reading, watched over by dear Prop.

Prop's picture is in pride of place in the library. On display too, are Paul's Oscar, his Bafta and a Golden Globe. Rebecca won a Golden Globe for her portrayal of Katherine. I am now a veteran of awards ceremonies and many premieres. After the Baftas, Paul's make-up artist sent me some waterproof eye make-up. Watching Paul collect his award I sobbed uncontrollably and after his speech I had to disappear into the ladies to clean the black streaks off my face. He thanked everybody who had helped him during his career and especially the team who worked on the film and then turned to look straight at me. He smiled and then told the audience how much he loved me and how his life had changed so much for the better since we had married.

Each film Paul chooses is different giving him scope to develop new roles. On screen I have watched Paul transform into a brutal gang boss, campaigning journalist, war hero, science fiction character, deaf mute and a star-crossed lover. He spends long hours working on the scripts with me reading the other parts. After years of loneliness I am loved and cared for by this wonderful man. I am so moved by him. He is worth my long wait.

No longer running my business, I have had time to pursue other activities. Research for my book has taken me to Germany, the Netherlands and Denmark. Hours spent in the state archives and family papers have given me a treasure trove of information. When I couldn't travel abroad, I visited the British Library, Prop's collection and the UK state papers. Soon my book on Elizabeth Stuart, Queen of Bohemia – the Winter Queen - will be finished. Through her daughter Sophia she is the descendent of the Hanoverian kings of England.

The last part of our renovation to the estate was the Lodge House at the entrance to the drive. Paul couldn't see a use for it as it stood. It was tiny, one room, a miniscule kitchen and an external outhouse toilet linking to a damaged septic tank. No bathroom.

As so often happens, fate offered us a solution. Walking Lilly and Teddy down to see Anna at the farm, I noticed three small children playing in the garden. Anna's two boys were old enough to be working. An unfamiliar woman was hanging up washing.

'Hello, Anna its Zoe, can I come in?' I called out. Anna came to the door looking stressed.

'What is the matter?'

'It is a long story. My younger sister Liz and her children are staying with us'. Anna's house only has four bedrooms and I could imagine it was a bit crammed for them all but probably okay for a short stay.

'I would love to meet her'.

'She is rather unhappy at the moment'.

'I am sorry, is there anything I can do to help?'

Teddy and Lilly ran into the kitchen followed by the children. The eldest girl was around eight years old and the two youngest boys were under five. They stood at the door not sure of their welcome. They were definitely hesitant.

'What are your dogs called?' Asked one of the young boys.

'Teddy and Lilly. Do you like dogs?'

'Yes, but our Dad wouldn't let us have one. He said they were dirty and would make us ill', the girl replied.

'Well Teddy and Lilly are very clean. I had to bath them yesterday because they got so muddy in the woods'. Anna shuffled the children to the table and gave them some drinks and biscuits.

Anna's sister came in from the back door. She had a large cut on her face and bruising around her neck. Her arm was in plaster. I could tell immediately what the problem was. She was here for protection. She was hiding.

Anna put the television on and sent the little family in to watch. She made some tea and we all sat down. She held her sister's hand.

By the time I had left I knew most of the story. Years of violence, then a few months where her husband tried to control his behaviour, followed by a gradual slide back into intimidating both Liz and the children. There was a lot of physical and verbal abuse.

Staying at Anna's farmhouse was only a temporary solution.

When I got back to the house, Paul was sitting in the kitchen with John, Anna's husband, discussing farm matters. Paul wanted the farm to become organic and John was very enthusiastic. I said where I had been and John looked up ruefully.

'I am not sure how long they can stay. It is very crowded. We tried to find a refuge but they were all full and Liz couldn't go back home. He has been a bad one since they got married. He drinks'. He got up and picked up his jumper. 'I had better get back'.

Paul was silent most of the day. I have got used to his 'thinking mode' now.

'Do you think it would help if we let Liz and the children stay in Phoebe, Tim and Becca's rooms? They won't be here now until the February half-term'.

'I think it is a great idea short-term but what happens when you want to fill the house up with your cronies when you fancy a shindig?'

'Well I think I have discovered a reason to re-build the Lodge House'.

'It will need to be substantially enlarged for that family' I said.

I will get Bob junior over tomorrow and chat to him. His architect mate can do some plans for us to submit to the council', Paul replied.

Another thing I now know about Paul is he likes a project.

His next one would be even more substantial and long-term.

It was really nice to have this little family sharing our house. Paul would spend hours playing with them. Maybe he saw them as a way of catching up on the years he missed with his own children. He had been so busy working. He had gone down to Anna and John's and explained his plan to rebuild the Lodge. Megan and Freddie were at the local primary school and Sam was in playgroup but Liz was taking a long-time to recover. I rang my counsellor and asked for his help. I drove her there twice a week.

We had converted one of the ground floor reception rooms into an office. I have an elegant Victorian office desk at one end, Paul uses a large table in another corner, his papers spread out. Both of us spend hours on the internet. He continues to be deluged with scripts. We had agreed early on that he would limit his filming to three projects a year but this was challenging. He was in such demand. He still had dreams too. He wanted to work in theatre and direct a film.

Returning from a trip to the counsellor with Liz, I noticed Paul's accountant's car parked outside. Probably telling him to spend more money, I thought. I wondered how much this time.

Liz went off to the kitchen to make some drinks and I heard Paul calling me to come to the office.

'Hello Andrew, here to help us spend some more money?' I laughed.

'It is your husband who is leading this one and it is me trying to control him for once', he grinned. I looked at Paul. He had been in thinking mode for several weeks. I had waited patiently for the outcome.

'I want to set up a charitable foundation'. Paul smiled at me. I wonder when I will be able to see him smile and not want to rush over and kiss him. Maybe when I was eighty.

'Liz's predicament set me off thinking. Why not use some of the money I earn to provide a refuge for women escaping violence?'

'You mean build a house?'

'Yes, but also fund the staff, counselling and its maintenance through a grant from the foundation I want to set up?' I looked at Andrew who was grinning silently.

'I think it is a perfect idea. I wish I had thought of it myself. Have you done the figures with Andrew?'

'Yes, that is why he is looking worried!. I want to move £5 million into the foundation'.

'Wow, no wonder Andrew is skittish'. I laughed. It seemed an enormous sum to me. I still had not got used to the money Paul earned. He was also a brand leader for an expensive watchmaker and a luxury clothes manufacturer. They paid huge sums for him to promote their wares. I knew, too, that he supported colleagues, who had hit hard times, through another charity. He gave what spare time he had to raising funds. At the local village fete he stood in the stocks being drenched by sponges thrown at him for hours on end, raising massive amounts of money for the community.

Paul was away filming when Liz and her little family moved into the Lodge so he wasn't there to hear her sweet little speech thanking him for being so kind. As usual I cried!

WEDDING BELLS

There is a large marquee up in the garden with staff setting up the tables. Paul is out there directing. Another wedding. Amy is marrying Angus. They have lived together for some years.

The church is at the end of our drive so we will all be walking up. Jake is due soon. Paul needs to put his clothes on so I will have to go out and get him.

A car stops at the gates waiting to be let in. The electronic gates are temperamental, very temperamental. This time they behave. The car pulls up and I watch Jake open the door to help his mother out. Robert and Andy are in the back seat. He hands Elspeth her stick and guides her towards the door. I must go down now and shout for Paul.

I haven't seen Elspeth for a very long time. She looks frail. Rushing out from my bedroom, I ask Amy if she is nearly ready. Angie is helping her. I love the fact that one of my closest friends' son is going to become part of my family. I knock on Varena's door. She opens it. She at least has her dress on.

'Varena, please can you go and drag Paul in, he needs to get dressed'.

'Your wish is my command'. Shoving on her shoes she

rushes off into the garden.

Anna is opening the door to Jake and his family. She and her sister are a godsend. When Paul is home the house heaves with his friends, they help me change beds ready for the next influx. Picking up my shoes I go down to my guests.

Elspeth is sitting on a chair. Jake turns to me and picks me up, kisses me then plops me down. I wave at Andy and Robert and then walk over to Elspeth. She looks up and I kiss her cheek. She pats me and says 'It is going to be a lovely day. I have been looking forward to it so much'.

I suddenly realise there are some guests missing. 'Jake where are Richard and Emily?'

'They have driven straight to the church.' Emily is Jake's new partner. She is a colleague at work whose husband died of Parkinsons. They have been together for nearly a year now.

Varena appears with Paul in tow. 'Get upstairs now', I yell. 'The bride is ready before you'. He bows deeply to everybody. 'Hello to you all. The Missus says I must look decent today'. He imitated a broad cockney accent and ran off up the stairs.

'Robert you need to get Elspeth and Andy to the church'. Jake hands over the keys to the car and helps his mother up. 'Jake, you come upstairs to see Amy'. I said.

Paul leans over the bannister. 'See how forceful she is'.

'Go and get some clothes on, you pest', I yell back.

Jake and I walk upstairs to Amy's room. I knock. Varena opens the door and lets us in. Amy is standing in her wedding dress and she turns towards us and swivels round.

'I don't look too fat do I?'

Jake shouts with laughter 'Given the fact that you are at least six months pregnant is it surprising? Your Mum was huge too'. Angie who is sitting on the sofa falls about giggling.

'We all need to go now to the church. Jake, you and Amy are going with Paul in the car. I am just going to find out what stage of undress Paul is still in'.

Varena and Angie start walking down the stairs then out and up the drive and I run off to find Paul. When I open the door, I can hear water running. Oh lord he is having a shower. It gets turned off and he emerges rubbing his hair which is now sticking up in spikes. He drops his towel and quickly gets dressed. I am still amazed at how he moves me, even when I am cross with him. I want to get hold of him but now is absolutely not the time.

Fully dressed and pulling on his shoes he aims for the door. 'Paul you need to comb your hair'.

'It is the unruly look'. I hand him a comb kissing him hard on the mouth.

Amy and Jake are waiting in the hall for us. I kiss them both and go to leave but suddenly Paul turns into the library. 'Wait I have forgotten something'.

'Paul we are late, if you are not quick you will need to get a speeding fine driving up to the church'.

He reappears with a chauffeur's hat, salutes them, and then opens the door ushering Jake and Amy out into the bridal carriage. Well, actually it is Paul's Range Rover which Varena and Angie have decked in flowers.

I run off up the drive across the road and into the church.

It is packed with the Chapmans, Angus' family and their friends. I rush up to the front, waving and blowing kisses to everybody and take my place next to Emily, Richard and Elspeth nodding a quick hello. A few minutes later Paul arrives, minus hat, and squeezes past me. They move up to make room for him.

Angus is waiting nervously for his bride. The organist starts to play and we all stand up. Jake walks his daughter up the aisle. The pride on his face makes me want to weep. After the vicar asks, 'who gives this woman to this man?' Jake says, 'I do', and then he returns to the pew beside me and takes my hand looking down, smiling. That part of the wedding ceremony always makes me laugh. As if Jake would ever totally give Amy away to Angus. A part of her will always be his. Paul holds on tight to my other hand. I am stood between my two loves.

We had an official photographer and Dad. His snaps were far better. My particular favourite is the one taken later at the reception with me, Jake, Amy and Paul dancing in a group trying to avoid Amy's bump. Amy was stone cold sober but the rest of us were paralytic.

Photos over, we start to make our way behind the bridal group when a piper arrives dressed in full Campbell regalia. Another example of Paul's thoughtful attention to detail. The guests cheer and fall into line behind him as he pipes us back to the house to the tune of Scotland the Brave. I bet he was glad the drive wasn't too long. He would have been out of breath if the walk had been any further. Robert will drive Elspeth down. Now the celebrations can begin!

Much, much, later in the early hours of the morning, snuggled in Paul's arms, I hear him chuckling. 'For somebody who will soon be a granny you are still very sexy'!

ACKNOWLEDGEMENTS

It just wouldn't be fair if I didn't thank my husband Philip for urging me to publish this book. Not only has he put up with me sitting at my computer for hour after hour with my headphones on listening to music and bashing away at the keyboard, ignoring him, but he has also offered plenty of sensible advice. We ended up talking about the people as if they really existed. Numerous adaptations took place before I was confident enough that I had reached the final manuscript.

The characters have been in my head for so long, but it took "lockdown" to give me time to get their story told. The months just flew past.

I am so grateful to Seb Soar for introducing me to Anne Holloway. Her editing skills have been invaluable, and the result is a much tighter and fluid story which I hope you have all enjoyed.

Thanks also to the many friends who have read the book suggesting tense changes and grammatical improvements.

Some of the proceeds from the sale of this book will go to two Romanian sanctuaries saving hundreds of abandoned dogs and cats, feeding and healing them and finding loving homes all over Europe. The dedication of these groups of people is awe inspiring.